Vibrational Passage

JENNIFER DUSTOW

AND

KIMBERLY MIYASAKI LEE

Copyright © 2011 Jennifer Dustow and Kimberly Miyasaki Lee

All rights reserved. No part of this book may be used or reproduced in any manner whatsoever without written permission from both authors.

First Paperback Edition: May 2011

This book is a work of fiction. The names, characters, places, and incidents are products of the writers' imagination or have been used fictitiously and are not to be construed as real. Any resemblance to persons, living or dead, actual events, locales or organizations is entirely coincidental.

Book design by Wesley Miyasaki of id8design

For information, contact us at: http://kimandjenn.blogspot.com

Vibrational Passage- Book 1 (Safe Passage Trilogy)

ISBN-13: 978-1461149736
ISBN-10: 1461149738

LCCN: 2011928310

Printed in Charleston, South Carolina

Manufactured in the United States of America

DEDICATION

I dedicate this book to my husband, who always makes me laugh, and continually inspires me to be more than who and what I am & to "C" and the new additions to our family "M" and "A".

Also I cannot forget Bev- thank you for everything.

-J.D.

This book is dedicated to my Mom, for her inner strength, kindness and generosity as she continues to nurture everyone around her, to W for the laughter and support, and to my two favorite alphabets: L and M-- lots of hearts, you bring love and light to the world; to Vonni for your enduring friendship,

and best of all to B.... I'm so glad it was you.

-K.M.L.

ACKNOWLEDGMENTS

Our deepest gratitude goes out to the angelic glass half-full gang and to those who guided this book along the way, especially when it all seemed like too much.

Thank you!

To our loved ones who have passed on, you live on in our memories, and in our hearts.

In addition, we thank you, the readers, for being open to our concept of fiction.

Cheers!

CHAPTER 1

Walden was supposed to be in Washington today. An unexpected email from his boss had changed all that. He rubbed his eyes, he was jet-lagged, tired, and wondering what Peter Lyceum had up his sleeves calling this emergency meeting. There was nothing random about any of Peter's decisions.

A call from Ian Hill, just moments ago, had felt more like a sucker punch to his jaw. Walden hated taking calls from Ian. Any conversations with him were full of expletives and blame. Ian had yelled at him about having to make last minute arrangements to board a Concorde flight just to make it back to New York in time for the meeting. He had tried to bully an answer out of Walden. When he did not get what he wanted, Ian had abruptly hung up.

Walden himself, had taken the redeye out of Miami, a hasty change of travel plans to accommodate the almighty Mendelrose CEO. Luckily, Hurricane Erin had not caused any flight delays despite the fact that it was churning just off the eastern seaboard.

The familiar façade of the giant tower he had worked in for almost ten years now towered over him, disappearing into the sky. He was not an expert on architecture, but he had an amateur's appreciation of it. Some days he wondered if the building's architect, Minoru Yamasaki, had meant the patterned steel frame that wrapped around the building to represent tuning forks.

Walden mused that the vibrational sound would be tuned to the sound of money. Or perhaps, the steel frame was meant to represent tridents. Neptune's tridents protecting, fortifying, strengthening the giant twin towers, surfacing from the murky depths of the Hudson, rising up above the earth, reaching, and connecting the ocean to the sky. In Walden's brief attempt to research the architect, he had not come across a satisfying answer yet.

He headed for the building entrance, and as he entered the spacious lobby, his BlackBerry sounded. A message from Peter's executive assistant read: *Your 8am meeting is rescheduled. Details to follow. -Felix.*

Walden let his briefcase drop onto the carpet as he furiously tapped out a message on his BlackBerry that he needed to speak to Peter immediately. Without thinking, Walden did the most curious thing. He just stood there looking at his phone, waiting. As if, his ever elusive and slippery CEO would actually answer back right away.

He had been traveling so much lately, the lobby was feeling like just another airport terminal. Silver casters lined up near the podiums against the wall could have been check-in counters for his next flight. Comforting sunlight streamed in through the giant lobby windows, filtering in as sunlight does into the open ocean. Without notice, that threatening feeling of danger returned, it happened anytime he had to deal with Peter lately.

Walden shifted his stare from the silent BlackBerry down over to his solid gold cufflinks, a gift from someone who truly understood his research. These small tasteful symbols were strengthening reinforcement of what Walden had discovered. It had been his work with honey bees that he had accidently stumbled upon, that would forever link him to these tiny creatures. He hoped the Merovingian's were right about bees… as the ever-enduring symbol of immortality and resurrection.

His cell phone rang, snapping him out of his thoughts. Walden glanced at his BlackBerry, the words stared back at him –

restricted. This has to be Peter he thought. Peter was notorious for blocking his number when he placed calls.

Going with that Walden answered his phone sternly, "Peter, what the hell's going on?"

The impatient, arrogant voice on the other end of the line was classic Peter. A question answered with a question. "Are you at the office yet?" Walden's gamble had been correct.

"I'm in the lobby...."

Peter interrupted him.

"Get upstairs right now and stay put. There is still a mandatory meeting."

Walden quickly fired off a set of rhetorical questions, not allowing Peter to take control of the conversation. "I assume you're trying to tell me you're sitting this one out? You never intended on making it to this meeting, did you? How long have you known...?"

Not responding to his, more like statements then questions, Peter laughed at him.

"You just do your part... your family will be safe. And, off the record, don't you think you've hurt your family enough already?"

Peter's voice dripped sarcasm.

"Remember Walden, you have been given a rare opportunity."

Walden despised Peter's ability to get under his skin. Yes, he admittedly made a mistake but he was paying for it daily. Peter cherished any opportunity of pouring vinegar in that wound. In less than two minutes, Peter had won the dogfight of dominance, but Walden was going to make sure he got a few good bites in before he hung up.

"If it works," Walden snapped back, making Peter laugh even more.

"Quantum physics is your field of expertise, not mine, Walden. You've kept to the agreement, haven't told anyone, especially Martha?"

Walden flatly stated, "No."

"Good to see that we understand each other." Peter hung up.

As Walden still held the cell phone up to his ear, a sinking feeling washed over him, it was as if he was standing on the deck of the Titanic just before it hit the iceberg, knowing a series of choices had led him to this moment.

Walden took a deep breath in and slowly released it out, as if surrendering to destiny... something he did not know whether he believed in or not. Reluctantly, he headed up to his office. It was easy for him to blame Peter for everything. However, in reality, his own blind ambition partly fueled his current situation.

Security procedures had changed over the years. Walden remembered the days when a security ID badge to get into the buildings was unheard of. Now without it, no inner access to the building's elevator took place unless, signed in by someone with a lot of political pull.

He swiped his micro chipped badge into a thin credit card device as he walked through the metal detector. The security guard waved Walden through after confirming his face to the ID badge. As he walked to the elevators, Walden briefly noticing the regular guard, Clarence, was not on duty.

The doors shut to the middle elevator. A thought whispered deep from within him. "It has begun." Without notice, the elevator lurched, startling everyone. The small group of men looked at each other with questioning glances, but then the elevator continued its smooth ascent, reassuring everyone's safety.

While the elevator steadily climbed, he felt raw and vulnerable, like a layer of skin was missing; Walden was venturing into the unknown. Today, he was not the man he envisioned himself to be at this stage of his life. Fear meant weakness and he was a man who would walk into any room knowing there was no one mentally stronger than he was. His heightened mental alertness and self-discipline is what gave him his unshakable confidence in any setting.

His father had frequently scolded him, 'Fear is an indicator that we lack experience with success. Successful people are not afraid. They are able to bend, transform, and replace the deafening chatter of doubt that paralyzes movement, to a heightened awareness of knowing that overcomes.'

He had heard this lecture; Walden swears from the moment he was born. These words would replay repeatedly as so many other 'words of advice' that had imprisoned Walden's childhood. He definitely did not radiate knowingness today... so fear was an obvious conclusion.

The well-dressed men in the elevator all nodded towards each another, but no words exchanged. Even after transferring elevators on the 78th floor sky lobby, no one talked.

Three of them, including Walden, exited on the 100th floor. Walden turned and walked left while the other two went right.

The hallway was quiet except for a small group of International Specialists who looked weary after a long overnight shift and appeared very ready to be going home.

Even though Walden felt in an emotional turmoil, he knew how to present himself. He walked with a confident but casual stroll from the elevator to his office. Growing up in a household that had a public figure for a father, and many years of corporate training made Walden a master of presentation.

His executive secretary, Ruth, better known as "Ruthie" by everyone in the office, had not arrived yet. Walden quickly glanced at his watch. She would not be in for another hour, if then. When he spoke to her on the phone yesterday, she sounded terrible so he had told, actually ordered her to take the day off. Ruthie had a mind of her own making her an outstanding executive secretary in Walden's eyes. Nonetheless, given the circumstances, he hoped she listened.

Keeping with his presentation he casually unlocked the door to his office, which he liked to call his glass box. It was a corner office, giving him an impressive view of the city, though he rarely ever looked out his windows. What prompted Walden's nickname "glass box" was that the other two walls to his private quarters were made of smoky beveled glass, providing him with adequate privacy from the rest of the office. Walden dropped his briefcase on his desk and fell back into his leather chair.

Flabbergasted by what was waiting there for him on his desk, left him dazed.

"This package should not be here," Walden whispered to himself.

He had gone to great lengths to have this parcel delivered two weeks ago. So therefore, what was it doing sitting on his desk. Walden began to examine the packet for clues. A big red stamp across it read: *Return to Sender*. The returning of the package meant only one thing. Someone had gotten to his contact. How many days had it been here, waiting unclaimed and vulnerable should the wrong person happen upon it?

Walden calmed his racing thoughts by rationalizing that Ruthie would have kept his office door locked and been a watchdog making it impossible for others to snoop around his office. Still, this was the last place this package needed to be. It was one of the keys to Walden's backup plan. Rather than focusing on what could have been, he refocused his thinking towards his next move. He immediately got up from behind his desk and went over to lock his door.

As he returned to his desk, Walden checked his watch again. He was not sure how much time he actually had left, but he was confident it was not much. His palms were sweaty when he reached for his phone and placed a call to Nicholas' cell.

Dr. Nicholas Lange was in charge of his team of geneticists. Nicholas was spearheading phase two of one of Walden's clinical trials. As the President of Research and Development, Walden had permission to hand pick his entire team of researchers. Over time, Nicholas became one of the few people who truly grew to understand Walden's drive to find one particular chromosome marker that would solve the mystery behind Autism's complex genetic architecture.

Walden tapped his fingers on his desk as he waited for Nicholas to answer.

"Bloody voice mail," he muttered. Without leaving a message, Walden hung up. He sat for a moment, rubbing his hand over his chin thinking. Picking up the receiver again, he had no choice but to place a call to Nicholas' home number.

There were two rings, and then a familiar voice.
"Hello?"
"Is this Emma?" He was brisk and straight to the point.
"Yes."
"It's Dr. Walden Sinclair." Walden could sense Emma's tone shift.
"Nicholas isn't here. Did you try his cell?"

The resonance of the tone in her voice was smooth and assuring, just as it always had been. It somehow had a calming effect on him. Not answering her question, he cleared his throat. "Did Nicholas fly to D.C. like I asked?"

"Yes." She paused. "He left early this morning. Is anything wrong?"

His voice lowered to a soft whisper, unable to stop in time, he uncontrollably uttered, "Wish, Kiss, Suicide." Understanding the ramifications of his slip he choked, "Oh, damn!"

"What did you just say?" She questioned.

Frustrated by this unplanned, uncharacteristic slip of the tongue, Walden felt he had no choice but to abruptly hang up on her. As much as he enjoyed his conversations with Emma, this was no time to get into something of this nature.

Walden was disappointed with himself. He was unraveling. However, what was said, - was said; there was no point to try to undo it now. Emma would eventually understand. He was counting on it.

When he had first encountered Nicholas' wife, Walden had been at a crossroads, one in which there would be no turning back from ever. Meeting her had only convinced him more that he was choosing the right path. Emma was an enigma to him. She had a complex and layered shy intelligence, she was attractive, genuine, and quietly confident, everything he had never imagined a wife in this type of profession could be.

On the other hand, his relationship with his wife Martha was that of rescuing. It began with Walden saving Martha from herself and then from her over-bearing family. He had made a grave mistake when he tricked himself into believing that the feelings he felt of neediness with Martha, were that of true love.

Observing Nicholas and Emma together showed him that he had settled.

Walden had first met Emma with Nicholas at a corporate party of some sort. It was loud, and she had had to lean forward to hear him. She could have pretended, like so many others, that she heard what he was saying but she did not. Emma had a way of treating everyone with respect. He could still remember the way her hair accidentally brushed against his face, and he caught the sweet scent of lavender. Emma was completely unaware of her attractiveness, which made her even more appealing.

Once, when he had taken his son to pick-up some books for a school project, Walden had witnessed Emma at the bookstore she owned. She charismatically worked a crowd of middle-aged bibliophiles into laughter, and then quickly changed gears to inspire a crowd of three-year-olds into a fit of infectious giggles. Emma had a way of putting people at ease and making them smile.

In the professional circle he swam in, a woman like her was nothing more than shark bait. While on the other hand a woman like Martha, born into it, knew how to navigate the waters. At least that is what he liked to console himself with, when he found himself enjoying Emma's company more than was appropriate. It was the sole reason why he kept Nicholas' wife at arm's length away from himself... always.

Walden's however unfortunate short conversation with Emma, had just jogged a memory. He had been feeling there was something that he could not quite put his finger on. In fact, it had been in his dream last night but had somehow slipped away when he woke up. There was something in the vibration of her voice that had triggered him to remember. That memory now validated the choices he had made over the past few weeks.

He yanked out a set of keys from his front pocket and immediately unlocked his bottom desk drawer. Walden then pulled out a large, thick, new brown envelope that was blank, with no company logo on it.

For one brief, second Walden stopped and closed his eyes before beginning to rub them, allowing him to breathe for the first time since he had stepped into his office. He took a deep breath with his mouth open. Then he got up, unlocked his office safe, and grabbed out a sealed envelope.

He hesitated when he returned to his desk; his heart started racing when he grabbed his palm pilot out of his pocket and searched his address book, while turning his computer on. He wrote down the address right next to the words "send to" and was still writing the zip code down when he picked up the phone and requested the in-house messenger. The round-the-clock service was a vital aspect to the corporation with so many international clients and contacts.

Walden placed the envelope from the safe next to the returned package. He hated the idea of placing one person in so much danger. Each piece on their own meant nothing, but the combination of them together, would control the recipient's destiny. He had no choice now. He placed both packages into the anonymous brown envelope.

Walden got up, opened his office door, and waited.

His eyes swept over the paintings against the wall, glad they were only lithographs. He would not be able to live with the thought of being responsible for the destruction of the original oil paintings. His desk was set in the far corner, his back somewhat to the windowing that was glass from the flooring to the roof. Along the bookshelves and filing cabinets, were his latest acquires.

Walden's favorite was a portrait of Lucas Cranach the Elder, it never failed to amuse him when visitors to his office assumed it was a painting of a famous family member. Anyone who knew art would know who it was, especially with the fact that next to the portrait was a blown up copy of the signature of Lucas the Elder. It was a sketch of a winged snake, holding a ruby ring in its mouth, and wearing a red crown. He liked to think the snake was sharing a sly smile.

To the right, the reproduction of Raffaello Sanzio da Urbino's, (better known as Raphael) *School of Athens* was always there supporting him when he looked up from his desk to ponder something or other. He had viewed the original at the

Vatican during his first trip to Rome. During moments of agitation, he would find himself looking at the central figures, Plato and Aristotle and somehow feel centered by the presence of the ancient Greek philosophers.

He had recently obtained a Titian reproduction, (his wife Martha did not want it in the house because she felt uneasy with the dark intensity of it) so now it sat on his bookshelf, leaning against the glass wall. It was the *Allegory of Prudence*, depicting the three ages of man.

There were the heads of three men facing in different directions, believed to be Titian, (the oldest on the left), his son Orazio in the middle, and a younger man (a cousin) on the right. Below the old man, who was facing left, was a wolf, beneath the middle-aged man who was staring straight at the viewer, was a lion, and under the younger man, who was facing right, was a dog. Above the three heads were the words, which when translated read, 'From the experience of the past, the present acts prudently, lest it spoil future actions.'

His son, Walden junior, fondly referred to as Wally, had been the only one to notice that all the artists were from the 16th century. Proud by his son's eagerness to learn about art at an unusually young age, Walden provided every opportunity he could for him. Wally noticed details, which made him smart, but Walden also knew it was hard for the little man, who did not seem to make any friends at school.

Walden nervously tapped his fingers on his desk as he began deleting files on his computer. He inserted a disk that would wipe clean his entire hard drive, and started a program he had been assured, would do some interesting things to the corporate backup servers. He was about to dial the service line again when Mylo knocked on his open office door. His wrinkled shirt not tucked in, along with his sun-bleached hair disheveled and still wet, Mylo started justifying that he had just started his shift.

Walden had heard that Mylo normally surfed out at Montauk before work and was reliably late. The only reason why anyone tolerated him was the fact that his uncle was Doug Mattheus,

VIBRATIONAL PASSAGE

Senior Vice President and Mendelrose's Chief Compliance Officer. Nevertheless, Walden liked Mylo.

Mylo seemed to brood when he read the address for the delivery, which frustrated Walden as he gave him concise instructions and told him he needed to leave right away.

"Can I take this out with my nine a.m. delivery?" Mylo asked.

Walden seemed amused and actually laughed. What he really wanted to tell the kid was that he was unbelievably lazy and ambition was not a dirty word. He was doing Mylo a huge favor that he would not understand until later. Instead, he repeated what he had just said.

"Make sure the only person who signs for it is the person it's addressed to."

"But… what about my nine a.m. deliveries…?" Mylo whined.

"If you leave now, you'll be back in time." Walden glanced down at his watch before he looked back up and shot him a stern look that he was clearly losing his patience with Mylo.

Mylo held his hands up and shook his head, walking backwards out of Walden's office. "Alright, dude, you got it. I'm going," he said in a singsong voice.

Even though Mylo moved at a different pace than the typical New Yorker, Walden knew that he would get the job done.

Just a mere fifteen minutes later, Walden was back to deleting emails, when a loud boom shook everything around him. The vibrational impact shifted everything in his office. A thunderous clap followed by a loud rumbling sound, accompanied by the smell of jet fuel seemed to happen in an instant.

An earthquake-like shake shuddered through him and the building swayed.

The smoky beveled glass walls of his office were shattered, no longer providing privacy.

Walden witnessed the chaos through the jagged shards of glass exposing him now to the rest of the office. He scanned the panic unfolding allowing himself these last few minutes as an observer - knowing that he would soon become a key player.

The sound of the impact was what seemed to rattle everyone around him. It was impossible to describe what it was; it felt like the building had been in a car crash - a deafening metal screech piercing the air around them. Walden could see the confusion on everyone's face - they all seemed to have a sense that something struck the building, but they had no idea of what it was.

As Walden watched, he did not recognize these people, running around like fearful animals in a panic. These were usually self-assured, confident men and women with more than enough arrogance and self-importance to go around. On the contrary now, encircled in chaos and confusion, there seemed to be a democratizing effect where everyone was acting out of survival instincts.

On every available phone, frantic calls were being placed; it was clear from the panic that no one was thinking straight.

The lights were flickering off and on. The evacuation alarm sounded... fire alarms blared all across the floor.

Walden was now sure, it had in fact, begun. Events began to unfold in slow motion.

Everyone flooded the hallways and several people were swearing and shouting.

"Call 9-1-1!"

A group of employees from the finance department was already in a meeting - someone from the meeting room motioned to Walden. It was Ian Hill, President of Mendelrose, he had just cursed him out earlier that morning on the phone.

Ian grunted. "So, where's Peter?"

Walden did not respond.

The struggle of betrayal clearly painted on the infallible Ian's face made Walden turn away. Ian's icy blue eyes, usually cold and ruthless, now filled with water. The half-brothers had always been a dominating duo over the years.

Peter liked moving his people around as if they were chess pieces. The reality was sinking in; once again, Ian reduced to a pawn for his brother's pleasure.

"A hundred floors down." Ian slammed his fist into the wall. "So what are the odds that I'll be able to kick my brother's ass after all of this?"

"Elevators are down!" Someone screamed out.

Ian coughed. "Where did all the smoke come from?"

"You think we should break the windows?" A voice pleaded somewhere amidst the haze.

Ian's assistant, Margaret, joined them in the hall. In one hand, she clutched an unfolded floor map of the north tower, and in the other, she held a red silk scarf over her nose and mouth.

"Maybe we should head up to the roof," Margaret suggested, her voice wavering as she pounded the map to her chest. "There's a helicopter pad up there, right?"

Without warning, she crumpled to the floor, and began to sob uncontrollably.

Walden, witnessing the unraveling and anarchy of chaos increasing around him, stepped forward. In a commanding tone, pulling in anyone within earshot of him, he established leadership right away.

He spoke in a slow, confident, and loud voice. "I need everyone to calmly, follow the emergency evacuation procedures! I need you to calmly, go to your designated exits. If those areas are blocked, I need you to calmly, wait in those areas for rescuers to arrive. Do you understand my directions?"

Walden started hearing the word, "yes" from different areas through the smoke.

It pained him that he was not going to be able to do much more for them.

Even though Walden knew survival was unlikely, he wanted to provide whatever little comfort he could.

Damn you, Peter... he thought, *you and your total disregard for the innocent...*

Walden stepped over to a desk nearby to place a call to his wife. When he got the answering machine, Walden did something he generally never does - he left a message.

"Martha, there's a fire in the building. I am okay. Give my love to Wally and Zoe."

He paused, uncertain on what else to say, and then he hung up.

Smoke was gathering around them, turning the normally brightly lit halls into a foggy London haze.

"The stairs are filled with smoke!" A disembodied voice yelled from somewhere in the gray mist.

"What the...!" Ian stared at his phone and started dialing. "I'm calling 9-1-1 again. This cannot be happening!"

Then something caught everyone's attention. At first, it looked like an object was being tossed out of the window, but then Walden realized someone from one of the floors above them had just jumped out.

A few people ran towards the window, looking down. After a few seconds, they turned away and groaned. By Walden's approximation, it would take about 10 seconds to hit the ground from the upper floors, going at about 150 miles per hour. He had read somewhere about bridge jumpers, how the moment of impact is what finally did them in.

Two more bodies dropped out of the windows to the left of him. It looked like they were linked together, holding hands.

"Oh... my... God...!" A woman nearby cried out.

Walden did not recognize her. She had a shocked expression on her face.

"Maybe he fell," someone said, a feeble attempt to console her.

Walden tried to call home again, but he could not.

"They've jammed the damn phones," he muttered.

He understood that they wanted to control the information that got out, but he still was not exactly sure who all the players were, other than Peter. Helplessly he shut off his phone. No one from the outside could help him now. The smoke continued to stream in through the shattered windows.

It was hot and wet. Sprinklers were going off, but they were useless. The smoke and heat was intense, making everyone cough and struggle for air. Walden pulled his shirt up over his mouth and made his way over to the lab, where he kept an extra inhaler. He was bound to have an asthma attack soon.

Walden's private laboratory was discreet, only a handful of employees knew it even existed. Anyone passing by his lab would understandably assume it was just another executive office - he wondered if the air might be less smoky in there.

VIBRATIONAL PASSAGE

It was difficult not to absorb the heightened panic surrounding him. It was strange, having the knowledge of the inevitable future and not being able to do damn a thing about it. When it came right down to it, staring death in the face was a daunting task, even when expected. He was having these strange thoughts when greasy Larry found him.

Larry was wearing that dreaded black leather jacket he always seemed to have on. His slicked back hair was so full of grease, hence his nickname. He was the man with the keys, he had access to ALL of the offices, but most of all he was the resident clean-up man.

His specialty was mistress-related issues. Find Larry and he will clean up your mess- grease his palms and he will never say a word. Anyone who Larry assisted referred to him gratefully as 'the magician' because he had a way of making your troubles disappear. Larry was proud of that nickname, which is why Walden preferred to call him 'Greasy Larry.'

Larry was all business and filled with self-importance as usual. "The Board just finished their meeting. They're waiting."

"I'll be right there." Walden's answer was curt and to the point, letting Larry know that it was in his best interest to leave immediately. Larry did not budge. He stood there staring at Walden, and motioned his head to the door. He had all the demeanor of a man with a gun. Walden knew he had no choice.

"Walden!" Larry's voice was firm and condescending.

Just to rub him the wrong way, Walden gestured for him to wait.

He turned his back on Larry, found his inhaler, and took one last dose.

Larry stuffed his hands into his jacket pockets and waited. Walden nodded at him when he was finally ready. Larry led him down a series of hallways.

They finally arrived at the end of a hallway. There was no visible doorknob; it appeared to be just a dead end if you did not know where to look. However, there was a thin electric slot.

Larry, as always, made a dramatic show of pulling out a card from his jacket, which he inserted into the nearly invisible slot. The two men waited until they heard the familiar hum and then click. Greasy Larry nodded, and pushed open the wall panel that was actually a door.

Walden walked into the private room that emptied into a discreet boardroom. He remembered the last time he was summoned here and how that act had sealed his fate. Under his breath, he repeated three words over, and over again.

When he placed his hand on the only doorknob, which was located on the internal boardroom's door, he had faith that the seeds of truth he had planted would grow. Walden had set in motion a chain of events so that the right people would be held accountable. He strongly believed that the power of knowledge did not belong to the select few.

He took a deep breath and gradually exhaled, firmly believing; now others will have the truth.

CHAPTER 2

Thousands of miles away in a rural military outpost in Alaska, at the Wavelength Octave Laser for High Frequency Research facility, codenamed "WOLF," transmitters were about to be powered up.

Alaska was the ideal site for a high frequency ionospheric heater because magnetic field lines, which extend to desirable altitudes, intersect the earth in Alaska. In addition, being in a remote region of Alaska, kept this large facility out of plain sight.

Within the entire facility, only the six men in the command control room knew of the plan for today's occurrence. Five of them had just received their orders one hour prior to this moment. Tension and concentration fueled the air, creating a tight pressure for all within the room.

O'Reilly looked down at his watch, "Now, Sir?"

His commander shook his head.

"No," Harris responded. He knew that firing up the array would draw attention to them, and he did not want his mission linked in any way to what was happening at the World Trade Center towers. He wanted to make sure the terrorists got full credit for the events unfolding.

"We fire up when we get the signal."

Harris was watching the twin towers burn on the computer screen in front of him. He saw bodies dropping out of the buildings, but they were just painful distractions. Another computer screen showed a zoomed in view of the North Tower. Everyone was waiting for the green light, and then there it was. Harris watched as panels were pulled away from the windows on the 100th floor.

Manning began grinding his teeth. They had cut it close before, but this time was different. His fingers twitched as he anxiously awaited his orders. He was not quick with his fingers, but today he had to be.

Harris nodded, "Power up."

Spiked alive as soon as the order left Harris's lips, the room was fully vibrating. As though a racehorse had just been released from the gate, the energy pulsed through the room, an electrical turbulence that was about to get even stronger. Calculations for this exact date and time took precise planning months in advance by a small team of specialists.

High Frequency, HF, Transmitter was switching on. At that moment, 180 antennas sparked to life over a span of about 35 acres in rural Alaska. About 3,600 kilowatts sizzled, sending out a high frequency signal ray. The antenna array programmed for the World Trade Center coordinates: 40° 42' 42" N / 74° 0' 45" W was up and operating as planned.

Engineers who were working feverously executed the computer commands - the classified series of numbers pre-programmed into the system awaited activation. It was not something they did every day, but it was not the first time they were doing it. Right now, it was just a race against time.

Ironic, since it was time they were about to alter.

Large energy emission drew microscopic attention. Today would be no different. The WOLF facility, closely watched by the locals, environmentalists, researchers, and of course the conspiracy theory crowd, would draw notice.

Timing would mean everything.

Harris paced back and forth across the command center, watching his men perform their function. He observed as

VIBRATIONAL PASSAGE

O'Reilly, with one executed computer command, wiped out the entire communications systems in New York City, while keeping the military's own communications systems up and running. This was phase two of information management protocol established an hour ago.

Viewing occurred at four strategic locations on the screen in front of them via satellite. It was a precise and controlled event - one with no margin for error. Molecular modifications according to each of their 'assets' were made by a team of specifically trained experts at the Texas facility. There were 33 assets in all.

When each of the chosen men had traveled to the Texas facility for testing, their particular molecules or molecular configurations were isolated through sets of calculations for their possible role in the temporal distortion field.

At 0847, Harris gave what would be his last and final order.

"Execute transport command."

The clicking of keys echoed, as security codes entered one by one, and each of his men shouted, "Check!" After the fifth, "Check" Harris placed the call.

They all concentrated on the screens in front of them when everything went to shit.

CHAPTER 3

In the boardroom awaited a group of influential men, CEOs, CFOs, Presidents from the most powerful industries who most days controlled the fate of millions, with the mere sweep of their pen. Top corporate world leaders - each of them billionaires.

A tall, slender bald man stepped forward. "Gentlemen, you have all been briefed."

He looked down at his watch. "When the next impact occurs, it will be time."

In the final preparations just weeks before, instructions to continue their daily routines included aspects such as, not to take out any last minute life insurance policies.

Phil Evans, Founder and CEO of one of the top international bond trading firms stood up.

"But how can you guarantee 'where' we will jump to?"

"There are three possible destinations. Your thoughts will determine 'where and when' that will be, so focus, and choose your objective wisely. This is no different from your earlier briefings. You all have the access numbers to the bank accounts each of you has established and the information with your new identities.

Each of you has been micro chipped with this information embedded behind your left ear lobe. You are here by selection.

This new beginning means there is no going back, no contacting your loved ones. Today, your past no longer exists. You all start with a clean slate. Earn it."

He took a sip of water, cleared his throat, while he turned and glared at Phil.

Walden noticed Frank Hyde across the room and understood why he was there. Frank had shared with him over countless martinis about that fateful day in July when Frank had been working in his office at home. The nanny was watching his son outside by the pool.

Frank had heard the splashing around, and had even considered stopping work to take a dip in the swimming pool himself. However once again, he had gotten side tracked with his work, until he heard the piercing scream from their nanny. A sound, he said he would never forget.

When he rushed outside, there was blood flowing everywhere and as their nanny tried to pull his son from the pool, she hysterically explained that she had only left for a moment to get the towels. The autopsy would confirm that his son had hit his head from falling or jumping into the family's pool.

Frank never forgave himself for not being there in time. His son's death was preventable - only if his emails had not been so important, he outwardly tortured himself. Walden knew exactly where he was going to jump to, and when, since Frank never forgave himself and neither did his now ex-wife. Walden watched as Frank stared down at the worn wallet-sized photo of his son that he was holding in the palm of his hand.

The bald man, who had yet to introduce himself, began passing out thin pieces of bark. He explained that the bark was retrieved from a Birch tree planted in a specific location, but he elaborated no further. Each man handed a piece of bark and a black Mont Blanc fountain pen set to work. The bald man placed an oxygen mask over his mouth and took a deep breath in. Then he began to instruct the group.

"There is a specific order in which this must take place. What you are about to experience is pure science based in quantum physics combined with sacred ancient knowledge. The ritualistic steps create a precise vibration, opening the passage. The higher vibration married with the magnetic pulse will ensure a successful jump. Each of you will write your last wish upon the Birch bark. This Birch is a symbol of Pentecost."

The bald man opened a bible and began reading portions of an earmarked chapter.

"And suddenly there came a sound from heaven as of a rushing mighty wind, and it filled the entire house where they were sitting. And there appeared unto them cloven tongues like as of fire, and it sat upon each of them.... the multitude came together, and were confounded, because that every man heard them speak in his own language."

The bald man paused, and looked up at the men in the room.

"Then they that gladly received his word were baptized: and the same day there were added unto them about three thousand souls."

He paused once again and then glanced at each of the men around the room.

"As John was baptized by water, so Peter was baptized by fire. Consider today your baptismal by fire, and may the Holy Spirit be with you." He made the sign of the cross and then gestured with his right hand for everyone to begin.

Walden quietly groaned, '*oh please*,' and rolled his eyes.

Why did people always have to drag religion into everything? He looked around the room and could not believe any of these men even kept one of the Ten Commandments. Yet here they were, comforted by faith. He hated the hypocrisy of it all.

Pens placed down, one after the other, indicated to the bald man that it was time for him to hand each of them a gold coin along with a silk pouch. The small bag attached to a braided, white silk cord was soft to the touch. Each man placed the bark into the pouch and hung it around his neck as instructed.

"The gold coin is your magnet," he explained.

"You will notice the various symbols on the coin and most certainly recognize a few. They will create the vibration you need for the jump. The coin will pull you in the direction of your thoughts. Our friends at WOLF will open the portal in a few moments."

Three months ago, taken by armed escort Walden visited a lab out in Brookhaven on Long Island. Once there, briefing on Operation Phoenix began. An all-star team consisting of a nuclear physicist, a psychologist and a medical doctor educated him on the process and procedures of Operation Phoenix. Walden participated in a series of extremely vigorous tests that took several days to complete.

Based on those findings, he received a coded message indicating his selection; it felt as if he had won the Nobel peace prize. In the weeks to follow, he learned that Operation Phoenix was a project based in technology from quantum physics, the experiments of Nikola Tesla, Albert Einstein's special relativity theory, and captured Nazi documents.

The government had discovered a way to produce electromagnetic fields to warp time. Assured that this was not a Philadelphia Project replication, Walden was still not completely convinced. Nevertheless, animals were the first test subjects before humans to demonstrate no psychological and physical side effects from the time jumps that were occurring.

A private jet flew Walden to Pearl Harbor in Hawaii where he toured of one of the time portals. He had boarded a large white dome set on a giant oil rig platform, and was provided with a private tour of the facility as it was towed out of the harbor and out to sea. His tour guide, a surprisingly friendly and eager Colonel Downing, explained that once there was no land in sight, the live demonstration would take place.

If they were too close to land, it would jam communication signals, and they had encountered a few mishaps where there were reports of computer servers crashing and garage doors mysteriously opening and closing on the occasions when they powered up too close to land, bringing unwelcomed attention.

To provide proof of what they were doing, Walden brought five unique and personal objects to the scheduled demonstration as per Colonel Downing's request. Instructed to place those objects in an envelope and seal it, Walden then handed a young officer the sealed envelope. A senior-looking officer placed the order for the facility to power up.

Downing proudly explained the science behind what he referred to as the 'jump.' Most physicists had always considered time travel impossible, because the amount of energy required to manipulate a wormhole would be too immense. Still, 'they' had found a way to harness the energy from solar flares in the ionosphere, and precisely send it to any location on the globe, thus, creating a vortex utilizing the earth's grid lines.

The high frequency transmitter located in Alaska would provide all the energy required.

Downing issued an order to begin.

A low hum began to echo throughout the massive, circular dome.

The young officer, referred to simply as "LT", received instructions to enter a glass-encased room, which was about the size of a tiny elevator. A flash of light followed another order issued, and the officer had disappeared.

Downing clarified that the glass room was merely a visual aid, nothing more. While the coordinates of where the officer was jumping to was predetermined, he also needed to focus his thoughts, so that his molecular vibration would not collapse the vortex.

Exactly three minutes and thirty-three seconds later, LT reappeared.

The envelope was no longer in his hands.

LT pulled his pockets inside out to show that he was not hiding the envelope, and opened his right hand to reveal a gold coin. A series of numbers along with symbols, engraved on the surface of the coin caught Walden's attention. Downing smiled and ordered LT to hand the coin over to him.

It was hot to the touch. Downing described to him that LT had traveled two hours back in time. LT's instructions were to place the sealed envelope in a designated area in Walden's New York laboratory.

Downing turned to Walden and directed him to call someone at his lab to confirm whether the envelope was in fact there.

Walden quickly took the cell phone from Downing and dialed. The only person at the lab that came to mind for him was Nicholas. He trusted that Nicholas would not ask questions. Nicholas was a master at the art of being discreet. Following the directions from LT regarding the location, he asked Nicholas to open the top drawer of the filing cabinet closest to the lab entrance, and look for a sealed envelope. Walden waited as he listened to Nicholas slide open the metallic drawer.

"Got it, boss, what do you want me to do with it?"

Walden asked Nicholas to confirm the contents in the envelope.

"Let's see here, it looks like I've got your car keys, a wine label, a photo of Zoe and Wally," Nicholas chuckled. "There's that tie clip you used the wear, the one with the honey bee on it."

There was a pause. "I'm not quite sure what this is. It is a torn piece of folder paper, with a sketch of what looks like a snake... no, maybe a dragon. I'm not certain; it's too blurry to tell."

"It's a dragon," Walden whispered. "Wally drew it," he paused. "Thank you just put the envelope back in the drawer. I'll be at the office by the end of the week and touch base with you tomorrow."

"Ok boss," Nicholas responded.

Walden hung up the phone and nodded. This was no hoax, and no sleight of hand, there was no possible way they could have gotten those five items to New York in three minutes. He was convinced, and for the first moment in a very long time, he was scared.

A proud smile stretched across Colonel Downing's face.

"Enjoy your stay in Hawaii, Dr. Sinclair. Believe me. Your life as you know it will never be the same."

That demonstration felt like years ago. Walden scanned the boardroom, knowing that each selected member present went through a classified vetting process. It was clear to everyone that their presence was a privilege, and one that came with a hefty price tag, at that. Peter had covered the cost for Walden. Nevertheless, from what Walden had heard, each man in the room had "donated" five million dollars, just for the chance to be there. Operation Phoenix was quite an expensive endeavor.

The bald man continued, "Focus on the words you have written, because they have now become your compass. And as you've been programmed, your thinking is your steering wheel."

Each member in the room received a set of objects, items, to visualize in their dreams the night before. They also were all required to listen to a series of CDs played in a specific order, while they slept. This music restructured the mind to respond to different frequencies.

The sound of a chain rattling against the mahogany doors and then a series of four clicks from heavy locks made everyone turn their attention to the loud noise.

A dark wall panel was pulled away to reveal four glass paneled windows. Two of the window panels were slid back, pulling wind and smoke into the room. Handkerchiefs were appearing; the real smokers among them seemed to cough the most. Then there was a large explosion.

The loud rumbling reverberation erupted, shaking the room and all the men in it. Whatever it was, it was something with such force that it could shake a tower 110 stories high. The panels of glass shattered, sending chards flying everywhere.

The bald man pulled out what looked like a military issued phone, one usually seen in combat zones, and answered it. "Harris. Assets are ready for transport," he informed the other person on the line.

He pointed towards the open windows. "This window is now active," he shouted over the gusting wind. "It is your portal through space and time. The gold coin will pull you towards your destination. I cannot stress enough. Center your thoughts! Or you will not make your mark."

Frank Hyde was the first one to go. He pulled out the piece of white Birch bark from the pouch hanging around his neck. Frank cradled the thin woody paper in his hands, reading the handwritten words scrawled out in black. He gently kissed before carefully cradling it, and placed it back into the silk pouch.

Then, Frank walked out of the window, like he was leaving the room and that was that. He did not scream, he did not look back, there was a blast of light, and then he was gone. The men were choking from the smoke, as one by one, they jumped.

"See you on the other side," Phil voiced to Walden.

Phil patted Walden on the shoulder; his damp hands betrayed the tears he had just wiped away from his face. Walden wished he had not done that. He was fine with how their relationship was. Now, Walden had to view Phil in a new light – someone that was capable of having feelings other than his own self-importance.

Walden stood at the window, staring out. He would always joke with his wife Martha that the architect who designed the twin towers was a kindred spirit because he too, was afraid of heights. Despite this, and the fact that his office was on the 100th floor, something about the repeating pattern of narrow glass windows and steel stripes made him feel safe.

When Yamasaki had designed the towers, the critics had blasted him. They called the giant towers, a blight, an eyesore, and criticized its minimalism. Yet, in the same case as the Eiffel Tower, the public quashed the critics eventually. Just as the Parisians had come to love their Eiffel Tower that became a symbol of national pride, so did the World Trade Center come to represent an unmistakable fixture in the New York City skyline.

What he did not share with Martha though, was why he really liked the architect. This man was an outsider, constantly criticized by architectural critics, despite the fact that the public at large seemed to like his buildings. He was a Japanese-American whose architectural talent had kept him out of the internment camps during World War II, and that was something Walden had to admire. Walden's grandfather had not been so lucky, who, within weeks of being transported to an internment camp in Colorado, had died of pneumonia, leaving behind his wife to raise three children alone.

Walden took a deep breath and coughed with an asthmatic wheeze. The path he had been on for the past five years had brought him to this point. Somehow, he knew that it was not finished yet.

He pulled off his favorite ring, pressing his family crest against his skin. Walden always liked the way it embossed itself onto his skin for just a few seconds, and then disappeared. He pressed it against his lips, whispered a few words, kissed it, and then tossed the gold ring that had been with him throughout his adult life into the gray willowing clouds of smoke.

Walden was amused for a moment by the thought of whether jumping out of a doomed, burning building technically qualified as suicide. It was either die of asphyxiation or jump.

Whatever the answer was, it did not really matter. Like all the others before him, he pulled out his own piece of white bark from the pouch hanging around his neck. Walden read the words he had written, and touched the bark to his lips, then slipped it back into the silk pouch.

At 10:27, Walden made his final decision of the day.

Bright lights surrounded him as he jumped.

CHAPTER 4

A pulse is what they would later remember it as, a temporary glitch.

"What the...?" Commander Harris shouted. "Where are they?"

"I- I- I don't know, sir," O'Reilly stammered.

They were all looking around at each other, shouting, "Where are they?"

The answers of, "I don't know," resoundingly echoed throughout the room.

"Shit! Shit! Shit! What the hell is going on guys?" Harris screamed. "Please tell me someone knows where they are!"

"I'm still locked onto ten assets, sir. I can see their molecular signature." Manning pointed at the screen in front of him to a series of numbers.

"But I can't get a visual on them. I do not know where they are. But they're there," he jammed his finger at the screen.

"Shit!" Harris slammed his fist into a keyboard shattering it, sending keys flying.

No one ducked.

They were all too busy checking their calculations, making sure they were not the one who had made a mistake. Thirty-three assets were no longer visible on the screen at location one. The locations two, three, and four, were void of any activity. It was impossible. All but ten of them had vanished.

Harris was blaring at his men, demanding answers.

"Maybe it's only temporal, sir," Manning suggested.

"Were the dB over 200?"

Vibrational decibels (dB) turn the human internal organs into fluid when above 200 dB.

"That's a negative!" O'Reilly shouted. "If they were just dead, we'd see them, if they made it to their target point, we'd see them, if they jumped back or forward in time, we'd see them. They are all tagged and tracked. There is no reason we shouldn't be able to see them!"

The commander's rage filled the room; no one dared move from their post.

"Was there a change in the ionospheric condition?" Harris barked.

"That's a negative, sir," Manning quickly answered.

"Please assure me," Harris bellowed, "That we did not, and have not cut it too close."

Clearly, by the way, the men were glancing at one another it was a rhetorical question.

The Chief Information Officer (CIO) rushed into the command room.

"Sorry to bother you, commander."

Harris raised his eyebrows and stared him down.

"Wilson. You are standing in front of me because...? That takes you away from the phones for what reason?"

It was protocol that whenever the station was required to power up, there was round the clock phone coverage and the CIO was on call. His job was to calm and assure the public that it was just another experiment occurring based on the ideal ionospheric conditions.

Usually, when the station powered up at full capacity, the phone lines immediately lit up, some demanding assurances of safety, some reporting interferences, while others spouting mind and weather control conspiracy theories. During other times, when lower frequency usage occurred, a basic pre-recorded message provided a statement that the transmitter was not in use.

"Commander, the senator is on the phone demanding to speak to you," Wilson stated.

"Does it look like I'm in a position to talk to him right now?" Harris snapped.

"I just thought," Wilson, stammered.

"Don't!" Harris shouted. "Man the phones, period. Maybe the senator needs to be more concerned with what's going on in New York."

Wilson stood at attention, but did not move.

"Get back to your station!" Harris pointed to the door.

Harris took a deep breath in, sighed, and shook his head. He knew in that moment that everyone in the room had just become expendable.

CHAPTER 5

Neat rows of colorful tulips cheerfully lined the cobblestone pathway to the church the Lyceum family had been attending for generations. Martha Lyceum-Sinclair caught her breath, not bothering to hold back the tears. Her eyes were red, and stung when she dabbed at them with tear-soaked tissues. She stepped into the church, remembering how spring was Walden's favorite time of year.

Martha scanned the standing room only church unable to distinguish who was who, among the friends and families attending the service. Martha liked the fact that the church was standing room only. To her it meant that Walden was receiving the admiration and respect he deserved. Although, none of them understood what it was like being married to Walden. Martha's mind began to wander back to the first time they met.

She had been lonely and isolated because she had grown up with a different disposition than her other family members. They were ruthless. At a very young age, Martha learned to stay out of their way when they locked onto winning or obtaining something.

Then one day he walked into her life. He, he was the one that saw and heard her for who she was, rather than what she was expected to be. Even from the first moment, she felt his protective intensity wrap around her. Like so many other women, she had been immediately attracted to Dr. Walden Sinclair's athletic physique, and overwhelming mental strength... he was a man who radiated confidence.

She was not even supposed to be there that night. It was an important fundraiser for Autism at the Metropolitan Museum of Art. At the last minute, her father was pulled away on emergency business and could not attend. He was the one who usually went to these events, the one who presented the check - a generous donation for Autism research, a cause Martha's family heavily funded.

Her father, Robert Lyceum, was over six feet tall, blue eyed, tanned, suave and smooth, a clear representation of their family's style. Martha on the other hand, petite just under five feet with raven black hair and the deepest emerald green eyes, possessed ivory skin that would burn at even the thought of going out in the sun. She hated getting dressed up and having to appear before a crowd of people, but her father had forced her to.

At that time in her life, she never quite understood why the family had taken on the Autism cause with such intensity. As cliché as it was, oftentimes for Martha, ignorance really was bliss.

Martha had been scared and nervous - her ball gown was plain and simple. Unlike the other women attending, she did not have a stylist and makeup artist to pull her look together for public appearances. As usual, Martha felt like an outsider who did not belong. After several glasses of champagne to calm her nerves, she thought she would be able to make it through the night - until she bumped into Dr. Walden Sinclair.

Actually, she had tripped on her gown, and then stepped on his foot with her heel, causing an ungraceful slip backwards, slamming her shoulder into the floor. Stunned by the fall, she was unable to get up right away. People around her asked if she needed help, but he, *HE*, was the only one who reached his hand out to her and actually helped her up. Finally, someone noticed her. One of the beautiful and smart people had not only noticed her, but also rescued her.

Walden was a research scientist on the Human Genome Project, one who she had read about from her father's files. He was one of the finalists on the list she helped her father cultivate for possible recruitment. It was her task to research possible candidates for her father. Except, this was the first time she had ever been face to face with someone whom she had profiled in a detailed report.

She knew Walden held double PhD's, one in Genetics and the other in Quantum Physics. She, on the other hand, struggled to decide what to do with her Master's in Philosophy. The thought of a job interview terrified her - which meant she would most likely continue the personnel research she did for her father and the family.

Martha was instantaneously drawn to the fact that Walden had an indescribable presence. Walden knew precisely what he wanted and who he was. He wore his confidence with ease. His focus was to change the world, while her objective was not to bring shame to the family name.

Dr. Walden Sinclair's genetic research was just faintly gaining a reputation in certain circles. He provided groundbreaking insight into genetic sequencing that did not exist prior to his unorthodox interpretation of human gene function.

When he had pulled her up onto her feet, he lifted her with ease. He had a look in his eyes that surprisingly made her feel instantly safe.

"Are you alright?" He had asked, still holding her forearm and her hand in his.

"Thank you," was all she could say.

He announced to the crowd of onlookers. "Thank you for your concern, she's fine." He did not release his hold on her and their eyes remained locked.

A gentle tingling sensation washed over the surface of her skin, unleashing a fluttering of butterflies inside her, by the way he had taken charge of the situation. Here he was smoothing over the shame she had just brought upon the family by her awkward fall.

"I'm Walden, Walden Sinclair," he offered.

She responded, "I'm Martha Lyceum."

"Of course you are," he teased. "Your family is hosting this event," he whispered as he leaned in with a grin.

Her face flushed. Trying to hide that she was still embarrassed, Martha looked away. She was so grateful that he did not leave her, but rather he moved the conversation to other topics. Martha gladly responded to Walden's kindness. In no time, he had her laughing, and her clumsy toppling to the floor was just a faint memory.

Martha studied Walden during their polite exchanges. Almost guessing what she was wondering, he added into the conversation with finesse that his heritage was a cocktail of sorts... of Swedish, French, Japanese, with a twist of Italian.

Whatever he was, she just thought he was the most handsome man she had ever met. Martha somehow knew that he was talking to her because he probably felt sorry for her, but she did not care. Being in Walden's presence for the rest of the evening was just like being in a fairytale for her. He had not brought a companion to the event to pull him away from her, so Dr. Walden Sinclair was all hers.

The boom of loud church organ music startled Martha back to her husband's memorial service.

Her father touched her arm and said, "It's time to take your seat."

Martha blinked away the tears, as she was jarred back to the blur of people surrounding her. He led her to the front pew, which indicated that it was time to start the service.

She rearranged her dress and fussed with her hat. Martha had spent weeks selecting the perfect black hat for this occasion because she felt she could hide behind the black veil that covered her eyes. Today, she hated the hat, she hated everything, and all she wanted to do was be at home with all the curtains drawn, blocking out the world, the pain.

Martha dabbed a tissue at her pale green eyes that were no longer a deep emerald. In fact, her eyes looked almost gray today. At the front of the church, there were enormous wreaths sent from family, friends, and colleagues, the grandest one looked ostentatious - it had come from her family's Mendelrose Corporation.

A large stone sculpture of Jesus hanging from a cross hung over the wreaths, Jesus with bowed head overlooking the flowers of Walden's past. There were no survivors from the Mendelrose Corporation offices in the World Trade Center.

The company's core group of researchers was intact because they were housed at the laboratory on Long Island, not the World Trade Center. Walden's was the last and final memorial of all the company employees presumed dead from 9/11. The lack of a body was what made it next to impossible to seek closure for her. It was the "what ifs" that plagued those left behind like Martha. As crazy as it sounded she had waited until spring for the service, holding out hope that they would still find Walden's remains.

Martha glanced down at her son, Walden, junior, Wally. He quietly sat beside her. She had barely noticed him up until this moment. It was unbearable for her to face the fact that he would now have to make sense of the world without a father, and he was only nine.

A tinge of guilt pulled on her as she faintly remembered promising her son a hug this morning. Like so many other things, she did not mean to forget about it, but focusing was next to impossible these days. Out of her two children, she knew he would somehow be okay. The one thing Martha admired best about Wally was his resilience - it was something he clearly inherited from his father.

Martha watched as her children's longtime nanny, Miranda, shuttled Zoe in and out of the church, trying to hush her. Zoe, who had just recently turned four, kept screeching, "Daddy," and pointing up at the framed photo of her father at the front of the church. Normally, Martha would be beside herself by Zoe's embarrassing behavior, but today, completely numb, she just did not care. The meds were doing their job.

When Martha did feel she felt intense loneliness, anger, self-pity, loathing, guilt. These carousels of emotions kept her a prisoner from moving forward. Martha's mind was in a reality of thick, dark tar molasses. She told grief counselors what they wanted to hear and they in return gave her what she needed, refills.

Martha kept fidgeting; she could not stop her mind from wandering from one random fragment of memory to another. Flashes of this and that, of faces from the past and present, she tried desperately to focus on the pastor whose voice droned on as he read ongoing bible passages to offer comfort. The pastor said something regarding love, triggering another memory of Walden and that first night when Martha sealed their fate by revealing some of her family's closely guarded secrets.

To this day, she remained astonished by her openness regarding that exclusive information she shared on their first magical night together. She did not know what would happen to her, if the wrong family members discovered what she had disclosed.

Out of all the possible candidates attending the event, she had stumbled into Walden. After that one singular embarrassing moment, she suddenly realized just how lonely her world was, and would continue to be without him. Martha had never allowed herself to want anything or anyone. It was the only way to keep safe. Wanting was neediness; a weakness that family members like Uncle Peter could use to destroy her.

This was different for Martha; she wanted to give Walden the edge that would secure his placement at the Mendelrose Corporation. He was no longer one dimensional, only existing in a file, he was now all six feet two inches of everything she ever needed or wanted standing right before her.

If Martha had not been a bit tipsy from champagne, she would not have been able to open up to him that night. Normally, she would nurse one glass of champagne, but on this night, she had had three.

He was explaining how he was searching for answers that kept eluding him.

Walden leaned in and lowered his voice, "I just need to find the key. You see, there is no commonality with children diagnosed with Autism, there might be a common reaction, but sensory processing triggers appear to be different among them, demonstrating that there is no scientific evidence linking obvious patterns."

He chuckled. "You know who has my answer?" Walden lowered his voice, "The Nazi scientists who abandoned Hitler, and who we snuck into the U.S. after World War II."

Even though trained since childhood on how to hold a poker face, the alcohol had rendered Martha vulnerable in front of Walden. She just did not care. In any other situation, she would have fled. Her face flushed red, for the third time in front of him that night.

"What?" She stammered, not quite believing she had heard him right.

"You know," Walden added, "all those human experiments. I bet those monsters discovered a thing or two about human genetics that have not been mainstreamed."

Regaining her composure, she tilted her head in a coy manner and smiled. "I wouldn't exactly call them monsters."

She was surprised when he did not flinch.

Walden retorted, "They say the secrets are sitting in a vault somewhere in America, waiting to be utilized by the right, *like*-minded person."

"Perhaps," she replied, clearly peaking Walden's interest.

"Some believe those files," he added, "are in the hands of one of the world's most influential families. A family who, let's say hosts events like this one." Walden raised his glass of champagne out to an imaginary audience.

Martha giggled, but did not answer him.

For the first time that evening, the tables were turned, and now Martha was the one holding out her hand to pull Walden forward in his research, placing him in a unique position.

Walden wanted access to those files, and now Martha was handing him the key.

There was a silence between them, but it was not awkward, like how it usually is when people back up away from her finding some excuse to be somewhere else.

He was fearless.

Walden leaned his head to the side and stared into her eyes for a few moments, and then he broke out into a smile that lit up the room. It was as if he knew her family secret, and he was okay with it. She did not panic about her slip.

Actually, it felt like they now shared a secrete place of safety. She did not judge his raw ambition and he did not judge the sins of her family's past. They continued to share the rest of the evening, discussing all sorts of things, but never returning to their initial conversation. In fact, even after getting married, there never was a reason to revisit that conversation. An 'understanding' forged between them. She would provide him access to the information he was searching for, and he would never have to ask for it.

The booming voice of the minister pulled her back to Walden's memorial service.

"In the name of the Father, the Son, and the Holy Spirit... Amen."

The minister closed the bible and introduced the first speaker. Martha dug into her pocket, searching for an unused, dry handkerchief.

Walden's boss, who was also Martha's uncle, Peter Lyceum, stood at the podium. Peter was clearly a foot taller than the priest was, and had to readjust the microphone before beginning. He had a way of gaining control and leading during uncomfortable situations. Before beginning the eulogy, he ran his slender manicured fingers through his short, blonde hair, placed both hands on the side of the podium, while leaning forward into the microphone.

Peter had a dramatic effect whenever he presented. Crisp, blue eyes scanned the audience as if he knew everyone intimately and was acknowledging them directly. He quickly nodded in her direction causing her skin to crawl.

Then Peter commenced his eulogy to Walden.

With her head lowered, she peeked around taking in the audience who seemed entranced by Uncle Peter's charismatic speaking skills. His low voice hummed reassuring the mourners that Walden was in a much better place now.

Uncle Peter was the definition of pure evil, Martha thought to herself. He was a monster. If only this audience knew how he possessed the cruel ability to get new mothers to poison their babies, and not be accountable. She had witnessed this firsthand in business dealings by Uncle Peter in South Africa. The company lawyers were still cleaning up that mess.

Martha chose to evade her Uncle Peter even more these days. She avoided him because she did not have what it took anymore to ward off his usual coldness. During their last conversation, his way of comforting her was by telling her that life is full of painful experiences followed by death.

CHAPTER 6

Since the incident on 9/11, the Wavelength Octave Laser for High Frequency Research facility, codenamed WOLF, had been on lockdown.

Sadly, Harris was correct. All the members in the control room that day were in fact, expendable. The Chief Information Officer, (CIO) Wilson, was the only one who survived with knowledge of events that day, not that he knew anything beyond that. Within a week of the incident, a series of freak accidents had claimed the lives of Harris and his entire team.

Wilson shifted in his chair, tapping his pen continuously on his desk, nervously awaiting Mr. Brown.

The young CIO had heard through a reliable source that Mr. Brown had appeared at WOLF sometime in the evening of 9/11. This same source had also let Wilson know that Brown was part of the unit originally assembled to execute Operation Paperclip.

Wilson was uniquely aware of Paperclip because he was born and raised in Texas. His father, an aeronautic engineer working at NASA, had worked closely with many rocket specialists who had emigrated under the supervision of the U.S. military from Germany following World War II.

Wilson had read dozens of books written on the subject, as well as the odd few underground publications on Paperclip. He was surprised there was never a public outcry despite all the evidence that was out there. Wilson's father had explained that NASA would not be where it was today without German technology and expertise.

It shamed Wilson that his father was so sympathetic to the ex-Nazis, who frequently came over for family barbeques. On the contrary, the advancement of science and technology meant more to the senior Wilson than politics, and certainly overrode past sins even if it included racial atrocities.

Operation Paperclip, a recruitment program of German scientists by the United States in the aftermath of World War II, had begun under the code name, 'Overcast.' From the beginning of Allied Occupation, the U.S. Joint Chiefs of Staff (JCS) managed to capture engineers who had worked on the German V-2 rocket program.

Since U.S. immigration laws forbade any former Nazi Party official entry into the country, President Truman had authorized Operation Paperclip on the condition that only "nominal" Nazis who had not committed any war crimes receive entrance into the country. Wilson's father had explained that the name Operation Paperclip was in reference to the paperclips used to attach the scientists' new identities.

Under the top-secret program, false employment and fictional political biographies created identities for the specialists, expunging their Nazi party memberships from public record. Among the Germans brought to the U.S. were nuclear physicist Werner Heisenberg and rocket scientist Wernher von Braun.

Von Braun would later go on to become the director of NASA's Marshall Space Flight Center and the chief architect of the Saturn V launch vehicle, the super booster that would make America's first launch to the moon a reality.

As the story went, on the eve of Germany's defeat, von Braun had fled the V-2 rocket plant located in Nordhausen, an underground complex built in the Harz Mountains of central Germany. Von Braun had relocated and hid truckloads of files, after that he had escaped before allied forces reached the plant. When the Soviets arrived, they took over the factory for occupation. Ultimately, however, the American military would claim von Braun - and the research he had secreted away.

Hubertus Strughold, once referred to as the 'father of space medicine' was also cleared for work in the U.S. and worked with NASA. Documents from the Nuremberg War Crimes Tribunal would later embarrassingly surface, linking Strughold to the human experiments at Dachau and Auschwitz.

More than 700 former Nazi engineers and their families moved into the U.S. under Paperclip. Those specialists received high-ranking positions on the cutting-edge defense and aerospace projects. Operation Paperclip continued during the Cold War era with the purpose of keeping the German technology out of the Soviet Union's hands.

Even though the American politicians guaranteed the people that, Paperclip, decommissioned and disbanded, was anything but that. On the contrary, the unit pushed even deeper into secrecy so that the American taxpayer could never discover that their own government had deceived them once again.

Wilson knew he thought about things excessively, to the point that he would get angry for days. He felt betrayed by his government but here he was working directly for his betrayer. Wilson bolted out of his chair when Mr. Brown marched into his office; he looked as if he were walking in formation, flanked by invisible soldiers.

Mr. Brown, clearly a code name, was five foot eight and stocky. On the contrary stocky, as in someone extremely fit from ongoing physical training. Wilson tried not to stare at the scars that covered Mr. Brown's face and arms. One particular scar on his left arm was clearly from a healed bullet wound.

Wilson stood at attention. "Welcome, Sir," he was not quite sure whether to salute Mr. Brown. "I'm unsure of protocol, Sir," Wilson stammered. "Am I to salute you?" Wilson knew he just had to stop talking, but this man made him so nervous.

Mr. Brown stood at attention with his hands clasped in front of him. He stared Wilson down, but did not respond.

Unclear of what to do next, Wilson stuttered even more. "Wh-wh-where would you like to begin, Sir?"

Mr. Brown stated with no emotion, "Explain to me what wasn't in your report."

"From the events on 9/11...?"

"That's correct," Mr. Brown nodded.

At that point, Wilson offered him a chair. "Would you like to sit down, Sir?"

Mr. Brown's intensity filled the CIO's tiny office.

"Walk with me," he commanded the CIO.

Wilson was relieved and temporarily freed from the overbearing tension that was boxing him into his own office. Wilson quickly came out from behind his desk and followed Mr. Brown out of his room. His relief quickly replaced with fear, as he wondered if he was standing out as a last loose strand in the cleanup.

Growing up exposed to how classified protocol played out, he was relying on the information he held back, which he believed would save his life. He had witnessed first-hand how the German scientists received safe passage because they had what the U.S. military wanted... knowledge of technology more advanced than anything America possessed. His father had taught him well... knowledge is power.

Almost reading his mind, Mr. Brown stated, "I require you to show me around and retrace your steps exactly as you recall."

As they stepped outside of his office, Wilson followed Mr. Brown out into the empty corridor. For a brief moment, he was free from Mr. Brown's microscopic scrutiny, allowing Wilson to be able to work through some of his paralyzing fear. He was finally able to take a deep breath.

CHAPTER 7

Emma Lange was so glad that this would be the last of a series of funerals and memorial services that had kept her in an ongoing place of darkness for several months. Just when Emma felt like she was climbing out of a black pit of grieving, she was required to attend yet another memorial service. She felt guilty about her selfish thoughts as she watched her husband Nicholas, lean in to give Walden's widow Martha Sinclair a comforting hug.

Fighting back tears from witnessing Martha's pain, Emma stared up at the rose vines weaving through the wooden trellis above them. She then politely looked back at the long receiving line behind them, which wound around the perimeter of the church as Martha and Nicholas exchanged a few words quietly.

This moment was just another reminder that it could easily have been her husband, instead of Walden. What if...what if Walden had not sent Nicholas on that business trip? Emma was emotionally exhausted by the 'what ifs' she tortured herself with at every one of these services for Nicholas' lost colleagues.

Nicholas gave Martha one last tight hug before stepping to the side providing an opening for Emma. She reached forward and gently squeezed Martha's hand. "I'm sorry for your loss," she managed to pull together enough to say. Emma was grateful that

Martha barely noticed her, because she could not and did not want to imagine what Martha must be going through.

Martha was the first one to let go of Emma's hand. Appreciative, Emma stepped slowly to the side and forward away from the receiving line. A young man with long hair introduced himself to the grieving widow.

"I'm Mylo Simmons Mrs. Sinclair; I worked in your husband's office as a courier. I owe my life to your husband," he said, shaking Martha's hand vigorously and almost knocking her down.

"Dr. Sinclair was a good guy, I mean a great man." He let out a deep breath and seemed to add reluctantly, "If he hadn't sent me out on an early delivery, I wouldn't be here today. I think I was the last one to see him alive."

Emma glanced back, noticing Martha's eyes glazed over even more as she shifted her gaze onto the next person in line, the young man's words did not even seem to penetrate her world of grief. Taken aback, Emma watched as Peter Lyceum, who had been observing the exchange, made an abrupt exit from the line and was dialing his cell phone as he rushed away. At least she thought it was Mr. Peter Lyceum. Emma had only met the man a few times.

She felt for the young man Mylo, who was trying to offer comfort to Ms. Sinclair. In reality, she could identify with him more than she wanted to. Emma's body shook with an eerie cold feeling as she reached for her husband's arm, once they were a few steps away from the receiving line. She did not recognize the tall, corporate looking man dressed in the mandatory funereal black, who waved Nicholas over from across the courtyard.

"I just need a few minutes honey, I'll be with you shortly, I promise," Nicholas said as he squeezed her hand. Emma meekly smiled and released his comforting arm.

Not sure what to do, she made her way through the crowd of mourners. Emma looked back for a moment, catching a glimpse of Martha once again. Martha was glaring at someone.

Her sudden hostile demeanor surprised Emma, who traced Martha's glare back to a young, neatly dressed woman in the crowd. At first, she did not recognize her. Then it dawned on Emma that this woman was one of the lab technicians Nicholas had worked with in the city.

Surprised, and uncomfortable with the exchange she just witnessed between Martha and the other woman, Emma looked around and was able to catch Nicholas' gaze near one of the trees at the far end of the courtyard. He held up his hand indicating he needed five more minutes.

"Damn," she sighed.

Emma knew that five minutes could easily end up being thirty minutes, so she pointed to herself and then over to the bench where Wally and his little sister Zoe were sitting. Nicholas nodded, and gestured that he would meet her over there.

When Emma approached, the nanny nodded and smiled at her. She was hovering over Zoe. That little girl, known for her bolting at any time, kept the nanny's full attention in situations like this. However, today Zoe was intensely playing with what looked like a ribbon in her hand.

The nanny seemed thankful to see her and happy that Emma would give some much needed attention to Wally. Ever since Emma first met Wally, she felt his craving for attention and the guilt that went with that need. The Sinclair family unit mostly focused on Zoe. Emma believed the day Zoe's diagnosis of Autism occurred - was the day Wally no longer existed. It was not that everyone wanted to forget about him, but rather Zoe's requirements overshadowed Wally's needs.

Wally was fiddling with a brown string hanging out of his pocket.

Emma greeted the children, as cheerily as she could. "Hi Wally, hi Miss Zoe."

Wally quickly looked up and smiled at her. He nodded hello, but did not say anything. Zoe ignored her as usual.

She had gotten to know the children over the years because of the friendship Walden and Nicholas fostered due to all the long hours they spent working together. In Nicholas' eyes, Walden was like family to him. During the summer, Walden's family would invite Nicholas and Emma to parties at their cabin in Southampton. Wally affectionately called Emma and Nicholas Aunty Emm and Uncle Nic, whereas Zoe had no interest in them at all. Both children were also frequent visitors to the bookstore she owned which was located near their home in the upper-east side of the city.

She watched the two small children at first. Wally was painfully aware of everything, while Zoe lived in her own world. It usually was not awkward like this between them but today it was. Emma knew she could not cheer up Wally, as that was always her first instinct when she saw a sad child. That feeling of powerlessness broke her heart. For a rare moment, she was at a loss for words.

Emma really was sad about their father's death, even if she thought Walden was somewhat arrogant and self-absorbed. In fact, she felt guilty that her last encounter with Walden was that of rudeness, him hanging up on her after an awkward phone conversation. Maybe her emotions were more about the disturbed feelings she felt by the last three words she thought Walden had whispered.

Yes, she grieved for Walden, even though he hurt her feelings regularly. Although, Emma never let Walden in on that secret as she felt sorry for him. In her eyes, Walden had come to a place in his life where he did not know how to be with others outside his work. Sometimes when she would ask him a question to draw him out, Walden would act as if he did not hear her. Those types of encounters with him chipped at her self-confidence.

Deep down she knew she was a people pleaser and she just wanted Walden to like her. Nonetheless, Emma could see the unhappiness growing within him and did not know how to help a man that did not want help. Walden repeatedly trivialized her presence. It made her feel as though her voice and thoughts were too small and insignificant. Because of Nicholas' close connection with Walden, Emma found ways to avoid him at gathering so as not to hurt her husband's relationship with him.

The nanny's cell phone broke through the silence bringing Emma back from her wandering thoughts. Looking at Emma while pointing at her phone, Emma nodded with understanding of her need to take the call. The nanny opened her cell phone and took a small polite step back.

Wally took the nanny's distraction as an opportunity to start a conversation.

"Aunty Emm," he mouthed loudly. "Um, when are you going to get the new *Dragon Kingdom* book? It's already been released in the UK, you know."

Emma laughed. Wally was one of her best customers. He spent hours in her bookstore, and consumed books the way most kids attacked a free stash of candy.

"Still a big fan of battling dragons?" Emma probed.

Wally nodded eagerly and smiled, "Faithfully. The Blue Dragon is my favorite."

"Why is that?"

"He has the keys to the ancient library. He is the smartest dragon. He knows the past, present, and future."

Emma smiled, "I hear he runs into some trouble in the next book."

Wally looked up in awe, "Really? What?"

She gave him a quick wink then turned to Zoe. Emma asked her, "Are you still a big Curious George fan?" She smiled at Zoe, not wanting to exclude her from the conversation. The little girl did not respond.

"Sorry, Aunt Emm, she's just in one of her moods today. *She's* not talking to any of us. But she's really into princesses right now," Wally offered.

Zoe stopped swinging her feet, and paused. She stared down at her black shoes, the patent leather was shiny new, and sunlight glinted off the smooth black surface.

"You haven't been in for your favorite raspberry hot chocolate lately. Are you planning on stopping by soon?" Emma asked Wally.

Wally nodded.

"With whipped cream," he said, licking his lips. "My mom says I can take your 20/20 workshop."

"Well, tell her to hurry, we only have a few slots left. The next time you are in my shop, I will have to treat you both to some hot chocolate. How does that sound?"

Emma specially ordered beverages for Zoe because Zoe was on a strict diet. Emma called it hot chocolate for Zoe, even though it was not.

An old man shuffled past them. Emma moved off the path and closer to the children so he could pass. Emma smiled and gave a friendly nod to the man who did not acknowledge her presence.

"That's Bruno Mahler... brilliant physicist," she whispered to Wally, then paused in thought, "Could use some manners though."

Wally seemed delighted by her comment, "He's okay. He's no Einstein, though."

Zoe giggled.

"That's Daddy's line," he uttered conspiratorially.

"You both like strings, I see."

Emma pointed to what was keeping two pairs of little hands busy for the moment.

Wally stared at her, apparently puzzled by the statement.

She smiled at Zoe. Zoe did not seem to notice.

Emma watched as the tiny girl swung her feet back, and forth, her beautiful blue flowery silk dress swished against itself with each swing. Zoe played with the matching baby blue ribbon tied around her ponytail, continuously wrapping it forwards and backwards around her index finger.

"Ohhhhh..., that thing in her hair," Wally flashed an understanding smile and stopped looking at Emma as if she was crazy.

"It's a bow Dad gave her; it's what Dad wrapped her birthday present in. Mom says Zoe likes the bow more than the gift.... It was a gold locket."

"Where's the locket?" Emma brushed her hand against her skin, feeling her own pendant between her fingers, a fleur-de-lis she had worn since her sixteenth birthday.

"Mom took it away," Wally, answered matter-of-factly. "Because Zoe put teeth marks in it, but it's only because she was nervous at her party that she chewed on it."

Zoe did not look up, she just continued gently rocking forwards and backwards, rubbing the worn velvet ribbon between her fingers.

Emma pointed to the string that dangled out of Wally's pocket, "What's, that?"

Wally pulled out something shiny and silver from his pocket. The object was tied to string that was fastened to his belt, which was also holding up his pants. In her eyes, Wally was too skinny for his age. That is why she was always coming up with ways of fattening him up with things like hot chocolates.

"So I don't lose it," he explained. "I promised Mom I wouldn't lose it." Wally held out the ring to show her. "You know they have not found Dad's body yet, but they found his ring. I heard mom say that pretty much means they are not going to find him. Someone at school told me that other kids had the same thing happen. They haven't found their Dads' bodies either, so I guess it's pretty common."

Overtaken by the little boy's inner strength she nodded, taking a seat beside Wally.

"It's our family crest. See." Wally held the ring out for her to see. She did not touch the ring; Emma did not feel she had the right to touch something so personal to Wally and his family.

Emma looked down at the ring, fascinated at how such a small object in that massive amount of debris at ground zero could even be located. Yet, no other trace of Walden turned up. It had been six months, and the cleanup continued at the World Trade Center site.

She watched as Wally ran his finger over the ring, tracing the grooves of the family crest.

"Dad put it in his will that Mom had to give it to me." Wally pushed it into Emma's hand, "See how heavy it is?"

Surprised by Wally's quick gesture she held it, feeling its weight. "Wow, it's pretty heavy."

"Yah, but I don't mind, one day I'll wear it just like Dad used to."

Unexpectedly Emma felt a tingling feeling in her hand. First, it felt like an electric shock sparking through her fingers, followed by numbness in her hand that held the ring. She felt the blood drain from her face and a cold shiver roll through her body.

From the corner of her eye, she caught a glimpse of a man standing next to Wally. He had a hand gently resting on the boy's shoulder. When she glanced over for a better look at the man, a bright light blinded her. Assuming it was just the glare from the sun, Emma blinked her eyes back into focus. No one was there. It was just her eyes playing tricks on her again.

"What's wrong? Aunty Emm... you okay?"

Emma's face flushed red with embarrassment as she promptly returned the ring to Wally's palm. "I'm fine, darling. Thank you. The sun just got in my eyes. I'm glad you have something very special like that to remember your Dad."

"You looked like you were about to puke," Wally looked skeptically at her.

Zoe was now staring up at her for the first time; she had stopped swinging her feet. She giggled, twirling the ribbon between her fingers.

"Daddy, Daddy, Daddy," she said, a barely audible whisper.

"Yah, I miss Daddy, too, Zoe," Wally fiddled with the ring, rubbing it between his thumb and index finger again, as though it were a genie's lamp.

Wally cleared his throat. "When I was small, I used to play with Dad's ring, you know, spin it around his finger. I liked the way it felt. Dad used to get mad at first, but when I told him it was because I was scared, he was pretty cool about it. He let me spin it whenever I wanted to after that. I think that's why he wanted me to have it." Staring down at the ring Wally was obviously fighting back tears." So I won't have to be scared, you know," he looked away, pretending to brush some dust out of his eyes.

They sat there sharing a moment of silence she did not want to break.

Wally looked up at her. "Can I ask you a question?"

His eyes were full of water, almost ready to spill into tears down his face, looking directly into Emma's eyes he asked: "What do you do, when you're not strong enough?"

Emma took in a deep breath, smiled back, and without hesitation tenderly answered. "You act like you are."

CHAPTER 8

He led Wilson to the command control room through a maze of corridors. The silence of the monotonous walk broken by the sound of a cell phone that echoed down the narrow hallway caused both men to stop. Mr. Brown abruptly pulled the phone out of his military issued pants pocket and glanced at the number. He glared at Wilson, making the young man take several steps back enabling him to take the call. Understanding protocol, Wilson respectfully turned toward the blank wall and waited.

"Yes," Mr. Brown flatly stated into his cell phone.

Only a select few had access to this line, and as far as he was concerned, Mr. Peter Lyceum used this privilege far too often.

"I have another lead I want you to take care of," Lyceum demanded. "I want you to interview one of the company's messengers, his name is Mylo Simmons. He was the last person to speak to Dr. Sinclair and I just found this out, Mylo delivered a package for him prior to the event. How soon can you take care of this?"

"Within 24 hours."

Lyceum barked back. "That's not good enough! Do I need to remind you who works for whom here?"

"Has it been cleared by the others?"

"I believe your focus should be on the task." Lyceum hesitated. "I'll expect a report within 24 hours," he then hung up.

Mr. Brown, left with the dial tone, had no other choice but to hit the end button on his cell phone. When he slid the phone back into his pocket, his mind was already calculating ways in which to make sure he would not have to continue enduring Lyceum's ongoing childish behavior.

*****

As he awaited orders, Wilson braced for the brunt of what he could only imagine was about to follow. The conversation was brief, but it was apparent that Mr. Brown's intensity had just doubled.

"I assure you," Mr. Brown said, "I do not want to hurt you. However, if you hold back any information, you will meet the same outcome of Commander Harris and his team. Clear?"

Wilson, promptly responded, "That's crystal clear, Sir."

When they walked into the control room, there was a new team of men running checks on the entire system. This had been going on since they replaced Commander Harris' team. Still unnerved by the news of what had happened to every member of the previous team, and being suspicious of the five newly reassigned men, Wilson kept his distance from them.

"I want this room cleared. Everyone, out, now," Mr. Brown commanded.

Wilson watched as the men looked between each other, obviously confused regarding Mr. Brown's role and the power that he held. He cringed and thought to himself, *Oh my God, I am about to witness a slaughtering.*

Mr. Brown, infuriated by the lack of their immediate response shouted, "I said out!"

One of the men stepped forward and said, "And you are, Sir?"

Wilson studied Mr. Brown from where he was standing, as Brown's eyes burrowed into the man who had made the biggest mistake of his military career.

Mr. Brown hammered his answer. "Right now, YOUR... WORST... NIGTHMARE...!"

The man shifted his gaze back and forth from Mr. Brown to Wilson, pleading for some kind of understanding.

Standing off to the right side of Mr. Brown, Wilson's eyes were wide with fear; he tilted his head slightly, gesturing for the man to get him and his team out now.

The man turned to other men. "You heard the man, everyone, out."

The men quickly got out of the room.

Once the large heavy door clicked closed behind them, Mr. Brown spun around to Wilson. "Retrace your steps, tell me everything you heard, saw, smelled and wondered," he instructed him.

Wilson, knowing that a secret is rooted in the fact that 'nothing is as it seems,' chose his words carefully. He understood the difference between having knowledge versus skills. Once extracted data occurs, disposal transpires in the covert military world.

However, the unique skill of mentally duplicating information makes a person irreplaceable. Over the last six years, having access to classified information, he had turned the knowledge he gained at WOLF into specialized skills. He understood the technical details behind what made the research facility operate.

WOLF included a system of powerful antennas capable of creating controlled modifications to the ionosphere. The mystery of the ionosphere fascinated Wilson, that delicate upper layer of the atmosphere ranging from about 30 miles to as far as 600 miles above the Earth's surface.

On-going experiences conducted at WOLF used electromagnetic frequencies to fire pulsed, directed energy beams at an area of the ionosphere, which ranged from a small patch, to a greater vastness of miles upon miles of area. Electromagnetic waves, then bounced back onto the earth traveling through anything in its path, had been recently stabilized.

Wilson often fielded calls from scientists involved in the public outcry against WOLF. They irreverently believed that the experiments were creating long incisions in the protective layer that keeps deadly radiation from bombarding earth. Needless to say, countless of those calls were not so pleasant.

Wilson was constantly defending WOLF, promoting it to the public as a necessary program for scientific and academic research development. Wolf was packaged and sold as a learning center studying the nature of the northern lights. The most difficult critics Wilson encountered were the well-informed ones who knew where to search in available military documents that revealed the Department of Defense's study of ionospheric modifications as a means of altering weather patterns, causing earthquakes and tsunamis, as well as disrupting enemy communications and radar.

An essential part of Wilson's job was to know the *'who and what,'* regarding the information he helped protect. Nonetheless, major aspects of the program deemed for reasons of "national security" remained secretive.

According to WOLF documents released to the public, "WOLF is a scientific endeavor studying the anomalies of the ionosphere, with the goal of improving and mastering communications systems."

It was not just conspiracy theorists Wilson had to deal with, he was tasked with making sure what happened in the late 90's didn't happen again. The European Union had called WOLF a global concern demanding more information on its health and environmental risks. Officials at WOLF claimed that the project was nothing more than just a "radio science research facility" monitoring the activity of the aurora borealis. It was Wilson's job to make sure WOLF maintained a low profile.

The CIO before him had invited locals to visit and tour the facility right before it opened. The final phase of the project occurred in 1997. The military had erected 18 towers, 72 feet in height, forming a high-power, high frequency phased array radio transmitter capable of beaming in the 2.5 - 10 megahertz frequency range, at more than three gigawatts of power (3 billion watts). The locals were excited and impressed, but had more questions than there were answers for, and that was the end of the friendly tours.

The most difficult question ever posed to Wilson came from an investigative reporter out of Chicago who had found out that during the 1980's, a Texas physicist working for the subsidiary contracted to build WOLF, registered for a U.S. Patent for an invention. According to the paperwork on file in the Patent office, that Texas physicist had discovered how to heat plumes of charged particles in the ionosphere, making it possible to selectively disrupt microwave transmissions of satellites, and cause interference or total disruption of communications over a large portion of the earth. The reporter also knew that the subsidiary in charge of building WOLF was a defense contractor that took over in the mid '90's, known, as Neotray, one of the world's largest defense service providers. Wilson had immediately routed that call to Washington.

His life revolved around the most prominent instrument at the WOLF station. Whenever the high power radio frequency transmitter facility operating in the high frequency (HF) band powered up, he was on-call 24/7. That transmitter was responsible for temporarily, disrupting a limited area of the ionosphere, and harnessing the energy.

He maintained contacts with other public affair liaisons at similar ionospheric heating facilities around the world. Wilson had contacts at the Fairbanks, Alaska site, the one in Puerto Rico, and Norway, but had to make a personal contact with anyone at the Russia facility.

"Wilson, anytime now," Mr. Brown's impatient voice snapped him back to the control room, and away from organizing in his mind what he should start with and what he should share.

Wilson quickly responded, "Yes, Sir." He started. "First of all, there was no geomagnetic storm that morning. No naturally occurring aurora borealis activity, either."

Mr. Brown nodded.

"Nevertheless, Sir, I believe we were not the only ones monitoring the event with the 33 assets located in the World Trade Center towers," Wilson said. "What I believe Sir, is whoever was monitoring us, jumped in, and took our assets. It started as a gut feeling. Because whoever did it, knew exactly what they were doing however they did not anticipate discovery."

"Who do you know, who would have that kind of technology?"

"Well, Sir, I believe you would know better than me."

Mr. Brown chuckled, surprising Wilson that the man was even capable of such an emotion. "Interesting hypothesis."

"Well Sir, it's actually not a hypothesis." Wilson walked over to one of the computer stations and punched in a series of buttons. He pulled out his card key, which hung around his neck, hiding under his shirt, and slid the security card through a slot. While the card was in the slot, he keyed in a series of numbers and letters, followed by quickly removing the card, returning it back to its hidden location. Wilson waved Mr. Brown over to the screen and began to point at what appeared to be a series of wavy lines.

"Mr. Brown, as you can see, this is from a conversation I had at a specific time. As you can also see, here is the vibration that is consistent with all the other phone calls being accepted and dispatched during that period. Look at the wavelength from our secured line compared to the wavelength from our unsecured line."

"You work from an unsecured line?"

"Yes, Sir. Whenever the HF transmitter is used, I field many calls from those monitoring our activity. Those calls from the public come in on an unsecured line only during those times. It is our friendly way of demonstrating to the public that we are not trying to hide anything. We mostly receive complaints about interference believed to be caused by the array."

"Who would know this protocol?" Brown interrupted.

He countered quickly, "Only a select few internally, Sir."

"Continue."

"As you can see, this is a phone conversation I had at that specific time. Observe what is happening with the connection .... it is faint and would have been hidden on the secured lines. On the contrary, on my unsecured line the wave patterns vibrate at a different frequency, as you know Sir, so at this different frequency," he pointed at the monitor, "it picked up that signature at the same moment the assets disappeared. I'm guessing whoever our guests were, most likely did not anticipate our use of an unsecured line."

Mr. Brown studied the monitor. "How come no one else discovered this, why are you the only one?"

"It would only show up in my area of communications. I'm in charge of the only unsecured line on premises."

Mr. Brown quizzed, "What made you look?"

"During the call with that faint signature we just talked about, the person complaining on the other end of the line became even more irritated about a feedback and a tiny echo during our conversation. This had never occurred, to my knowledge on the unsecured line before," Wilson answered. "You and I both know, Sir, there are no accidents especially in the line of work we do."

Mr. Brown raised an eyebrow, "We do?"

"Sorry, Sir," Wilson apologized. His confidence had led him to accidentally step over an invisible line.

Mr. Brown leaned forward, squinting at the monitor.

"I'll play it for you again. Do you see it, Sir? If I remove this," Wilson clicked a few keys, leaving only one curvy line on the screen. "There it is, Sir. At that exact moment in time, we had unwelcome guests."

Mr. Brown nodded.

Wilson felt the watchful eyes of Mr. Brown studying him once again.

"You figured this all out on your own?"

Wilson replied sheepishly, "Yes, Sir. When something doesn't make sense, I can't let it go."

"Well, that's a good thing for us, isn't it?" He paused. "Have you told anyone about this?"

Wilson quickly answered, "No, Sir."

"Do you think you could locate the signature wave again?"

"Yes, Sir, I can."

Mr. Brown smirked. "Then I guess we're going to require your skills."

VIBRATIONAL PASSAGE

He did not trust Brown. Nonetheless, he still wanted an answer for himself because it was not going to be one of those mysteries that he would take to his grave.

CHAPTER 9

"Can you believe Gabriela showed her face?" Emma asked. "That was a bit awkward, huh?"

Nicholas shifted uncomfortably behind the wheel, as they made their way home from Walden's memorial service through heavy traffic.

"Don't tell me you're taking her side? You men all stick together," Emma teased

"Emma, we talked about this remember, for lengths. We do not know all the details, and it is not fair to pass judgment. Besides, Gabriela moved back to Connecticut after that incident. Did I tell you her place was trashed? She said she felt like she was being watched."

"When did you talk to her?" she nervously asked.

"Honey, I am not going to ever have an affair on you." Nicholas gently answered her real question.

"You're right, let's just drop it and talk about something else."

They had already gone through all of that when he had told her about Walden's affair. At least Nicholas was talking more these days. Emma did not want her insecurity creating a fight with her husband.

For a long while, he had mentally floated away from her into a foggy mist, Nicholas had become unreachable, no matter what she tried to do. Emma could even remember the exact moment when it happened. A few weeks after 9/11, they had gone down to ground zero. It was as if he just needed to see with his own eyes that the towers were no longer there.

They had obviously seen the in-depth TV coverage, but seeing the giant gaping, dusty nothingness, where once stood two skyscraping giants, had altered both her and her husband at the inner core level. Walking silently along the crowded sidewalks of Wall Street, gray dust covered everything, giving the ominous feel of Armageddon.

Passing by abandoned cars covered in concrete dust in parking garages, she had wondered if their owners were still alive, or whether grieving family members would eventually have to claim these sad relics. Nicholas and she had been standing near Trinity church when she felt her husband shift away from her. He had been strong, logical, and talkative about everything up until that very moment.

They returned home with very few words shared between them, and then... nothing. He even stopped making small talk; he became distracted and always seemed to be in a bad mood. He blamed it on the stress from work, the restructuring, transition to offices on Long Island, and all the changes he was now facing.

Emma understood the weight of such pressure, so she did the only thing she knew to do, she left him alone. Then one day she realized, they had become roommates. They barely spoke.

She did not know it at the time, but Nicholas under the direct orders of the company's HR department was seeing a grief counselor. Only when the grief counselor signed off on his paperwork could he return to full-time employment. It seemed to have worked; he was doing better this month, more open and conversational. Not the equivalent to before, but at least he was beginning to share his feelings again with her.

She looked over at Nicholas as he drove. Emma smiled with pride at how hard he was working on overcoming the pain, and his guilt of being one of the survivors. She took a deep breath in and sighed. He was focusing on the heavy traffic situation and did not even notice her gazing at him.

Nicholas put on his indicator and pulled off the road, stopping for gas. Due to all the day's emotions, Emma felt famished. She quickly walked into the convenience store to buy a drink and some snacks.

How strange the total cost was $9.11. Those numbers seemed everywhere for her these days. She would look up at a clock and it would be 9:11 or she would get lunch and her change would be $9.11. It kept happening so much, she started wondering what it meant. Was it just a coincidence? Nothing made much sense to her anymore. Her world was upside down most of these days for her.

Once back in the car, Emma stared at the receipt.

Tears began to run down her face.

As he was merging their car back into the intense traffic situation, Nicholas glanced over at her. "Honey, you okay?"

Emma did not know why she was crying. Then it occurred to her. "The morning Walden died," she began to confess, "Remember I told you he called the house looking for you?"

Her husband nodded while keeping his eye on the road ahead.

"Well, I didn't tell you everything," Emma nervously admitted. "He said some really strange things even for Walden and then rudely hung up on me. I was so upset that he had been so disrespectful. Today hearing Wally speak about him and Zoe calling out for her Daddy broke my heart. To see how much they loved him, and miss him makes me feel really bad for judging him."

"Emma, you're one of the kindest people I know," Nicholas said glancing in her direction briefly. "So stop beating yourself up over it. Walden can be abrupt. It's logical that it would hurt your feelings that he hung up on you."

"It's just that he was saying some crazy stuff. Something about suicide, I think. He didn't seem to me like that kind of guy."

"He wasn't. Granted he was pretty serious, well no, I'll say really focused," Nicholas insisted. "Walden was all about business and projects and goals. There was only one time Walden ever surprised me."

"Really, what did he do?"

"It's not what he did. It's what he said."

Emma fished in her pocket to find an unused tissue, wiped the tears away from her eyes, and then blew her nose. "What did he say?"

"I can't remember exactly what we were talking about. We were in the lab finishing some work, when he said the most pessimistic thing I had ever heard from him. He said, 'Life is about a series of painful experiences strung together followed by death.' It was so out of left field, it made me laugh."

"So did you tell him how morbid that sounded?"

"I think I said something about how life does include pain, but, it also includes happiness, joy, and love. If we avoid pain, we will also avoid love. I explained that life to me was more than that. It was about what we do with the time given to us, the relationships we foster, and goodness, we choose to see. You know Walden; always trying to poke holes in my belief system, as any true scientist does. So rather than getting into a debate I shifted the discussion to my definition on stress."

"Did it work?"

"Talking about nature always perks his interest. I told him that when a bud transforms into a flower, there is enormous stress before it becomes all that it can become. That flower can choose to focus on the stress or the beautiful outcome."

"So what did he say to that?"

Nicholas sighed. "As usual, Walden made fun of me. According to him and in his world plants did not share in human feelings and emotions."

They both laughed picturing Walden's logical approach to life, and then it was completely quiet in the car.

She reached over and rubbed Nicholas shoulder. "You really miss him, I'm so sorry."

"That's ok," Nicholas shrugged.

She stared out her car window.

"What is it?"

"It's nothing."

"Come on tell me," Nicholas teased.

"It's just that I can't believe anyone could view life so negatively and miss all the beauty that life has to offer." Emma sighed. "It's like focusing on the thorn rather than the rose itself."

"But Walden wasn't like that." Nicholas' tone turned defensive. "He was always focused on possibilities."

"Well, I believe you," Emma said. "But that phone call just didn't make sense."

"I agree. Even though he liked to tease me about my approach to life, he understood the importance of every moment. Walden was a scientist that comprehended the importance of time and he did not waste a moment of it. Maybe you didn't hear him correctly."

"Maybe." She did not want to upset her husband any more than she had.

Nicholas and Emma stared straight ahead at the road in front of them. Neither knew what to say.

Feeling bad about disagreeing with Nicholas, she closed her eyes, and let her thinking drift. Emma found herself remembering the second and last lengthy conversation she ever had with Walden. It was at a company party held at an Italian restaurant once frequented by various mob bosses.

Emma and Walden were talking about the latest Broadway version of Macbeth. It was a stripped down version with paltry set design and costumes. A famous Hollywood actor was playing the lead role.

The play was so bad that it had closed after a mere two-week run. Emma had begged her husband to accompany her to the opening night. He had agreed to go weeks in advance, however when the night finally arrived, Nicholas attended exhausted from putting extra hours in at work. Apparently, Nicholas had shared with Walden that he had fallen asleep halfway through the third act.

Walden appeared annoyed that Emma had dragged her husband to the performance, especially since Nicholas did not enjoy Shakespeare. Emma on the other hand, had a love-hate relationship with Shakespeare. Her father had made her write essays on Shakespeare as part of her punishments from the time she was thirteen. Even so, Macbeth and The Tempest became her favorite plays.

"Out, out, damn spots," Emma defended herself, in response to Walden making her feel defensive for getting her begrudging, overworked husband to see a play he did not want to watch.

Walden droned on about how Shakespeare was not for everyone. Then he had recited the witches' lines from the first act of Macbeth: "*Fair is foul and foul is fair: Hover through the fog and filthy air.*" She had expected him to recite the more popular lines of "*double, bubble, toil and trouble.*"

He told Emma that it was one of his favorite plays when he was younger. Walden revealed to her that he used to wonder about fate and prophecies back then, as well as whether the three witches were merely mirrors of fear.

Walden had quizzed Emma, wondering if she believed the witches were good or bad.

She retorted, "Bad of course."

He, on the other hand, believed they were neither. They were a reflection of the desires of the person stepping up to the cauldron. Walden was pensive and in his own world, as if he did not need her to have this conversation. Being unconcerned with her point of view was no surprise to her, Walden, could be discourteous in Emma's opinion.

Before leaving the restaurant where the office gathering was taking place, Walden recited lines from *Love's Labor Lost* to her:

"*To seek the light of truth, while truth the while doth falsely blind the eyesight of his look. Light, seeking light, doth light of light beguile. So ere you find where light in darkness lies, your light grows dark by losing of your eyes.*"

A car horn blared causing Nicholas to mutter under his breath.

Emma rubbed at her eyes, trying to wipe the recent memory of Walden away. Her husband was focusing on maneuvering through the traffic jam. She decided not to reopen the Walden conversation again and tell him about what she had just been remembering.

Nevertheless, Walden stuck with her, haunting her thoughts, making her feel uncomfortable in her own skin - again. They sat in silence for the rest of the ride home.

When they finally arrived home, Emma was physically exhausted. She knew it was due to all the emotions from the memorial, plus the tears in the car ride home, coupled with the witnessing of two adorable children who will grow up without their father.

Nicholas had some work to do in his study so he kissed her on the forehead, before Emma dragged herself upstairs and into their bed. She was asleep in mere seconds after placing her head on the fluffy pillow.

She saw Walden. He was standing in an empty whitewashed hallway.

He wanted her to go with him.

Confused, she refused.

"This is just a dream, I'm dreaming about you," she told him.

"You've got much to learn," He motioned for her to follow him. "I must show you something."

"But Walden, you're dead and I'm dreaming."

"Our friend Shakespeare said it best, *To die, to sleep; To sleep: perchance to dream: ay, there's the rub; For in that sleep of death what dreams may come When we have shuffled off this mortal coil, Must give us pause.*"

Not even giving her a choice, he pulled her through a doorway without even touching her. They walked towards a dark forest. A terrible garbage stench engulfed them, and Walden pointed for her to look through thin branchless trees. The trees had white bark - with an iridescent look to it in the dark.

Emma began to repeat to herself, this is just a dream; this is just a dream...

Walden pointed to the trees. Not feeling like she had a choice, she began to look in the direction he was gesturing at, past a forest of thin tree trunks. There were three creatures around a large pot, with a fire blazing under it. The creatures were dancing around it, the foul stench was coming from the pot, and the trees without leaves were the fuel for their fire.

Walden told her it was important for her to remember the type of trees they were. They had white bark. Emma recognized them right away from her childhood, she used to peel off the bark and write on it as a kid. They were Birch trees.

"Why are you in my dream? Why am I here? And what in God's name is that smell?" Emma asked making Walden laughed.

"You are here because you see things with your heart instead of your head, so you have the ability to see more of the truth," he explained.

"However, you must discipline your emotions because they blind you to the full truth. Remember these two keys Emma, when you blame others, you give them your power and, what you hate consumes you until you become what you hate."

Even in her hallucinations, Walden chose which questions to answer while scolding her like a small child. Emma just wanted to wake up – as if reading her thoughts Walden told her, "Not yet." He made a gesture towards his ear. "Listen to what they're saying."

Giving in, she leaned forward trying to hear what these putrid smelly creatures were saying, but it was in an unfamiliar dialect. They kept saying three words, repeatedly. Emma did not care at this point; she just wanted to wake up.

Walden drilled her, "What are those three words?"

"Walden, I don't care," she groaned.

"Remember them," he insisted.

"I don't understand."

"Say the words to me."

To get him off her back she repeated the three words.

"Remember them, save the children, and you must find me."

"What... save whose children...? Walden... you're dead," she pointed this out again, as if reminding them both.

"There are many realities within reality," he explained. "It's like the rings of a tree trunk." He took her hand. "It's time for you to go back."

Before she could ask or say anything more, Emma was awake in her bed, uncontrollably shaking. Everything looked different, colors were different, and smells were more vivid. She could clearly smell the lavender sachet that was tucked inside her dresser drawer. Emma saw light radiating off the things in her bedroom, even after rubbing her eyes several times.

Every aspect rattled her about the dream but the comment about the children upset her the most. She picked up a notebook and wrote down the three words. Those words were familiar, but she could not put her finger on why. As the delusion of seeing Walden began to fade, she was able to find strength to leave the comfort of the cozy bed.

Emma's hands were still shaking as she made her way downstairs to get a glass of water. She was trembling from what she had just experienced, but kept reminding herself that it was merely a hallucination based on all the emotions of the past several months.

She began to rationalize and analyze her apparition, trying to make sense of it. Emma concluded that she was dreaming about Walden because they had just come from his memorial service. Therefore, he was on my mind, Emma reassured herself – that is all. She went on to rationalize that it was her unconscious mind making sense of everything.

Then again, Emma could not shake the fact that the dream had been so vivid, as if she had been awake through it. She scratched at her left arm uncontrollably before looking down to discover a flaming red rash running up her wrist, snaking its way completely up to her shoulder. Her skin felt as if it was on fire.

She could hear her husband's voice coming towards the kitchen. It sounded like he was on the phone, and it did not sound like a good conversation.

Emma poured a glass of water and handed it to him just as he was ending his call. She turned back to the sink and poured another glass for herself.

"What's wrong, Honey?" She secretly scratched at her arm, trying to bring relief to her irritated skin, but the more she scratched, the more it hurt.

Nicholas just shook his head and combed his hands through his hair.

"They've yanked my project."

"What?" Emma inquired.

"The dedicated server for the project was in the lab. That is gone, of course. It simply does not make sense why they cannot find any of the backup data at the Brookstone lab. Three years of work, just gone, like that."

Nicholas looked devastated. His face had turned white and ghostly. "I can't believe it."

Emma stifled a yawn.

"You've never really talked about what you've been working on."

"I signed confidentiality papers," Nicholas explained. "But I guess it doesn't matter anymore."

"I'm so sorry, honey," she repeated, trying to offer comfort.

"We were so close." Nicholas dropped himself into a chair. "I just cannot believe the Birchwood Project is dead."

The glass slipped out of Emma's hand and shattered on the floor in slow motion. She turned her head to the left and saw an image of Walden standing in her kitchen. She blinked her eyes, and gradually began to hear Nicholas' garbled voice. When she looked back again for Walden's image to her left, it was gone.

Nicholas was on his feet rushing towards her. "Emma, are you okay?"

Without hesitation, Emma replied, "I'm fine."

However, she was far from being fine. Her life as she knew it was beginning to unravel.

CHAPTER 10

When Mylo woke up, he could not move. His body felt raw and every part of him throbbed with unspeakable pain. Even though he felt disoriented, he knew he was sitting in a metal chair, with his hands tightly bound together behind him; a cloth blindfold prevented him from seeing anything other than faint slivers of light.

The room he was in had an oily, musty smell, it was cold and damp, and Mylo could hear distorted voices around him. He could not quite make out what they were saying to each other. These muffled voices echoed, as sounds would in an empty warehouse where the tiniest noises travelled great distances up and around the vast high open ceiling.

He could feel that there were several men surrounding him with demanding voices, one in particular, aggressively barking orders. Mylo could not understand any of their words; his head ached and pounded too much for him to concentrate. In fact, he could not seem to focus on constructing a whole thought at all. Unexpectedly someone struck his face twice, and then again, once in each direction. The forceful impact against his jaw brought forth jarring, agonizing explosions of stinging pain.

Cold, freezing water hurled on his face, caused him to gasp with shock and surprise.

VIBRATIONAL PASSAGE

As the water dripped from his face, the words slowly began unscrambling. He could hear the word 'package' followed by other words, until finally, it was making sense.

"Where did you deliver the package for Dr. Sinclair?" a voice demanded.

Mylo was confused again.

"What? Dr. Sinclair is dead," he countered.

"Sir, I think he's telling the truth. He doesn't remember."

Someone loudly snapped his fingers and barked another order. I know that voice, Mylo thought to himself, but his thinking was too fuzzy to make any connections.

Mylo could feel the intensity of someone quickly approaching him. He winced, half expecting another blow to his face but instead he felt a sharp prick to his upper inside arm. He struggled and tried to pull away, but the wire only tightened around his wrist, cutting into his skin even more than before.

It stung and burned in the section of his arm where they had just injected something. Whatever it was, it felt very icy as it entered his blood stream.

His heart began to race followed by his stomach flipping as if he were on a roller coaster amusement ride. Mylo, for a split second, thought he was going to hurl. Subsequently he started to experience a calmness that permitted him to focus his thoughts. The agonizing pain that engulfed his entire body had just vanished. He began to laugh. Mylo's body experienced the sensation of riding one of the best waves of his surfing career. Without hesitation, all he sought to do was divulge to these men anything they wanted to know.

Mylo continued laughing. This was surely just a hallucination. Nothing of this could be real.

The pain was gone, where it went to, Mylo had no idea. Nevertheless, he liked this feeling, except the sensation of the sweat trickling down the side of his face. If he could only wipe it off, he thought to himself.

He shook his head, "Oh that wasn't a good idea, now I've gone and found that headache again," he laughed. The liquid continued dripping slowly down the side of his face, it was thicker than sweat.

"I think one of you may have gone and hurt me. Anyone got a handkerchief?" He laughed again.

Out of nowhere, in the back of his mind, he could hear Dr. Sinclair's voice as if he were standing right behind him.

"Mylo... Mylo focus on my voice, this is Dr. Sinclair. I know you can hear me. I need you to concentrate on my voice. The last day I saw you, when I had you deliver that package. That is the information they are after. You cannot tell them where you delivered it. Lives depend on it. Zoe's life depends on it. Remember Zoe, Mylo?"

Walden faded away in Mylo's thoughts.

"Not cute, funny, Zoe," Mylo whispered, suddenly struck with a wave of emotions.

"What the hell is he talking about now?" One of the men standing near him snapped.

Mylo, in spite of everything still in his own world, was now remembering that day he first met little Zoe in Dr. Sinclair's office... it still made him laugh. She had climbed up on her Dad's desk. The Executive Secretary, Ruthie left in charge of her had clearly lost control of the situation within minutes after Dr. Sinclair's departure to an unexpected meeting.

Half-naked Zoe had punted off all the files as well as the other items on her Dad's desk, making it her personal stage. She was belting out at the top of her lungs, *Twinkle, Twinkle, Little Star*, repeatedly as if performing encores at a concert hall, while gripping her Dad's state-of-the-art stapler as her microphone.

Ruthie kept trying to pull her down off the desk, but she was quick at moving back and forth just out of the woman's reach. What Mylo found was so hilarious, was that this woman who was used to dealing with some of the most powerful men in the corporate world, could not get this 25 pound little girl under control. Zoe was definitely uncontainable. She continued scuffing up the polished mahogany desk with her one shoe she still had on, while avoiding Ruthie's grasp.

VIBRATIONAL PASSAGE

A painful punch to his jaw jolted him back to the present and the obscurity that wrapped around him.

"Where did you deliver the package to?" The voice demanded.

Mylo could feel the compulsion to give this man his answer he was seeking. He had to stop himself from telling these men anything. How... how... Mylo searched what was left of his mind for a solution. Then he began to sing Zoe's favorite song, *Twinkle... Twinkle... Little Star...*

"What the hell," someone to his right retorted.

"I'm telling you Sir, we've tried. He is a dead end. This delivery boy doesn't know anything," someone else added.

"Look, we're not going to go through this again. You made a delivery for Dr. Sinclair. Where did you deliver the package to, and who received it?"

"Hey I know your voice," Mylo blurted out. He was not good with names, but he could always remember a voice. At that point, he felt the energy shift in the room. The sound of feet shuffling echoed, but no one said a word. He could make out the distinct resonance of a gun chambering, and then he felt the heaviness of cold metal pressed against his chest.

"Package... Where did you deliver the package?"

Mylo concentrated on singing Zoe's favorite song. *She would be proud of me*, Mylo thought. He knew in every cell of his being, whether he told them or not, they were going to murder him. His last thoughts were... *he gave me extra days on this planet to surf a few more big waves, and now it's my turn to save his little girl's life*. Mylo was not good at many things but he was loyal.

He smiled as he pictured funny, little Zoe in his mind.

A sharp burning sting to his chest tailed an ear-piercing echo; everything went black.

CHAPTER 11

The Brookstone Laboratory for the Mendelrose Corporation (BLMC) was a sprawling campus encompassing a majority of the seaside property in the sleepy town of Glacier Bay. Millions of dollars from the Lyceum Foundation poured into this research facility situated on the northern shore of Long Island in New York.

The Lyceum family wealth achieved by means of mining and oil production occurred in the late 1800's. Their philanthropy was world renowned, so it came as no revelation in 1913, when other notable industrialists added additional funds to help establish the Brookstone Laboratory as a haven for scientific exploration. Twenty years later, the Lyceum family acquired the Mendelrose Corporation, and placed the Brookstone Laboratory under its financial umbrella. Ever since then, a revolving door of distinguished scientists from around the world awarded with Mendelrose grants took up temporary residence in Glacier Bay throughout the years.

Scientists in molecular biology and genetics at BLMC have been responsible for many discoveries in cancer, genetic diseases, stem cells, and neurology. All those groundbreaking breakthroughs happened in that laboratory facility.

VIBRATIONAL PASSAGE

In an effort to appear as transparent and family-friendly as possible, BLMC hosted school field trips to its laboratories, demonstrating what a DNA strand looked like to the oohs and ahhs of school-aged children. As well, on weekends, public tours took place in the main part of the vast property. The quaint settlement created an ideal environment for BLMC, giving it the feel of a relaxed chic college town.

At a highly secured section of the BLMC labyrinth of buildings, Peter Lyceum sat at his desk, furiously looking through documentation, which was not his. He had had them secretly removed from Dr. Walden Sinclair's lab at the World Trade Center, on the eve of 9/11.

Walden's notes were sporadic. Peter was searching for *the* answer. He knew Walden had succeeded in breaking the genetic code for these children labeled with Autism.

Peter got angrier by the minute, as he flipped through the documents. He knew Walden had discovered his intentions. Peter could not explain how Walden had figured out how he was going to apply Walden's research findings. This knowledge, Peter believed was likely the source for causing Walden's retreat into profound secrecy.

What infuriated Peter most about Walden was that he could not figure out his incoherent files, plus the fact that he was not able to locate the bastard. As Mr. Brown had briefed Peter, Walden and the other assets from the twin towers had just vanished from WOLF's radar. The Lyceum family was one of the top private funders of the WOLF project.

WOLF was a joint venture between the Mendelrose Corporation and the U.S. government. They forged an equally deeply classified partnership, because of the sensitive nature surrounding the arrangement. Mendelrose had obtained Nazi research medical files, which were married with data acquired from Nazi engineers through Project Paperclip. Peter and several Mendelrose scientists acquired and maintained unique clearance as consultants for the WOLF project.

In the medicinal and scientific field, the Lyceum family held a highly distinguished association as movers and shakers in the world of academic circles. While on his mother's side of the family, were famous and highly successful gun manufacturers and bankers.

Peter was a child prodigy, reading by the age of two, by the age of six, he read Shakespeare for pleasure, and had a reputation to quote the Bard at great length. His parents pressed him to enter the medical profession and like a good son, he complied. He followed it up with studies in International Finance, which is how he met his beautiful wife. She was everything he was not and he worshiped her for that.

Left emotionally crippled after the death of her during childbirth, Peter focused on all that he had left of her, their child. Then only two days later, his newborn son just stopped breathing while being cradled in his arms. The medical field was unable to provide closure with answering the *why*. Never psychologically recovering from their deaths, Peter focused on his work of strengthening and building the Lyceum family empire. He became a rock, smashing anything that got in his way.

Peter knew that Walden had broken the DNA code because he had strategically placed an attractive female lab assistant in Walden's presence to spy on him. He was aware that Walden had been spending many hours at the lab away from home, which isolated him from his family support system, especially his wife. Not missing an opportunity, Peter plotted quickly and precisely. He knew that this isolation meant loneness making it easy for someone to gain his trust and seduce him.

Gabriela Sheen was the ideal individual for the task. She was sharp, intelligent, with an understated exotic beauty to her. She barely wore makeup to work, but when she actually put some effort into putting herself together, she was breathtaking. Gabriela was also young and ambitious. Peter had prided himself on finding the perfect person for the mission.

However, he had not calculated Gabriela turning against him and falling in love with Walden. Peter, confronted with this fact at their last meeting became infuriated. Gabriela had refused to help him any more even after he threatened to expose her complicity to Walden. Peter could not believe he had underestimated her level of determination in advancing her career.

He also did not foretell Walden reassigning Gabriela to another department in the lab, subsequently ending the affair. If Walden had not admitted to the affair, Martha would never have reached out to *Uncle Peter* for help in saving her marriage. Martha had come to his office, asking him to fire Gabriela, which of course, he would not do. Nonetheless, if that chain of events did not take place, Peter would never have known how far Walden's research had taken him.

Peter did not comprehend why people felt the need to absolve their conscience and be so honest.

He could justify anything he did, because he believed that there *was* no truth. Truth was just a matter of perspective.

One thing he was sure about was that Walden had not told Martha *everything*. Otherwise, Martha would not have turned to him for help had Walden exposed what he had discovered to her.

Peter enjoyed being the puppet master. He would always have Martha's loyalty because he was instrumental in making sure Walden and Martha got together. He was the one who had run interference with Martha's father, who had been against the marriage from the beginning. Without him, Martha would be an aging-spinster, and both uncle and niece knew that as an unspoken fact.

His observation of Martha was that she was a loyal, hard worker, but she failed living up to the family name because she was just that, a worker and not a leader... a huge disappointment in Peter's judgment. However, she was a useful pawn to utilize at his discretion.

He still could not believe Gabriela had shown up at the memorial service. What was she thinking? Peter sighed and thought... *one could always rely on the unstable and erratic nature of women.*

All the same, she had been somewhat useful to him. Gabriela's surveillance had been fruitful. Now, he conjectured whether she had withheld more from him. Peter made sure there had been a thorough search of her apartment.

Something is missing...but what? Peter thought.

Because of Gabriela, Peter knew that Walden had broken the cryptogram on how to influence these children diagnosed with Autism. Cracking that code would materialize to the scientific world and make the appearance that the scientists at BLMC discovered a cure for Autism.

What it really just meant was that they would end the current global 'programming' which made information processing impossible for these children. Peter smiled to himself with the thought of making history with Walden's findings. He would have it all, the controlling of the minds of these little powerhouses, while making him an international hero to the world.

In fact, that releasing of a cure would compliment all the current prestigious awards lining the office walls, recognizing Peter as a generous man for everything he achieved in the Autism cause. Not only did he consider himself handsome and charismatic, but also a master manipulator of people. He would have it all.

He spearheaded the Center for Advancement of Autism Research (CAAR) located on the Brookstone Laboratory campus. CAAR was a collaboration of treatment and research centers conducting accelerated clinical trials. CAAR had international acknowledgment as the principal Autism research centers in the world.

Its program involved children that ranged in age from infants to young adults (18-year-olds) diagnosed with Autism and related disorders. CAAR integrated highly qualified professionals from the fields of clinical psychology, neuropsychology and neuroimaging, child psychiatry, speech-language pathology, social work, genetics and the biological sciences, stem cell research, as well as psychopharmacology.

Peter was pleased with his own brilliance. CAAR was an ingenious way to disguise itself as a clinic helping children diagnosed under the Autism Spectrum Disorders (ASD). No known cure for ASD existed. Even the huge intercontinental support groups for Autism could not agree upon a universal definition.

Parents were panic-stricken from the moment they heard the word Autism in connection to their child's existence. For that reason, there was great demand for the most effective treatment to develop their child's skill levels - to help him or her talk, interact, play, learn, and care for his or her own fundamental needs.

CAAR had become the hero to these families, even providing partial scholarships to parents. Peter was a genius because the parents paid half the cost to further Peter's personal research agenda. It always made Peter smile when a grateful Parent would thank him for helping them with the pricey treatments. *If they only knew,* he snickered.

Peter had discovered a way of reinforcing the value of his treatments. Parents wanted calm children and therefore he provided just that. Calming entrainment music piped into the therapy rooms for the children right before the end of their 'rehabilitation sessions' guaranteed the parents' unquestioning endorsement.

On a couple of occasions when parents started inquiring too much Peter eliminated them from the program immediately. It was quite easy. He simply had his team of therapeutic experts frame the situation as if the parents were getting in the way of their child's recovery. Shaming was the best way to quiet already fractured parents.

Never permitted beyond specified points in the clinic, caregivers were enlightened in the Federal law for privacy and the clinic's own security reasons, of course. It was difficult for the parents to comprehend that they were dropping their child off at a scientific lab because security officers were dressed in nice, casual clothing and no one wore lab coats. It had the feel of a large healing facility that supplied hugs to parents that needed them.

The 'team' presented to parents included friendly and welcoming speech therapists, occupational therapists, psychologists, and other specialists who had impeccable qualifications in their areas. In spite of this picture perfect presentation; speech therapy was not what was occurring during speech sessions.

These children never received the therapy listed in the brochures or written up in their treatment plan. They were the human lab rats tested against vibrational waves. The hidden objective behind the clinical research was to see how the scientists could take control of these children through brainwave entrainment - the ability to change brainwaves and states of consciousness with sound waves.

The reason for Peter's interest in these children was due to discoveries based on the Nazi's exploration coupled with brainwave detection. These overly sensitive children access and process information through the mental organizing and understanding of patterns, making them more open to higher frequencies.

He had uncovered this through findings from previous research. Files concealed and secreted out of Germany had provided Peter with a rare treasure trove of systematic examinations that the world believed had been lost. His family had simply referred to them as the 'family files.' The world believed that Josef Mengele's research files destroyed by the Nazis no longer existed. Peter completely amused by this cover-up and was actually surprised that people supported this obscure story. But then again, he had discovered, people would believe anything....

Boxes and boxes of information contained data on Mengele's experiments with twins and the various human experimentations performed in the effort to create the perfect Aryan race. Mengele, dubbed the "Angel of Death' (*Todesengel* in German) conducted human experiments at Auschwitz.

The files even contained research data from Mengele's mentor, Dr. Otmar Freiherr von Verschuer. Von Verschuer was a leading scientist known for his exploration in genetics with a particular interest in twins. He worked at the Kaiser Wilhelm

Institute for Anthropology, Human Genetics and Eugenics in Berlin.

Hitler had wanted his scientists to create a race with particular physical features, such as blonde hair, blue eyes. However, Peter had taken the research one-step forward. He believed he could not only create a hidden master race, but also manipulate their rare abilities.

The family had inherited many obscure items from the Nazi regime, including looted artwork of famous masterpieces, but the technical research was what fascinated Peter. These German scientists advanced knowledge, by making amazing discoveries in genetics that would remain a mystery to scientists in the West for another decade.

In the 'family files,' Peter had found out that through experimentation, Nazi scientists had stumbled upon the fact that certain children were more intuitive to certain vibrations. He believed those files were describing children with the unique learning approach known today as Autism; they just did not put those pieces of the puzzle together as Peter had.

Consequently, the research Peter had been involved with at WOLF afforded him access to the most up-to-date results. At WOLF, *they* had discovered that the magnetic field on earth was altering. As the magnetic field changed, it was causing the earth to shift on its axis creating the world to spin faster increasing the earth's vibrational pulse.

Peter discovered that the children with ASD intuitively understood the significance of this change. In spite of this, until he could figure out a way to control them and make sure they did not communicate what they knew, he had found a way to scramble or jam their frequency. The Mendelrose Corporation's majority ownership of a global pharmaceutical distributor, made it easy to have an inhibitor placed into specific Mendelrose antibiotics administered when the immune system was underdeveloped or overloaded. An unexpected outcome of the inhibitors, created a new set of variations of Autism in children, which was fine by him.

In addition, through a media outlet subsidiary, subliminal vibrations placed in certain popular children's programs caused hypnotic trances. When these trances were broken, the children would act out aggressively, similar to a drug addict looking for their next fix.

This was the safety mechanism Peter had put in place for parents that refused to put their infants or young children on the Mendelrose's antibiotics. When he figured out what Walden had hidden in his files, he would have the information he required to make sure he was 'the one' who controlled these labeled children.

Bottom-line, Peter believed that these children due to their mental processing abilities held the answer to controlling the earth after it shifts.

He had seen too many things that had occurred through the research at WOLF to tell him otherwise. Technology now made it possible to change the weather, and travel through time. Even though WOLF had messed up the latest mission at the twin towers on 9/11, Peter had witnessed several successful trials. One particular trial involved two assets who had created a lucrative outcome through time jumping, of which Peter was still reaping the financial benefits.

As Peter opened up another set of Walden's files, he spoke aloud to himself.

"Alright Walden... where'd you hide it...?"

CHAPTER 12

It was Sunday, Emma and Nicholas' favorite day of the week, the one day they allowed themselves the luxury of sleeping in late. This was such a routine that even when they were infuriated with each other, which lead to no talking, they always stuck to their Sunday schedule. Whoever got up first would make the coffee and bring in the breakfast tray.

Nicholas was usually the lucky one waking up early, today was no different. He confessed to her that he did not mind because he was able to select his favorite breakfast items. They shared breakfast in bed along with three different Sunday papers. He preferred to start with the crossword puzzles, which is what he was doing when Emma disrupted his thoughts.

"Honey, what was the Birchwood Project?" She quizzed.

"I'm sorry. I cannot tell you. It's classified." Nicholas laughed and glanced up at his wife. "I could tell you, but then I'd have to kill you."

"Oh yah," Emma challenged, "well, maybe I'll have to kill you if you don't tell me."

"Well, aren't you the spunky one?" Nicholas smiled and the two of them shared in an intimate laugh.

"I thought it didn't matter anymore after they shut it down on you," she pressed. Emma pushed herself up, backing into an upright position against the headboard, as she curled her knees into her husband.

"Seriously, it's not something I can discuss." Nicholas made a face indicating the subject was off limits.

She could not push him; she knew from experience that it would only make him retreat into his own world. "Okay, okay. I will not ask about the project. But what do you know about Birch trees?"

"Birch trees..." Nicholas put down the New York Times crossword puzzle, leaned his head back and sighed.

"Let's see, for one, Howard Hughes," Nicholas chuckled. "Not everyone knows this but the Spruce Goose, was actually made mostly of Birch, not Spruce." He smiled and paused. "And, number two, the bark peels off between seasons, making it an ideal writing surface. Number three, this type of wood is perfect for campfires. It burns evenly, and even when it's damp, you can still start a decent enough fire."

Nicholas was in his element, "Oh, and um number four, 'birching,' a form of corporal punishment back in the old days." He pretended as if he was a game show contestant, spouting out the answers.

She rolled her eyes, and thought that she should have known better that he would turn this into a playful sport. Her husband got a thrill out of showing off his encyclopedic abilities to her. Secretly, Emma was impressed with Nicholas' intelligence but rarely told him so.

"Number five," Nicholas excitedly held up another finger. "I hear Birch is really good for speaker cabinets. There is something about its natural resonance, peaking in the high and low frequencies. If my memory serves me, the resonance compensates for the high and low frequencies, evening the tone. Number six, they use Birch for drums because it gives a boost to high and low frequencies."

Nicholas stroked his chin as if he had an invisible goatee.

"And then, there's number seven. Birch is the New Hampshire state tree. This takes us to number eight, as Birch is a symbol for Pentecost in Europe."

VIBRATIONAL PASSAGE

"Whoa... whoa... encyclopedia boy," Emma interrupted.

"Actually, I'm more interested in the part about Pentecost and the music stuff. You said something about Birch boosting the low and high vibrations and frequencies."

"Wow, my lady is only interested in numbers five, six, and eight."

This made Emma laugh and shake her head. "I'm sorry, honey, but what is Pentecost?"

Nicholas took a sip of his favorite coffee he special ordered from the Big Island in Hawaii. Sunday was his day for enjoying the 100% Kona coffee, a rich indulgence that always reminded him of their honeymoon.

Her husband playfully imitated the Catholic ritual of making the sign of the cross, tapping his forehead, his chest, and then each shoulder. "It's the celebration 50 days after Easter Sunday," he began. "Hence, its name, let's see if I remember Sunday school correctly, it commemorates the descent of the Holy Spirit upon the Apostles after Christ died. About three thousand souls received baptism on Pentecost. I always remembered it because John had his baptismal by water, while Peter had his by fire."

"What do you mean baptismal by fire? Do you mean literally by flames?" Emma inquired

"I'm a little rusty, but you can read about it in the book of Acts. I'm sure we have a bible in the study."

Quickly hopping out of the bed, she said, "Well, let's see smarty pants." Emma had no trouble locating the King James Version of the bible and quickly returned, tucking nicely back into bed next to Nicholas. He was back to solving the crossword puzzle when she found what she was looking for in Acts 2. Just as Nicholas had said, Emma read the part regarding the baptizing of three thousand souls. She shut the bible and looked up.

"About how many people died on 9/11?" She asked her husband, stammering.

Nicholas, startled by her question and the way she was acting, answered slowly.

"I don't know, about 2500, maybe 3000. They still do not have an accurate account. Are you asking just about the twin towers, or about the Pentagon attack, too? And then there was that fourth plane that crashed in the Pennsylvania field."

Emma opened the bible and pointed to Acts 2:41.

"Don't you think that's uncanny? The number of people in the baptismal by fire is 3000 souls, also the same number if we add up the 9/11 assault."

"You're being creepy," Nicholas studied her face. "What's going on here? Anyway, 9/11 did not transpire on Pentecost. Pentecost is usually in May or June."

"I don't know honey, but I have to use the washroom. I'll be right back."

She slid out of bed, and headed to the bathroom to splash some water on her face. The random dream of Walden and the Birch trees was starting to take on new meaning. Emma could not make sense of this on her own, but she knew just the person who could.

CHAPTER 13

Emma was cleaning up in the kitchen since Nicholas had been the one to make breakfast this morning. She was hurrying to finish because it was about time for her call.

Besides spending mornings in bed with her husband on Sundays, Emma was also committed to another routine that had not changed since she was a teenager. Wherever she was in the world, Emma would always have a phone call with her best friend Maddy on Sundays. When Emma's father received orders for a three-year stationing in Hawaii at the Hickam Air Force Base, she would never have guessed that she would meet and remain best friends with Madeleine Yanagi.

Seventh grade was the first year at Punahou School for both of them, and the two formed an instant friendship. They clung together in fear of the bossy eighth graders. Emma had made the unthinkable mistake of sitting on the eighth grade wall on her first day of school. Quickly shoved backwards off the wall, and warned about kangaroo court, Emma quickly learned her placing as a new comer to the private school.

Maddy was the one who joined her in the mocking of the stupid eighth graders and their dumb rules, together they gigged. It was a friendship borne of survival, which blossomed into one each of them nurtured with love, throughout the years of boyfriends, first jobs and traveling around the world.

Once, Emma had been in a rural part of India and could not get to a phone in time, but she found a little hut with a sign outside it that simply said 'Internet.' Inside the hut, there was a foldout table with a computer on it, making it possible for Emma to email Maddy. Sunday contact was important, necessary, and non-negotiable for both of them.

This Sunday rule had all began after the two of them received continual groundings for dominating the phone lines, preventing other family members from using the phone. In an effort to keep the two friends off the phone on weeknights, their parents had devised a plan allowing them to talk on the phone for a whole hour on Sundays. Therefore, every Sunday morning, in the Thompson and Yanagi households, everyone knew when the telephone lines were not available.

Ever since the age of thirteen, they continued this ritual. There were lean years for both of them, where they would have to spend all their savings on long distance bills. None of that mattered; neither of them could bear to give up this habit. So all significant others in their lives would always have to plan around the "Sunday talk zone."

She had moved around a lot when she was young and single, but these days, Maddy made Hawaii her home on the island of Kaua'i. She had two young sons, a husband who adored her and one cat and a dog. She lived the perfect family life Emma knew she could never have. Emma and Nicholas had tried to conceive, to no avail.

Maddy owned a small spa in a posh hotel in Poipu called 'Mind Your Spirit.' She was an amazing massage therapist, specializing in Lomi Lomi. She had even trained under a famous Kupuna on the Big Island. Lomi Lomi was unique because it was a type of massage conducted with prayer and intention. Maddy trained in the old ways approached her work very seriously. Touched and profoundly moved by her friend's dedication to her work, Emma was grateful she made the time to be there at Maddy's spa opening.

She watched as Maddy prayed while picking herbs - as taught to her by her mentor. It was hard for Emma to remain quiet; Maddy had explained that she had to focus on the healing, and any distraction would break the vibration.

Emma patiently watched her friend out in the garden, communing with nature. Maddy received teachings regarding the power of the spoken word. Her friend used this knowledge as she gathered and created the vibration needed for the healing just as she had learned as an apprentice.

"The healing flows from God through me," Maddy had explained.

She had silently observed Maddy pray as she worked; it was only then that she realized her friend of many years was now a modern day healer in the old Hawaiian traditional way.

The reason why Maddy had chosen Lomi Lomi as her specialty was her strong belief in 'Mana.' The Hawaiians believe thoughts contain 'Mana' or energy. When thoughts combined with touch and breaths are in line with the creator, the receiver will experience healing. However, the receiver must ask with gratitude. Hence, for one to perform Lomi Lomi, one must be able to focus on love and healing aligned with divine energy.

It was Emma's turn to call Maddy this week. She picked up the phone and dialed her number.

Maddy picked-up on the second ring with a cheerful "Hello?"

"Hello, back."

Maddy paused. "So... *what's* up?"

"What do you mean, what's up?"

"Come on, I know pretty much every one of your tones."

Somehow, Maddy's voice provided the support for Emma to release everything she had been holding. She choked back tears. Embarrassed, she began to share. "I am so sorry. I don't know where this is coming from."

Maddy warmly consoled her oldest and dearest friend. "Well, let's try to figure it out."

"I feel like I'm going crazy," Emma said. For the next ten minutes, she recounted the memorial service, her dream, and the glimpse of Walden in her kitchen.

Maddy took a deep breath and paused. "Okay, I'm going to walk you through this and you're *not* crazy." Intuitive and calm, Maddy began with her approach regarding time. "Most indigenous cultures believe we're all connected. Connected in an agreement of the concept of time, whereas time controls the space we're in."

She slowly began pulling herself together, "Well, I don't know Maddy, I don't know if I believe in all that stuff."

"It doesn't matter what you believe," Maddy replied, "it appears *it* believes in you. So just, hear me out. You ever notice when you do not wear a watch or when you are sick, you have no idea of time? When you have no concept of time you are actually more in touch with what you are feeling? Because rather than your feelings leading you, time leads you and regulates you."

"What do you mean by that?" Emma asked.

"Think about eating. How many times are you actually hungry at noon, versus knowing it's time to eat and therefore you're meant to be hungry?"

"You're saying we are all trained mice?"

"As children, we learn in preschool about time," Maddy explained. "And time begins to regulate our senses which affect our vibration. Our vibration, at whatever level we vibrate at, determines what we are able to see. During circle time, children learn today is... yesterday was... and tomorrow will be. It is the beginning of the framing of the time concept in our lives. The time concept creates files just like the rings that you would find inside a tree. For children, life is one ongoing event, where the introduction of time in their lives begins to provide file dividers." Maddy went on.

"Some cultures believe the present, past, and futures are all happening at one time. I watched this amazing documentary. It was a documentary on how much of our mind we actually use. They studied brainwaves in adults and children and the interesting thing is that they included children with Dyslexia and Autism. What was so amazing was that the children with Dyslexia and Autism process information in different parts of their brain than others. There's controversy on how much of the brain we actually use, but everyone's in agreement that we don't use the mind to its full capacity."

Maddy continued. "You know what I believe? It is that as children, we use more of our brain. However, once imprisoned in the concept of time, we have to let go of what we are capable of seeing. In fact, we start building walls in our consciousness to protect ourselves. That is how we lose our sixth sense. These walled in senses are our way of functioning within the framework of time." She chuckled and went on.

"And that's why people like *me* are sought out. We help them remove the bricks from their built-up walls so they have a better understanding of self. When someone understands who they truly are, they can relate to and understand others. This is how they open up to having healthy relationships. Time is no longer the most important aspect in their existence, relationships are."

"I'm sorry," Emma said. "But I still just can't wrap my thinking around it yet."

Maddy giggled. "Well, let's figure out how to apply this to what you're going through."

She proceeded for the next twenty minutes, to explain the 101 guide of how not to appear crazy to others, especially should Emma be in a situation where she encounters Walden again. The discussion also included Emma finding safety in her visions. Rather than having her dreams control her, Maddy explained how Emma could maintain her personal power and make clear choices in her trances. She walked her through a couple of breathing techniques to help Emma maintain focus.

Before ending their weekly conversation, Maddy assured her, "It sounds like this man Walden has left bits and pieces behind for you to find. Just know that I'm here if you need anything." She paused, "By the way, welcome to crazy land, my friend."

They both giggled, and then reluctantly hung up.

CHAPTER 14

Emma was in a boardroom surrounded by men dressed in suits. Her back was against the wall and she was standing next to an entrance. The room was murky with blurs of light. There was dust and debris everywhere; somehow, she knew it was 9/11.

Everyone looked scared, as if these men were waiting for something to transpire. They did not seem to detect her at first. Emma thought of the play, *Waiting for Godot*, because she had a gut feeling they were waiting for something or someone who was not coming. It appeared as if they all had the flu by the way they were slowly moving around the room. Intuitively she knew these men, wounded at a molecular level, were dying.

A trapped, state of terror surrounded her. Scanning the area, she was shocked to see Walden, situated amidst the chaos. He did not notice her at first, but when he did, he locked his eyes on her. That is when the other executives in the room were suddenly aware of her existence. A state of alarm gushed through her body. She instantaneously began to do one of the breathing exercises her best friend Maddy had taught her during their most recent phone conversation. Out of nowhere, a man with gray hair grabbed her upper right arm, squeezing so tightly, she shrieked.

VIBRATIONAL PASSAGE

Then she could hear her husband calling her name. He was next to her in bed, gently shaking her arm, trying to get her to wake-up.

In a frantic state, Emma yanked her arm away from Nicholas. All of a sudden, a stream of light blinded her. Her husband had switched on the lamp beside the bed. Narrowing her eyes until they adjusted to the brightness, she examined her arm. The crimson rash she had earlier disappeared almost as fast as it emerged, but now her skin was red again; her arm was throbbing with soreness.

Nicholas peered over to see what she was looking at.

"Oh-my-god, did I do that?" He stammered.

Emma stared in disbelief at her arm. "I don't think so," her breathing began to calm.

She did not want to alarm her husband with her nightmare. She knew Nicholas was still dealing with balancing his survivor's guilt, and the last thing she wanted to do was to make things worse by mentioning anything more about Walden in association to 9/11.

Emma took a deep breath and as calmly as possible whispered, "It's nothing, Honey, everything's okay. Just go back to sleep."

She looked over at the clock on her nightstand, and froze. It was 9:11. Emma quickly closed her eyes and began to compose her thinking by taking in long slow breaths before opening them again.

She turned back over to watch as Nicholas switched off the light.

The deep throb was now a faint ring of tenderness around her arm.

Emma spent the next few minutes tossing and turning. She shifted her pillow here and there, moved her blanket around her in every possible direction, in desperation of finding that perfect spot to relax. Gradually, she eventually drifted off.

Once asleep, Emma found herself participating in one nightmare after another. Each nightmarish dream was more intense than the one before until Emma forced herself awake.

She bolted up in bed struggling to breathe; her heart was racing out of her chest. She was hyperventilating uncontrollably.

Nicholas quickly switched on the lamp next to the bed for the second time that night.

As her eyes adjusted to the light, Emma could see the concern in her husband's face. Now, Nicholas was demanding to know what was going on as he stroked her shoulders and arms to reassure her that he was there to protect her and that she was perfectly safe.

"This is the second bad dream tonight," Nicholas yawned. "Maybe you need to talk about it."

If only she could divulge to him that this was not just the second petrifying dream, it had been an entire evening of nightmares, one after another. "Honey, I'm fine. Really, I'm fine."

"Well then, humor me," he insisted.

Clearly, he was not going to let it go.

"I'm just going to sound crazy."

"Well," Nicholas grinned, "that was the number one quality that drew me to you." He teased her, "I've always found crazy sexy."

Emma giggled.

Nicholas leaned back against the headboard, his arms wrapping around her. She rested her head on his chest, feeling the tenderness and security of his embrace. Emma slowly stopped trembling.

"Okay," Emma murmured, anxious and still afraid. "I saw Walden in my dream...and you," she waited for a response from Nicholas.

He remained quiet, so she continued.

"Walden was standing on a football field. He was wearing a white lab coat; you know the kind you wear at work in your lab. When I looked over at what Walden was gesturing towards, he was pointing at a player who was faking a pass. The player's face, it was Walden's.

He faked the pass, but when everyone was looking where the football was going, he passed the football to you, and then it was a briefcase. Sounds ridiculous but the football just turned into an attaché case. He kept showing me this same football play repeatedly in a loop. I had no choice I just kept watching this replay, which I could not stop. Remember that movie we watched a long time ago with Bill Murray, *Groundhog Day*. It was like that," she hesitated catching her breath.

Before carrying on, Emma gently rubbed her husband's arm.

"Honey, I know I am rambling but when he passed the ball to you, you stuck it under your jersey. Then that football turned into a briefcase, the sort of case that a military agent might use when transporting secrets. You know the one that you see in movies, which has the launch code for nuclear missiles or something like that. I know it sounds outrageous. Just know I feel really crazy right now."

Nicholas' body seemed to tense against hers. In spite of this, he remained silent, so she persisted on. "Out of nowhere Walden had that attaché case back from you and was trying to handcuff it to me. I flatly refused because I had no idea what was in it, and it scared me," her heart began to race as panic set in.

Nicholas instinctively seemed to feel her anxiety. He began to massage her back in a calm and soothing manner, which helped her relax her racing heart.

She went on. "When Walden realized I wouldn't take the case he walked towards this door that just appeared. I followed him through the doorway thinking it was a way out but we were in someone's study. Expensive looking books lined the walls; those shelves were made of this luxurious mahogany wood. There was a judge's robe hanging on a coat rack. Three men were sitting and talking. One man was behind the desk, while the other two were sitting on the other side facing him."

"Did you recognize any of them?" Nicholas questioned.

"No, I couldn't really see their faces. I did notice that one of them looked like he was out of the 50s. He was wearing a thick leather jacket, while his hair was dark and slicked back, greasy like. Then all three men disappeared. I was trying to figure out where they went when a book dropped on the floor, half scaring the wits out of me. Walden then emerged back in the room and he gestured for me to pick up that book and open it. It was so heavy. He then told me; 'Ask Wally,' as he pulled a piece of paper out of the book I was holding, gesturing as if he were a magician."

"Did you see what was written on the paper?"

"I'm not quite sure, but I think it was a grouping of numbers."

Emma rubbed her eyes, and prepared for her husband to tease her. Nicholas said nothing. Even though her nightmares were disturbing and they deeply scared her, it felt good to talk about it.

Subsequently, Emma pushed on, telling her husband the rest.

"I saw a river of blood. Just blood everywhere. Then Hitler, yes Hitler, he was holding a large oil painting of a naked woman standing next to a child. The woman had on this unusual hat, and the child was holding a honeycomb. He was just staring at the painting."

Emma could hear Nicholas rub the stubble that was starting to grow on his chin. He always rubbed his chin when either stressed or worried. Her husband remained quiet.

"There's more," Emma quietly added, wondering when he was going to stop her. Since he was not, she carried on. "I saw a room full of children, and they seem frightened, but it's as if I'm on the outside of the room looking in. No one is helping them. Walden wants me to help them. But I don't know how to help them or why he wants me to help them." She paused.

"But Walden let me know that these kids are in enormous jeopardy."

Knowing Nicholas felt the same way about children that she did, she spared him the horrifying details from the unspeakable experience. She decided to keep the rest of the particulars of what was happening to these children from him. "I think that's all I can remember," she lied to him.

Emma waited for Nicholas to tease her. It was his usual way of lightening up a situation. At first, he did not say anything; instead, he pulled her up into a sitting position so that she could see his face.

He spoke slowly, choosing his words carefully, "I think I need to show you something."

Nicholas guided her to the study, but not before taking the top blanket off the bed and wrapping it around her.

Once in the study, he removed the large Degas oil painting from the wall exposing a concealed wall safe. After dialing several numbers in different directions, he then pulled down on the lever, which exposed the contents.

Emma watched her husband as he pulled out a black briefcase that had a shiny silver chain with a handcuff attached to it. The blood rushed out of her face, as she realized it was the exact same attaché case from her unnerving nightmare earlier that evening. Emma's knees went weak; she fell into the chair behind her.

Nicholas placed the briefcase on the desk and began to explain.

"Three days before Walden died; he stopped by when you weren't home. He asked me to hold this for him. Walden instructed me not to discuss this briefcase with anyone, ever. He gave explicit instructions on that. It has been under my care ever since," Nicholas halted briefly.

"He said if he didn't come to get it, he'd send me a message one way or another. I always assumed a messenger would stop by one day to retrieve it. I never actually thought he would send me a message, which appears to be through *you*."

"So you believe me?" Her voice had a pleading tone.

Assuring her of his support he answered, "I've learned in my work over the years there are no accidents."

"What's inside it?" Emma inquired.

"I don't know." Nicholas blushed. "After Walden died, I tried to open it. I was curious. But I couldn't figure out the right combination to open it."

Emma's skin got all bumpy instantly, "You think that book Walden showed me in the dream, the one where he shows me the scrap of paper with numbers on it. Do you think if I find that piece of paper it's the code to unlock this briefcase?"

"Perhaps..."

"So you actually believe me?"

"Yes, honey I do. You have too many details for this to be coincidental. The man you described with the slicked back hair in your dream," he explained. "They called him the magician. His name was Larry, and he always slicked his hair back with gel, so that it looked wet. Larry liked to wear this black leather jacket even on hot days. He enjoyed telling anyone who would listen, that his grandfather knew Houdini."

Emma interrupted, "Have I met ever met this Larry?"

"No. Larry was one of Peter Lyceum's personal assistants. He actually behaved more like a bodyguard. The way he made it impossible to approach Peter got on everyone's nerves," Nicholas hesitated, "You know they haven't found his body yet, either."

Emma bit her lip, trying to fight back tears, because someone believed her, and that someone was her husband. She could feel Nicholas watching her, so she tried to hide her tears of gratitude underneath the blanket, which wrapped around her.

It was pointless; he saw right through her attempt and walked over to hug her.

"I'm actually glad that this is happening, honey," Nicholas confessed. "Because there have been so many incidents left unanswered and unexplainable things still keep occurring. I don't know who to trust anymore."

"You have me," she beamed.

"I'm a bit on the crazy side, but I am cute," she teased.

"That you are – I mean the cute part."

She smiled to herself.

They were back to being the team they used to be, before 9/11.

CHAPTER 15

Emma soaked in the delicious aroma, as she poured herself a cup of coffee. It smelled heavenly this morning. Through the kitchen window, she looked down onto the building's courtyard where a gloomy, cloudy day in the city awaited her. Nicholas had already left for the day, but not before brewing a fresh pot of coffee for her.

She always appreciated this because it took a while for her to kick-start her day. Emma was not a morning person like Nicholas. He was usually out the door to make the commute to Long Island, at least an hour before she awoke. She did not know how he did it, but he always seemed to manage on a lot less sleep.

Emma looked towards the fridge hoping to find a note from Nicholas. There it was a post-it stuck to the fridge door, which read: 'I'll call you later. Have a good day, honey.' The note ended with his signature sketch of a heart. She smiled, feeling the warmth of his thoughts, making her feel loved and safe all over again.

There was a time when she knew he would never leave the apartment without providing her with a romantic note, reminding her how much he loved her. However, Nicholas had been so preoccupied with other things these last few months, that it was a pleasant surprise to see that he had remembered this morning. Last night, for the first time in a long time, she had felt truly connected to him. Emma contentedly sipped on her coffee.

As she drank the last few drops from her favorite blue mug she reflected back onto the previous night, her nightmares, Nicholas showing her the briefcase, and Walden's son. Emma's thoughts then drifted to Wally. Why would Walden say his son would know what was on that piece of paper?

She then wondered if Wally did know, but without knowing, just like her. Worst yet, how would she even broach such a subject, especially with a child who was still grieving over the loss of his father? Emma sighed. She looked down at her watch deciding whether she had time to pour another cup of coffee or not. "Oh no, I'm going to be late again," Emma stammered. She swiftly placed her mug in the dishwasher.

Emma had to get to her bookstore to oversee the final changes on a crucial exhibit. The latest book in the *Dragon Kingdom* chronicles was about to be unveiled today, which meant mass chaos for her and her staff even with being prepared. She reached for her keys and purse.

Just as Emma was about to walk out the door, the phone rang. *Who would be calling her on her home phone line,* she thought. Everyone usually knew to call her on her cell. Maybe it was Nicholas. A sinking feeling came over her.

What if the discussion around Walden last night, touched on unhealed wounds with her husband? She could not suffer through that isolation again if he chose to retreat into that profound state of sadness. That silence was excruciating. Overcome with fear and regret Emma rushed to the phone hoping she was wrong.

"Hello...?" She was about to say 'Honey', when a booming voice echoed out of the receiver.

"Emms! Guess where I am right now?" It was her brother, Jake. Thank God. Then again, she had to hold the phone earpiece away from her because he was yelling. *Why was he so vociferous?* She wondered. "Jake, stop shouting! And what's all that noise in the background?"

Jake, slurring his words continued to yell, "I'm on a flight to Washington!" His voice dropped to a loud whisper. "I'll be there for a few days and then I thought I'd stop in and see my little sister."

Emma agitatedly rubbed her palm into her forehead, and thought, now was not a good time for a visit from Jake. Visits from Jake were always complicated. She sighed. "Shall I book you a room at the Plaza?"

Jake, garbling his words hooted, "You're so *fun-ny*, Emm."

"Have you been drinking?" she probed. "Or better question, are you *still* drinking? Is Helen with you?"

Jake did not say anything, he just laughed drunkenly.

In the best compassionate tone, she could muster knowing he was intoxicated, Emma prompted, "Is everything alright, Jake?"

Jake did not answer right away. For a few seconds, she listened to the annoying static on the line.

He finally spoke, continuing to slur. "What can I say? I am Mister Relationship."

She looked down at her watch, knowing this was going to make her even later. Jake would probably remember very little from this conversation but she took a deep breath and inquired, "What happened between you and Helen?"

"Emm, she's gone."

"Gone where?"

"Helen moved out," Jake answered flatly. "She moved to New Zealand. The wedding's off."

Emma took a deep breath in and sighed. She wanted to ask him what he did wrong this time, but knew it was too harsh to ask right now. His breakups were becoming predictable. He was yet to find a woman who could actually get that ring on his finger. "I'll let Nicholas know you'll be gracing us with your company." She smiled, actually happy to be seeing him. "We'll dust off your sofa bed for you."

Jake laughed. "Thanks, Emm. Love you."

"Love you, too. Be safe."

Emma hung up the phone, wondering how she was going to tell Nicholas about Jake's latest. Oh, the non-refundable tickets she groaned, and the fact that Nicholas was unhappy with having to make special arrangements to take time off to travel to Australia for his wedding. He is going to flip. If this was happening for the first time, that would be one thing, but it was not. Right now, they had a drawer that contained several non-refundable plane tickets to Jake's other failed wedding events. Emma had really hoped Helen was the one.

As exasperated as she was with Jake's love life, Emma could not help but feel protective of her big brother. Jake had been sick most of his childhood. One specialist after another poked and prodded the tiny scared little boy, but none of them could figure out what was weakening his immune system.

The medical experts were trying various cures, which meant Jake was constantly taking different types of drugs. Each drug treatment had its own side effect, causing him to be in and out of hospitals his entire youth. Emma was his only companion throughout the whole ordeal. She would distract him from the ongoing torturous treatments by making up elaborate stories, which he could eagerly escape into and sometimes become one of the characters.

With only a year separating them, most times she felt like *she* was the older sibling. They had been through so much together; Emma held a sadness regarding Jake. She felt he was still trying to fill that emptiness inside himself for a childhood of isolation, but it was like trying to fill a black hole with light.

Both their parents, preoccupied with their own interests, pretty much left them to raise themselves. Their mother was busy at the club for officer's wives. She was usually unable to offer comfort, as she was engrossed with examining the bottom of her martini glass. Meanwhile, their father took every opportunity to move up the ranks; constantly receiving promotions meant extra training and the moving of the family from Air Force base to Air Force base around the world.

Emma was the one that taught Jake how to be an explorer and look at each new experience as a fun new adventure. He took that skill and developed his persona to the point where lost souls gravitated to him because of his magnetic personality. He was like Peter Pan. In fact, the real Peter Pan could learn a few things from him.

While on the other hand, a lot had changed also for Emma since their childhood. The pressure from the death of their Aunt Gertie had left Emma fractured. She had always had numerous friends, but when she made the choice to take care of her dying aunt, she quickly learned that she only had one true friend who was there for her - Maddy. She did not blame them because she knew how emotionally draining she must have been. Nonetheless, Emma had learned an important lesson about loyalty.

During her grieving process, Emma withdrew, no longer able to relate to others as she used to. Only a few, like Jake, Nicholas, and Maddy could see her pilot light of charisma still glowing, waiting to ignite once again one day. She was grateful for that.
Meanwhile, Jake was now the charismatic one. He could figure people out pretty quickly, and they liked him easily because of his nonjudgmental ways. The problem was he would get restless, with his female companionships. That is why most of those relationships ended badly.

When he loved, he loved with all his heart and could make a woman feel like the most special person in the universe. Although, when he grew restless, he tended to wander off and get himself into more trouble and mischief than he should. As cautious as Emma had grown over the years, Jake on the other hand had become more adventurous.

She scratched at her elbow, bringing her back from her immersion of thoughts. Emma, reminded of the red welts up and down her arm from the night before, continued to scrape at her irritated skin. She had scratched so hard, a few dots of blood seeped through her blouse. It was too late to change; she figured that no one would notice anyway.

Emma glanced down at her watch and hurried out the door. She knew she was fortunate that her commute to work was a short one. Their apartment took up the entire eleventh floor. It consisted of seven bedrooms, a living room that faced a tree-lined street, and a dining room overlooking a European courtyard. Her commute consisted of an elevator ride down, a three-minute walk through the lobby, followed by several steps outside to her bookstore.

When Aunt Gertie died, she had willed Emma this entire building in an exclusive neighborhood on the Upper East Side. The eleven-story building was residential from the fourth floor up. There were several storefronts on the bottom floor, making Emma a tenant as well as the property owner. Her bookstore took up most of the square footage, however.

Her bookstore became very popular over the years. In fact, from all over the world, bibliophiles flocked to the 'Rue de Royales' bookstore. Emma had designed it to be a book lovers' oasis, 'a swank bookstore that was like a fancy, yet comforting blanket to wrap around oneself'. At least, that is what a magazine writer had once written about her store in a review.

The bookstore had an extensive children's section, one of the biggest in Manhattan, with a reading nook where children could sit in beanbag chairs. There were daily story time sessions where the children could meet the authors and dress up in their favorite story characters.

At the far end of the bookstore was a little cafe to feed Emma's addiction to caffeine. She preferred French Cafe and a croissant or a scone with jam for brunch. The cafe only sold desserts, fruits, and an array of exotic drinks.

The hot chocolate bar of a hundred flavors was very popular with the kids. The flavorful drinks always had a generous portion of whipped cream that came in a dozen different shades and flavors. During the previous week, the bestseller had been the 'purple grape spectacular' whipped cream. It was a pastel shade of purple, with a rich grape flavor. It did not matter what time of the day it was, the cafe was always busy and crowded.

Although Emma had meant the hot chocolate bar for kids, there was always a good crowd of adults indulging their inner child at the café, making long lines of those waiting to get in during the evening hours. Whenever there were leftover desserts, Emma would package them up for a local homeless woman who would come by at the end of the day with her companion, a small scruffy dog.

She remembered the initial time she met Ester digging through Emma's garbage bin. It broke her heart watching the old half-blind woman excavate through the trash to find something edible for them. When Emma approached the elderly woman the first time, the woman was afraid that she was going to call the cops on her. After a few minutes of reassuring her, she began to open up to Emma.

Emma learned that Ester and her dog Frank had been traveling together for the past three years. Ester found Frank abandoned at an empty house. It looked like the family had moved away without him. Frank would not leave the dwelling. Consequently, Ester remained with him until he gave up on his family ever coming back for him. Ester and Frank had been traveling together ever since.

She called him Frank after her late husband. In her mind, they shared the same type of loyalty. Ester made it clear to Emma that 'her and Frank were not looking for handouts'. She assured Ester that, in fact, they were doing her a big favor by taking the leftovers. Emma made a point of there always being leftovers every day. It was one of her strict rules with her pastry chef.

Another one of Emma's strict rules was no mixing foods and beverages with books. Emma loved her books and taught the children to respect them and treat them with kindness. To her, novels provided wonderful new worlds with amazing possibilities.

In order to enter the bookstore from the cafe, anyone and everyone had to wash their hands at the rainbow sink. The process was actually fun for children and adults enjoyed using it as well. There was a foot pedal, which when pressed, released what looked like a colorful shower of warm water. However, the colorful rainbow effect was actually the sink basin made of specialized glass. The pressing of the foot pedal activated the different colored light bulbs, which in turn created the rainbow experience.

Along with the usual staff needed to operate a bookstore, Emma also employed three security guards. They had been with her since the opening of the bookstore nine years ago. They were friendly but took their jobs seriously. Part of their duties was to monitor the rainbow sink, making sure everyone washed their hands before entering the bookstore. It was Nicholas's idea for the security guards. At first, she felt it was ridiculous, who hires protection for a bookstore?

In spite of this, her husband had been able to repackage the idea by convincing her that by hiring retired veterans as security guards, she was helping them regain a sense of duty. Emma could not argue with that and hired the men. She was so glad she had, because over the years these men became an important part of the bookstore's charm. The children loved the security guards and could not wait to tell them about their school day, a party they were going to, or a new pet they just got.

At last, Emma reached the bookstore and unlocked the front door. She was feeling a sense of jumpiness. The lights were already on. Riley had begun arranging the final display items for the *Dragon Kingdom* books. He had done an amazing job as usual. Riley exuded creativity; he had an eye for design and could place items so that they looked even better.

Emma nurtured his natural set design abilities by encouraging him to go back to school, but he insisted that he liked working at the bookstore. He was a rare find. A manager she could depend on and trust. He was her eyes and ears there, and gave her the freedom to come and go as she pleased.

There was only one other person she had trusted like this, and that had ended quite badly. In fact, she was still picking up the financial pieces from that mistake. The thought of Suzanna, better known as Suzy, still stung. Emma had not quite figured out how to move on from the betrayal. How could she have been so blind?

Emma glanced around the bookstore, when her eyes fell on the orange tablecloths in the cafe. Suzy had ordered them last fall, pumpkin orange. Emma had wanted a more neutral color, but as usual, had deferred to Suzy, because, after all, they were just tablecloths. Little did she know then, that these covers would be constant reminders of all the times she should have stood up to Suzy.

Before Riley had taken over the daunting task of managing the store, it had been Suzy's responsibility. She was in charge of all the bookkeeping and employee schedules. Emma was frequently told that one of her greatest strengths was also, her greatest weakness. In fact, when she trusted someone, she entrusted completely. Generally, with no questions asked.

Shortly after that catastrophic day in September, when everyone was still reeling from the tragedy of it all, Suzy had told everyone that she had had enough of New York City. She gave Emma two-hour's notice, by scribbling on a scrap piece of paper, letting her know that she was quitting and moving 'abroad.' Suzy never really specified where *abroad* meant, and as Emma would eventually find out, there was a good reason for that.

Unbeknownst to Emma, Suzy had been skimming money off the book sales. She was also able to hide unpaid invoices by asking the venders for extensions that included hefty interest and pocketing the cash. In a final coup de grace, she cleaned out the business account, leaving a balance of around a hundred dollars.

If she had not stolen the business credit card, Emma would not have been able to trace her to the last place she had used them, the Bahamas. Even though she canceled the cards, she was still accountable for the charges because Suzy had signing rights, making Emma legally answerable.

The worst part was the public humiliation that went with Suzy's betrayal. There was not enough money left in the bank account to pay the electricity bill and the company was threatening to cut power off if she did not pay immediately. Come to find out, the power bill was overdue by three months. On top of that, Emma was now required to put down a $1500 deposit because apparently, they no longer trusted that she would pay her bills in a timely manner. All her vendors were treating Emma this way due to Suzy's embezzlement.

When Emma had originally hired Suzy for the manager's position, it was only supposed to be temporary. Suzy had planned to get her master's at NYU, and she needed money to go back to school. Emma and Suzy had been roommates in college, so it had been a lot of fun working at the bookstore together. It was like the old days, they talked about everything.

Even until this day, if someone warned her in advance of what Suzy's intentions were, she would not have believed them. Nicholas had warned Emma about the danger of letting Suzy have carte blanche access. Riley had also mentioned that a customer had noticed Suzy pocketing money instead of putting it into the cash register. Emma had trusted Suzy, believing there was a logical explanation for it all.

She took a deep breath in. Emma could do nothing about it now; her feelings were severely hurt along with her business. Someone she felt was her friend had betrayed her. Emma verbally made a mental note, "Order new tablecloths and burn those ugly orange ones." That statement made her smile.

Riley greeted her cheerfully as soon as he saw her walk around the display he was creating. Nothing seemed to get him down; he was always so chipper and positive. After a few minutes of small talk, together they quietly worked on finishing the staging for the novel's release. Actually, Emma just assisted a little, while trying to stay out of the way of his 'vision' for the layout.

Over the next few minutes, the rest of the workforce arrived. Adam, the first shift security guard, provided access through the employee entrance. As soon as they pinned their nametags on, they helped ready the store by addressing last minute details before the barrage of children flooded through the doors. As specified by the two authors of the chronicles, the books were to go on sale at exactly noon.

Riley had devised a plan of two separate lines. There was the pre-order line; customers received numbered gold cards, which had reserved their place in line ahead of time. For the customers who had not prearranged purchase in advance, they received numbered royal blue cards. The numbered cards would prevent anyone from cutting in line, which unfortunately happened frequently.

Emma glanced down at her watch; it was two minutes to noon. She scanned her store to make sure everyone was in place and ready to go. She took another deep breath in and slowly released it. It was exactly noon. Emma signaled to Adam, standing next to the front doors, that it was time to open them.

From noon to closing, there was a constant crowd of customers eager to get their own *Dragon Kingdom* copy. Emma and her staff were so grateful when the hectic day was finally over.

Riley tilted his head and gave her that look. The one that said her perfectly happy and cheerful manager had something serious to discuss. "Um, Emma, do you have a minute?"

Emma nodded; she was half hoping it was about his personal life, and not about the bookstore.

She followed him through the store to the back where the main office was located. It was the area where all the company's files were stored. He motioned for her to have a seat, and then it became obvious what he was doing. He pointed to two piles of paperwork he had neatly stacked side by side on the desk.

Emma frowned. "And here, I was thinking of giving you a raise."

"No, no, no. You cannot afford to do that. Not yet, of course," he smiled. "I know it's been a long day, but I've needed to talk to you. I know you're avoiding it..."

"Stop," she held out her hand and waved it in front of her. "Just rip the bandage off and tell me where we're at."

"Those are the bills I've paid," he said, exuding optimism. "And those," he pointed to the much taller stack, "are the bills we've got to pay..., all passed due with the interest mounting. How shall we handle *that* stack?"

Emma rubbed her forehead with the palm of her hand trying to relieve the tension that came with powerlessness. Riley was sweet, even when he was making her deal with stuff. He had a way of taking something that was so overwhelming and split it up so that being held accountable was manageable.

"I'll have some money transferred to the business account. Can it wait until tomorrow?"

Riley nodded. "Have you told Nicholas, yet?"

"No."

Riley shook his head. "I'm not your accountant, but I'm sure it's obvious that you've got to cut costs."

"Where...?" She moaned.

"Look, you have no overhead as far as rent, so that's helpful. But you have payroll, electricity, gas, inventory costs are going through the roof and don't forget, I filed your extension, but you've got to get the paperwork together for your taxes."

"How much do we need to make it through this month?"

Riley licked the eraser end of his pencil, and then began punching in a series of numbers into a calculator handset in front of him. He looked up, but did not say anything.

"Well?"

"You need an extra five-thousand dollars. You need to pay the suppliers, and, I know you love Stacy, and she is the best pastry chef in Manhattan, but I do not think you can afford to keep paying her salary. Have you thought of bringing pastries in from other bakeries to keep your costs down?"

Emma frowned.

"I can't let go of Stacy. Riley, come on. She just had a baby; there is no way she could find another position right now. Plus, our customers just *loooove* her pastries. The cafe seems to be the place where we are making most of our profits. Where else can we cut costs?"

Riley shook his head and gave her a sad smile. "Emma, you are bleeding money there are all these interest charges." He cleared his throat. "Have you considered selling the business? You'd be able to collect rent, and have some sort of an agreement with the new owners to keep the current staff employed."

"I don't know."

Her eyes were getting watery; she did not want him to notice, so she stood up and started tidying up a stack of books on the corner bookshelf. "Let's talk about this tomorrow," she checked her watch. "I'll have the money in the business account by tomorrow morning, okay?"

He nodded, with a wary look of defeat. "Okay," Riley sighed.

The past several months had been an uphill struggle. It seemed that at every corner she turned, something even more difficult was occurring. First, there was 9/11, and then as if that was not dreadful enough, her husband withdrew into his own world leaving her alone, which was followed up with, one of her close friends robbing her blind.

She had had to start paying for the business disaster using her own personal funds. Emma felt she could not tell her husband about it, he had enough on his plate. In addition, Emma was deeply embarrassed.

On the other hand, the one thing that was looking up was that she felt she and Nicholas were back on the same team again after last night. Emma hated the days when Nicholas had withdrawn into his own world, in which she was not invited. At first, it was understandable. He had lost many colleagues that morning. If Walden had not sent him to Washington, Nicholas would have been right there with him until the very end.

At first, she felt supportive by letting him process his pain and guilt, his way. Then, she believed deep in her heart that she just needed to cheer him up. Emma wanted to make things better for him, but it had achieved the exact opposite. She felt powerless as she felt her husband drift away.

He would get home from work, and not be in the mood for any type of conversation. Nicholas preferred to sit in front of the TV watching something on the sports channel. Other times he retreated to the study to read a magazine or the newspaper.

The company policy after 9/11 was that everyone had to undergo what 'they' called a debriefing from the September tragedy. A list provided to all employees, included psychologists, clergy members, rabbis, and grief counselors, approved to sign-off on paperwork so employees could return to their normal work schedules. Nicholas had chosen a grief counselor from the list, but she did not know anything more than that.

Even though she finally felt closer to Nicholas, Emma still knew she was having a pity party for herself. She did not care, besides no one else was invited. The nice thing about pity parties is that only one person needs to get the party started and keep it going.

Emma made her way home. Exhausted, all she wanted to do was drag herself into the shower before crawling into her bed for a very long time. She was emotionally and physically exhausted.

She had spent the day nicely avoiding any thoughts about the nightmares from the night before. Emma had reveled in the happy smiles of the children, which helped push back images of the reality of that briefcase sitting in their safe in Nicholas's study. The briefcase from her dream was in their study. How was that even possible?

Then sweet Riley had to go and cheer her up with a reality check of how deep she was in debt. She felt for Riley, he was a good man that did not have to help her but he did and she was grateful. How would she ever get back in the black? Emma continued on her way home not wanting to think about any of it anymore.

She knew there was something she was forgetting, but she could not figure it out as she greeted Paulo, the night door attendant. He tipped his hat to her and smiled. Emma stepped into the elevator and that is when she realized what she had forgotten. Jake was coming for a visit and his wedding was off... again.

"Ugh," she muttered to herself. *Could this day get any better*, she thought, as she rode up the elevator. When Emma reached for the door it was unlocked, which meant Nicholas was already home. She was excited that he beat her home.

Emma found herself standing in the foyer, going through a stack of mail, still milling over the possibility of putting off talking to Nicholas about Jake. She always felt that she was a respectable problem-solver. However, these days, she felt more like a problem-avoider, not a very attractive attribute.

Her husband called out from the living room.

"Welcome home, honey. Hope you are in the mood for Italian. I got your favorite Gorgonzola bread from Angels."

Emma's stomach growled and she was suddenly famished. She quickly found her husband in the living room amid containers of take-out he had arranged on the coffee table. She leaned in to give him a kiss.

"What's wrong, honey?" Nicholas asked.

Emma was startled, and unprepared for his question. "That's a pretty broad question," she joked with him.

Nicholas lowered his chin, and studied her. "Are you still thinking about what happened last night?"

That was not quite all of it. Emma shook her head and sighed. "Jake phoned this morning," she confessed slowly. "He says he's coming to New York and wanted to know if he could stay with us. Is that okay?"

Nicholas gave Emma that usual look. The one of amused annoyance, the one that did not have to ask aloud, if this meant that once again, another engagement expired.

"Thought you'd say that," Emma joked, grateful that he did not put into words what he was really thinking and just left it at one of his disapproving looks.

Nicholas finally interrupted the silence. "So when exactly will Mister Casanova be here?"

"I need to pick him up at the airport on Thursday."

"Is he still working for that crazy guy?" Nicholas, trained in Emma's loyalty to her brother shifted the topic away from Jake's latest allergic reaction to the altar. She and Nicholas had many heated discussions regarding Jake's behavior that usually ended in not talking for a few days.

Emma nodded.

Jake was the one and only financial advisor to a reclusive billionaire from Japan who had a thing for real estate investments. They only knew of him by his reputation and stories shared by Jake.

Emma looked at her husband. "Nicholas, just say it and get it over with."

He laughed. "I was actually looking forward to Jake finally settling down. Maybe he'd grow up a little."

"Ouch," Emma winced. "That's harsh."

"What can I say," he chuckled. "Jake has a way of bringing out the best in me." Nicholas paused, "Remember when we lost our best lab tech, because the words 'I do' aren't in your brother's vocabulary?"

Emma promised Nicholas to keep Jake on a short leash.

As they started to eat dinner, Nicholas inquired, "Have you figured out how you're going to talk to Walden's son, Wally?"

Emma heaved a sigh, "Not quite yet."

CHAPTER 16

Wally and Zoe returned to school the day after their father's memorial service. Wally had begged his mom to let him stay home, but she would not listen to him. As usual, he thought aloud, "Mom doesn't care how I feel about anything." His dad's memorial had reopened his emotional wounds of loss and he felt extremely vulnerable.

He hated facing the others at school; he found their sympathy drove him insane. Monday was the worst and Tuesday was not much better. *"Oh Wally, how are you doing?"* If he heard that question, one more time he was going to scream in someone's face.

Even when he told his mom about his stomachache for the third day in a row, she conveyed to him that he was still going to school.

"What, no doctor?" He whined.

She rationalized with him, that he would feel much better once he was sitting in his desk learning just like Monday and Tuesday. Arguing with her was always pointless. Subsequently off to school he went, miserable.

It was Wednesday, Wally's mom had been in to see the school's Principal twice this week already. Once when Zoe bit one of her classmates, and then when she had screamed for ten minutes straight during circle time. Apparently, Zoe was not a big fan of the circle time concept. Wally was not sure why his mom was back yet again. He sat outside the Principal's office, but the one thing he knew for sure, Zoe was in trouble for doing something outrageous again.

Wally pulled out his father's ring from his pocket, and examined the family crest. He squinted, wondering if it was three lions or three dragons on the crest. His father had never really explained what all the symbols meant. He was examining the skeleton key beneath the... dragons he decided. Dragons sounded much cooler. Breaking through his thoughts, he heard someone call his name.

He looked up, "Aunty Emm."

She was whistling a tune that sounded familiar.

"What are you doing here?" he asked.

"I should be asking you the same thing. So, what are you in for?" She gestured towards the Principal's office.

"Not me," Wally shook his head.

"It's Zoe. She spends more time in the principal's office than she does in her class. I think she's going to be the only one in our family history to get booted out of preschool."

"Oh, I see," Aunty Emm nodded.

Wally made clear, "they just don't get her. She doesn't like it here." His voice had a note of protectiveness. "You still haven't answered my question, what are you doing here?"

Aunty Emm laughed and began to give the specifics. "You're quite right. I am just dropping off a book order form. I guess I can give you the inside scoop, you are about to have a book fair in a few weeks. So save up your allowance." She gave him a friendly wink.

"Do you still have any copies left of the *Dragon Kingdom* book? I hear it's sold out."

"Well, young man," she teased him, "you happen to know the right person. Come by my bookstore tomorrow, I have your *Dragon Kingdom* book, plus there's a cup of your favorite hot chocolate with your name on it waiting for you."

Wally was silent. His smile slowly vanished. His stomach began to ache again; he wrapped his arms around his tummy and began to cry. Big deep sobs overtook him. He could always count on Aunty Emm, she never forgot about him. Then all the stress from the past few months and the weight of all the grief, his, Zoe, and his mother's pain burst through him like a crumbling dam that could no longer hold in the anguish.

"Everything will be okay. Trust me, everything will get better," she soothed Aunty Emm sat down beside him and gently patted him on the back.

Wally held his head in his hands, trying to push the booming headache back before the pain became too much to bear. She handed him a clean tissue to blow his nose with, which he gladly took. Wally began to feel a little embarrassed by his uncontrollable outburst. Uncontainable eruptions were Zoe's style, not his.

"Thanks, Aunty Emm," he whispered back to her and wiped away his tears. "I'll be there tomorrow."

The Vice-Principal ducked his head out of his office. His eyes seemed to light up as soon as he noticed Aunty Emm. He motioned her into his office. He did not even seem to notice Wally – just like everyone else. His aunt gave him a wink and smiled back at him, before disappearing behind a closed door.

A few moments later, Zoe and his mother exited the Principal's office. He was so thankful he had had a small amount of time to pull the rest of himself back together. Zoe appeared unfazed and skipped the whole way to the car. His mom's tension filled the air, making Wally's stomach throb even more as he followed behind them to the car.

On the ride home from school, his mother shouted most of the way. She was clearly embarrassed and wanted to take it out on someone. She usually yelled at Dad, but now that he was gone...

After ranting for a while, she turned up the radio blasting some song Wally did not recognize.

Wally stared down his sister, who was looking out the window, fiddling with the buckles on her car seat, unaffected by their mother's recent rambling and delirious raging.

Zoe turned to look at him and said, "I have something for you."

Wally did not answer.

Zoe pulled out a tube of ointment from her pocket. Their nanny used the aloe salve whenever they had cuts or scrapes.

"Look, I got this for you. This is what Gama puts on my owies to make better."

Gama was her pet name for their nanny.

"Eat it," she said, pushing it in his face. It looked like she had already eaten part of the tube, which looked brand new.

"It'll fix your tummy owie and you will feel better."

As much as Zoe drove him crazy most of the time, moments like this made it clear how much she loved him.

Wally grabbed the tube out of her hand. "Don't be stupid," he snorted

Zoe giggled and looked him in the eyes. He could tell by the way that she looked at him that she knew how much he loved her.

Why don't you just stop it already, Wally thought to his sister. Wally did not know when it started, but it was sometime before she was two, he could hear Zoe inside his head. Then he found out she could hear his thoughts inside her head.

I can't, she thought back to him. *It's like I hear lots and lots of different things in my head all at once, and it hurts.*

Well, now Mom is angry, and you know what that means.

Zoe nodded, and began whimpering softly. She cradled her face in her hands.

I am sorry, Wally thought to her.

Then Zoe just went off like a siren.

"No! No! No!" Zoe began screaming repeatedly. She stuck her fingers in her ears and screeched like a wild animal, while kicking the back of their mom's driver's seat. Wally watched his mother's eyes in the rear view mirror. She was looking at Zoe, and now she looked frightened. She quickly turned down the radio.

"Calm your sister down right now," his mom, snapped.

Why was it always his job to fix everything, he contemplated.

"Zoe, look, here's your favorite book," he evenly spoke as he handed her a princess picture book.

She whacked the book out of Wally's hand releasing it into the air where it proceeded to bounced off his forehead. Wally was angry now, while Zoe was laughing hysterically. He looked straight ahead out the front window upset, as Zoe initially licked her window and then drew designs with her fingers. The rest of the ride home had an uncomfortable silence to it, but Wally was just fine with that.

After the car pulled into the driveway, everyone got out of the vehicle without speaking a word. Zoe stomped upstairs to her room, while Wally snuck into his father's den. His mother kept the door locked now, but Wally knew where the hidden spare key was.

A long time ago, Zoe had locked herself in the den. Their father had rushed to the linen closet to retrieve the extra key. Wally remembered where he had seen him grab the concealed key from the rear of the closet. He just loved the way his dad was good with secrets.

He tiptoed into the den and closed the door quietly behind him so no one would know he was there. Wally jumped into his dad's favorite leather chair; hands spread out on the armrests he looked around the room. Nothing had been touched or changed in the study since his dad died.

In truth, his mom never came in here, so it was simple for her to keep everything precisely the same. The only difference was the growing layer of dust. He pulled his father's ring out of his pocket. Wally began twirling the enormous ring around his finger, thinking it would be a long time before he would actually ever be able to wear it properly.

The air was musty with a faint smell of old cigar smoke. There was a cigar still in the ashtray on the desk. Wally remembered sadly, about the talk his father had with him the night before he disappeared.

Wally had been asleep in bed when his father woke him up.

"Hey, little man," he nudged Wally on his arm. "I've got to talk to you."

Wally was always happy when his dad was home from work. He was usually sound asleep when his father got home therefore Wally mostly saw his dad in the mornings and on weekends. Wally rubbed his eyes and yawned as his dad pulled a chair close beside his bed.

He leaned forward, placed his hands on Wally's shoulders, and squeezed before releasing. He did not have to say it aloud, but Wally knew that that was Dad's way of saying, "I love you."

Wally tried to sit up straighter now, wanting to show his father that he was listening.

"You know because I work long hours, I don't get to see you as much as I want to, right?"

Wally nodded, tentatively.

"Well, I need you to be the big guy of the house when I'm not here, okay? Zoe Ann looks up to you, and she really needs you to be there for her. Your one job is to protect her, okay?" His Dad held up one finger, to make his point.

Wally nodded again, but he was doubtful. Was not that his dad's job? He was only eleven. "But..."

His Dad held his hand up to stop Wally from interrupting. "I'm always here for you, so if you need any advice or help, just asking...okay?"

"Okay."

"Did you figure out my latest clue?"

Wally's face broke out into a big smile. Now he was wide-awake. "The word jumble," Wally murmured.

He jumped out of bed and grabbed a scrap piece of paper covered with scribbles. He pointed down to the paper, so his dad could see his answer.

"Magic Hat," Wally triumphantly announced. "Am I right?"

His Dad gave him a great big hug, "How'd I end up with the smartest kid in the world? Huh? Tell me, because I haven't a clue." He tousled Wally's hair, and then reached beneath the bed, pulling out a large magic hat, with a magician's élan. "I hope this is the one you wanted."

It was exactly what Wally had wanted. The hat was sturdy, not like one of those fake felt ones. It had a white satin ribbon around it, and was just the right size to fit Wally's pet bunny, Fluffy in it.

"Oh-My-God, Thanks!" Wally oohed and aahed over the magical gift.

"You earned it, that wasn't the easiest jumble. It was a bit cryptic," his dad proudly stated. "You're really getting good at this game. I think I'm going to have to make it more challenging for you."

"Noooo," Wally complained. "It was hard enough. I had to spend hours on the Internet looking up the clues. We're not studying Renoir at school yet, Dad."

"Well, that's a shame, you should be." his dad laughed. "What are we paying all that money for you to go to a fancy school for, anyway, right?"

His dad winked and gave him one last great big bear hug of a hug. Wally liked the way his Dad smelled like honey. He had honey in his tea, honey on his toast, and best of all honey on his Sunday morning pancakes.

Tears flowed from Wally's eyes. His heart ached with that memory. There would be no more games with Dad, no more bear hugs or piggybacks. He wiped away his tears on his sleeve and blew his nose on his shirt. That was the last time he saw his dad. Wally felt so lost and alone. His life was changing who he thought he was supposed to be, he longer had the luxury of a childhood.

He sat in the dark, looking up at the paintings on the wall. Something did not seem right. The paintings were different somehow from the last time he had been in his dad's office. How was that possible? It did not seem like anyone else had been in the room. A chill ran down Wally's spine, he jumped up and tried to make a quick exit.

Just when he opened the door, a heavy, old book fell from one of the shelves that lined the walls. Wally was too spooked to take a closer look. He shut and locked his dad's office door, and returned the spare key before sprinting back to his room where he immediately turned on the lights, and then dove under his covers.

He decided that his eyes were just playing tricks on him. Nonetheless, Wally was too tired to go downstairs and eat dinner. He fell asleep curled up in a tight ball beneath his blanket. Crying and being scared was tiring. He had no idea why girls were not tired more. In no time, Wally was asleep. He dreamed vivid imaginings of his father the entire night.

CHAPTER 17

Wally eagerly entered the Rue de Royales bookstore, hoping Aunty Emm would not be too busy and would have some time to chat with him. It felt like Wally had been to the bookstore hundreds of times. He was generally too bashful to approach Aunty Emm, and she was usually too busy.

Nevertheless, she always waved at him, and he would with enthusiasm wave back. On occasion, she made time for him, making him feel extremely special. However, he tried never to take up too much of her time.

Wally had been to several of her story time gatherings, and he found her to be an exceedingly funny storyteller because she would do exaggerated voices that made everyone laugh, including him. He enjoyed the fact that she was always smiling. Somehow, it made him feel as if everything was going to be okay.

When he normally entered the store with his nanny, she made a beeline to the cafe, while he went to the young fiction section. Wally had just enough time to pick out one book prior to having a small snack at the café, before they were required to leave to pick up Zoe from piano lessons. That was the routine.

Although, today was different, his aunt had promised yesterday that there would be a copy of the *Dragon Kingdom* waiting for him. He could not wait to read it. Wally was so glad that she noticed him as soon as he entered the bookshop. She waved while giving him a big smile. Wally excitedly waved back and headed over to his favorite spot in the store to wait for her.

When Aunty Emm approached him, he was secretly appreciative. Unlike the other adults, she always came through with her promises. She had not only vowed a copy of the *Dragon Kingdom*, she had also mentioned a hot chocolate yesterday. He could already taste the raspberry flavored hot chocolate.

There was a faint aroma of warm apple pie in the air. Wally had not noticed it when he initially arrived but now he hungered for a slice of Dutch Apple pie with a scoop of vanilla bean ice cream. That would go so well with the hot chocolate.

At first, he was a little embarrassed, the last time they spoke Wally had cried, and he was not going to do that again. All the same, it did not seem to matter, because his eyes instantly lit up when he saw his Aunty Emm coming towards him with his very own copy of the *Dragon Kingdom*. She was now officially, his hero.

"Thank you!" Wally gushed. "Mom wouldn't let me come on Monday, and I heard all the books were sold out."

She opened the front cover to show him that both of the authors signed his copy. His eyes went huge, and his mouth dropped open. He thankfully accepted the book and clutched it close to his chest, hiding it a little. He was not sure why, but he was afraid someone would try to grab it from him if they saw it.

"Come on," she gestured for him to follow her. "I believe there's a hot chocolate I promised as well. Correctly me if I'm wrong."

Wally smiled and eagerly followed her. "Are you baking an apple pie?"

She smiled back at him and then laughed. "Good nose, young Sherlock. I'll grab you one of those, as well."

She gestured for him to take a seat, and then he watched as she placed an order with the woman behind the front counter. His nanny, sitting at her favorite table in the corner, began to stand and walk towards him to retrieve him. Quickly, he pointed to himself, and then to Aunty Emm. His nanny nodded and smiled, before returning to her coffee and chocolate croissant.

Wally's fingers were crossed that Aunty Emm would have time to sit and talk to him for a few minutes. He was excited that he got his wish when he observed as she gestured the number two with her fingers to the server. He assumed this meant that she was ordering for the both of them.

Aunty Emm returned, followed by a café staff member who had a tray full of desserts and two steaming mugs of hot chocolate.

"Choose anything you want," Aunty Emm offered.

The server nodded and smiled. Wally stared for a moment, wanting everything. On the other hand, he did not want to seem greedy, so he pointed to the apple pie, the hot fudge sundae, and the mug of hot chocolate.

"Wise choice, my friend," Aunty Emm nodded with approval. She scooped up a bowl of crème brulee and the other mug of hot chocolate. "Thanks, Shirley," she responded.

"My pleasure," Shirley nodded and headed back to the kitchen, her tray still half-full of other tempting deserts.

Aunty Emm slid into a seat opposite him and told him to "dig in."

Gladly, Wally obeyed.

He did not even notice that they had not spoken a word, until he was halfway through the apple pie. He looked up at his aunt, who was smiling at him.

"So, how did you get the book signed by the authors?" he asked. "I thought the authors weren't going to be here on Monday."

"They weren't here," Aunty Emm assured him. She went on to explain that whenever they had a new release of a book, the author or authors always sent a few signed copies.

"Wow, and you gave me one of those copies?" he grinned with pride. "Dad would've thought this was really cool."

"Interesting that you mention your Dad," she added. "He's been coming up in my thoughts lately."

"I dream about him all the time," Wally was eager to share. "It's as if he's in my room talking directly to me. It doesn't even feel like a dream sometimes."

"I know how you feel, because I've been having dreams regarding your dad, too," she causally said.

Wally eyes went wide. "What happened? Was it a good dream?"

"I don't quite know. It was really part of a series of dreams, but in my dream, he says, 'ask Wally,' but I'm not quite sure what I need to ask you."

Wally did not say anything. It did not sound like much of a dream. "Did anything else happen in your dream?"

She told him there was something about a football that turned into a briefcase, and Wally was not quite sure what to make out of any of it, until she mentioned the book.

Wally sat and digested what he had heard. "Was the book one of those big, heavy old books?" he excitedly asked.

She went on to describe the exact book that Wally had witnessed unexplainably drop to the floor in his Dad's study. Goosebumps ran up and down Wally's arms. He started to tug at the string hanging out of his pocket, and he pulled out his father's ring. He twisted it around his finger as he thought.

He was not sure yet if he could completely trust her. Yet, since she was the only one who had ever talked to him about his father, he was aching inside to tell her. Wally was surprised when his words tumbled out of his mouth uncontrollably.

"The last time I was in my dad's study, a book fell from the shelf. It was spooky, but I wasn't supposed to be in there. Promise you won't tell my mom… Promise?" he paused, and stated again. "Promise…?"

Emma raised her hands and nodded in an effort to calm him.

"I'll get into a lot of trouble if Mom finds out," Wally explained. "I feel close to my Dad when I'm in his study."

Aunty Emm made the motion across her chest, 'cross my heart, hope to die,' you have my word on it. She hesitated. Then Aunty Emm inquired, "Do you think you could get me that book? I think it's really important."

"Do you think it has to do with your dream about the briefcase?" He watched her shiver as she stroked her arm, now she was the one with Goosebumps.

"I'm not sure," she answered.

"I'll have to sneak in again." Wally looked down at his Dad's ring. He did not want to cry again. "I had a dream, too," he blurted it out.

Wally wanted someone to listen so badly. He hoped Aunty Emm would let him tell her. Adults always liked to interrupt him and tell him to be quiet. She looked at him with compassionate eyes, so he felt safe to continue.

"My dad, he's running from these two guys. The men are walking oddly. They lift their feet up and walk with stiff legs, as if they are one of those tin wind-up toy soldiers. Then they have these red bands around their arms. One man has a mustache that looks like a caterpillar. The guy next to him, has on a white coat, the kind Dad used to wear in the lab.

These men are trying to gather up a bunch of children, who are all wearing light blue. Dad keeps trying to keep the angry mean men away from the children, and Zoe's one of the kids. I want to help my dad, but I cannot talk, I am too scared to move. Then I wake up. It feels so genuine, like it really happened. I have had that exact dream so many times, it won't go away. This dream just won't stop no matter what I do."

The color seemed to drain out of Aunty Emm's face.

Worried, Wally inquired. "Are you okay, Aunty Emm?"

"I'm fine, but I need to show you something."

Without speaking again, they got up and washed their hands at the rainbow sink, then quickly held their clean hands up for the security guard, Mel to inspect. Wally followed his aunt as she made her way to the history section. She pulled out a book with the words World War II on the cover, and quickly flipped through the pages to the middle where there was a section of photos.

"Is this the angry man from your dreams?" she posed.

Wally was scared now. It looked exactly like the angry man from his nightmare. "See, he's got that caterpillar mustache," he pointed at the photo. He gulped down a short breath, "Who is he?"

Aunty Emm did not answer him.

"What do you think this has to do with my dad?"

"I don't know yet," she answered back. "It sounds like you and I have a mystery to solve young man."

What kind of answer was that? Adults are supposed to have all the answers. Wally's stomach was aching again. It always hurt when he felt anxious.

"Hey, I said we're in this together, right?" she smiled and winked at him.

He straightened up and took a big, deep breath. Wally's eyes suddenly lit up, as he realized what was happening. It felt like he was playing the game with his dad, but now he was playing it with Aunty Emm. It was another game of puzzles. The difference this time was that unlike his dad, Aunty Emm did not hold all the answers.

"Perhaps our answer can be found in that book in your father's study. In my dream he pulled out a slip of paper from it," she explained. "You know, like how a magician pulls a rabbit from a hat?"

Wally nodded, "My dad and me used to do magic tricks together. He taught me that not everything is, as it appears to be. He told me; *Don't always believe what your eyes are showing you. Everything is explainable. You just have to be open to what the answer is. It's easier for people to believe it is magic, versus what it actually is.*"

Wally fondly remembered the last time he saw his Dad, and the perfect magic hat his Dad had given him. Now Wally winked at his aunt. "I'll come by after school tomorrow. I'll tell my nanny that I need to pick up a book for a research project."

Speaking of his nanny, Wally looked up in time to see her making her way over to them. It must be time to go get Zoe. Picking up Zoe from piano lessons was always a nightmarish experience for everyone, except the piano teacher who was excited to send Zoe on her way. Aunty Emm gave him a great big hug and a small kiss on his right cheek.

Wally left the bookstore, stomach filled with the best apple pie and hot chocolate in Manhattan. He glided through the wind, feeling lighter than he had in a long time. He did not feel isolated and alone any longer.

CHAPTER 18

The following day, Wally was so preoccupied with thinking about how to get the book out of his dad's study that he did not notice or care that Zoe was not with him and the nanny on the ride home from school. Once he got home and opened the front door, he could hear his mother shouting and Zoe screeching. Wally assumed the preschool finally suspended his little sister, which was the reason why she was home earlier than he was.

"Do you know if you keep it up, they're going to kick you out of school?" Mom was shouting at Zoe in the kitchen. She had a stack of letters in her hand that she was waving around while ranting and raving at Zoe. While Zoe on the other hand, did not seem fazed as she parked herself on a stool playing with a light blue ribbon.

Mom finally opened a letter with her finger from the stack she was holding. She jumped from the sting that she received from a paper cut. She waved her bleeding finger in the air, and seemed to be getting even more upset – *if that was even possible*, Wally thought.

"Why? Why can't you just behave like the other kids?" She was now furiously pacing back and forth, while Zoe stared at the light blue ribbon.

Zoe did not say anything, which only seemed to infuriate their mother even more.

"Wally! Where is my letter opener? Were you playing with it again?"

He shook his head. "I didn't take it," he softly added.

Wally knew his Mom was venting and the only way to escape was to lay low.

"Well find it, please," his Mom snapped at him. "How can that school be so irresponsible?" she expressed even louder. She continued opening the rest of her mail with a tissue, which wrapped her bleeding finger and was slowly turning crimson red. Surprising everyone in the kitchen, she slammed the opened mail onto the countertop. "I can't deal with this anymore." She turned to Zoe and screamed, while waving her hands at her. "Where am I going to send you? If you get kicked out, what school is going to take you?"

At first Zoe just sat, and continued to fiddle with her favorite faded velvet light blue ribbon. Then in true Zoe style, began belting out defiant screeches at their mom.

"Stop screeching!" Mom shouted back.

Wally hated witnessing situations like this with his mom and sister. He could see both sides of the circumstances but he did not have the knowledge and grace that his dad did to defuse the situation. These states of affairs were now becoming a daily occurrence.

The nanny walked into the kitchen with bags of groceries from the car and began putting them away. Their nanny had a way of soothing their mom without saying a word. Miranda was so different from Mom. She generally approached life much calmer. Wally often gratefully felt that Miranda was like a ray of light that came through dark clouds

Wanting Zoe out of her sight, his mom demanded that he take her up to her room.

"But Mom, I've got to get the book for my research project, I only have the weekend to get it done."

His mom stared him down.

"Fine," she snapped.

VIBRATIONAL PASSAGE

"You can go with Miranda in about twenty minutes."

Taking her hand, Wally took his sister upstairs to her room as commanded. Zoe screeched the entire way up the stairs.

Once in her room, Wally thought very strongly in Zoe's head, *just stop it please.*

She stopped right away and began to giggle inside of Wally's head.

Zoe, I need to sneak into Dad's office, do you think you could keep Gama and Mom busy downstairs? He pleaded inside her head. *I forgot something in there.*

Zoe glared at him.

Come on Zoe, Something's not quite right. I know this sounds weird, but I think Dad is still alive and needs our help.

She shook her head defiantly.

Wally concentrated on his sister and thought hard, *Come on Zoe, help me, please?*

She quietly pretended she could not hear him.

Please! Wally thought again, this time focusing every brain cells as hard as he could to get through to her.

Zoe folded her arms tightly around her and turned her back to him. *Why should I help? Daddy doesn't even talk to me anymore. I think he hates me; he only wanted me to do those stupid tests.*

What tests?

Saturday tests... stupid Saturdays...!

What are you talking about...? Dad used to take you on all those outings to have fun, and he wouldn't let me come. You were the lucky one. I hardly got to do anything with him.

No! They were stupid tests at his work.

Wally was shocked.

He had always been so jealous of his sister. He had imagined all the fun places and ice cream he was missing because Dad would only take Zoe out on weekly 'daddy-daughter outings' leaving Wally behind. *What kind of tests?*

Stupid tests! She screamed in his mind, giving him a sharp pain at the back of his skull.

It hurt inside my head the whole time. There were others like me, some boys too.

133

I don't believe you. If Dad were doing tests on you, it would only be to help you.

No. He hurt me inside my head and he hurt other kids inside their heads. Him and the other bad men in the white jackets, they're just mean.

Okay, okay, Wally backed down.

He knew that he was not going to get anywhere with her because that is how she got when she was in one of these moods. Wally could not believe that their dad would be doing anything to hurt Zoe or any other kids. Zoe just had it wrong. Nevertheless, he was running out of time. Wally had to get the book from the study to Aunty Emm. *Could you distract Mom and Gama for a while, please? I just need to get a book from Dad's office.*

No, I should just tell on you. Then Mom will be mad at you instead.

Wally sighed.

He stared at his sister, and then looked away. It was no use. He felt defeated. Wally had tears running down his face. He did not even care anymore that he was becoming a crybaby.

Wally's sniffle caught Zoe's attention. The way she looked at him, he could see that she felt sorry for him. He also knew she resented him because he did not have Mom shouting at him all the time the way she did.

Even when he tried to help her with Mom, she did not seem to want his help. Zoe just seemed to enjoy winding her up on a regular base. He waited as she folded her hands over her knee, resting her chin on her hands as she watched him.

My big brother, cries like a baby. Maybe you need to be in preschool and not me, she laughed at him. Then Zoe took a deep breath. "Yes," she said aloud.

Wally wiped his tears away on his shirt. *Really...Thanks*, he thought, as gently as he could so that she would feel how grateful he was.

Zoe slipped out of her room and down the stairs.

She was much smarter than anyone ever gave her credit for. A few minutes later Wally could not help but smile when he heard a commotion downstairs. He looked out the bedroom window. Zoe was running around naked in the terrace garden and screeching at the top of her lungs.

VIBRATIONAL PASSAGE

The nanny and his mom were trying to catch her, but Zoe was slippery and fast. Wally knew that Mom would be furious because now all the neighbors in the penthouses nearby would be able to see Zoe in her birthday suit.

Zoe had just given him the chance he needed to get into their dad's office. He rushed to the hallway closet to retrieve the key before unlocking the door to the study. He quickly closed the study door behind him.

Everything remained covered under an undisturbed layer of dust. He located the book that was still lying on the floor. He kneeled down and shoved the book into his backpack that he brought in with him. It was a lot heavier than he expected. As he was leaving the room, he looked up at the paintings hung on the wall and gasped.

The paintings had changed yet again.

However, this time he knew for sure that they had.

His father had a vault of paintings, and he would move his collection of paintings around whenever he felt like it. Sometimes it was for a holiday, other times it was for a new season, and then occasionally, it was because he wanted Wally to solve a new jumble puzzle.

Everything was still in its place like before except the paintings. Wally knew for sure that at least two new paintings from his Dad's vault were replacing the others that were hanging on the walls from yesterday. No one had been in the room other than him, he was also sure of that because of all the undisturbed dust. Wally could not worry about that now; he was running out of time.

He rushed out, locking the door behind him and returned the key before proceeding downstairs. He knew he owed Zoe big time. Mom was already mad at her; he prayed she would let the nanny handle Zoe tonight. Wally was already down the stairs with his backpack when they were bringing her in with a large mint green towel wrapped around her mostly-naked body.

As it turned out, Mom decided to walk with him the three blocks to the bookstore, instead of sending him with Miranda. She needed a break from Zoe's most recent unclothed expedition. His mom appeared to be lost in her own thoughts. They did not speak at all during the entire walk.

He observed that when adults existed in their own stuff - self-absorbed in their own dilemmas they perceived very little. Wally was grateful for this, because it meant she would not notice the bulge in his backpack, and catch him with his dad's book. If Mom found out he had been in Dad's study, she would hide the key.

Once at the bookstore, his mom went to the cafe to order herself a cup of coffee. Wally found Aunty Emm right away, next to the bestseller shelf. He unzipped his backpack and held it open for his aunt to see.

"It's the book," he whispered.

"Can I see it?"

He opened his backpack a little wider, not wanting to pull out the book just yet. He felt like a thief.

"Relax, Wally. You are in a bookstore. It'll blend in," she teased, her expression was reassuring, and he somehow felt safer.

Wally also felt a little embarrassed. He grabbed the heavy book and handed it to her.

"Do you mind if I borrow it for a while?"

Wally shrugged, and tried to act nonchalant about it. No one would know it was gone, but he still felt nervous.

"Don't worry, we'll figure this out together," she reassured him.

Wally looked up at her and smiled. He wanted to believe her. "I saw you in my dream," he said. "You took me to see my Dad."

Aunty Emm smiled at him. Her eyes filled with sadness, "I wish I could, dear."

"Just promise you won't give up because I think Dad needs your help," he paused. "I know with my head that Dad's dead, but I believe with my heart that he's not."

"Wally, I'm beginning to feel the same way," she agreed. "I think your dad somehow needs both our help."

CHAPTER 19

Later that evening, Emma had been excitingly waiting a good half-hour before Nicholas walked through the front door. As soon as he had shed his coat and put down his briefcase, she handed him a glass of red wine. He followed her into their study. Once he settled himself into a leather chair beside her, she showed him the old worn book that Wally had given her earlier that day at her bookstore.

"Of course, Shakespeare," Nicholas laughed and rolled his eyes. He flipped through the heavy, leather-bound book. It was the complete works of Shakespeare. "Walden was always joking and quoting lines from Shakespeare," he explained. "I told him he was just being a show-off."

"Honey, you've got a photographic memory. You could quote those lines, if you wanted to."

"Now there's the rub. The key is *if I wanted to*. I deal with numbers and data all day. If I am not at work, I want junk food for the mind. I want to relax. Now, magazines... short, to the point, *and* best of all, big, glossy pictures."

Emma giggled. "Um, Honey," she pointed at the book. "It's exactly like the book in my dream."

She flipped the pages to the place where she had earlier found a piece of paper. It appeared to be a receipt of some sort; the numbers on the paper were beginning to fade. It had a barcode, and beneath that, there was a black box. There were a series of white numbers on the black background.

"Honey, I think I'm going mad."

Nicholas grinned. "Honey, you already are. You married me, right?"

They glanced at each other, grinning.

Then she gave him *that* look. The *let's be serious* look.

Nicholas nodded, and proceeded to remove the Degas painting that hung over the now unlocked safe. She had purchased the oil painting of Edgar Degas' *Before the Race* for him as an anniversary present since he loved horses so much. The gold-leafed frame had cost her a small fortune.

He explained to her that the case lock had exactly six numbers on it. Nicholas had noticed that the numbers on the slip of paper had a series of six numbers as well. Then again, he also stated that the likelihood of these numbers on this piece of paper matching up to the briefcase lock was highly improbable.

Emma moved a stack of magazines out of the way making space on the desk, for him to set the attaché case down.

"Ready?" She stared down at the numbers, then back at her husband. "If I'm wrong, then it's all your fault, okay?"

Nicholas laughed.

"Just want to make that clear before we proceed," she pointed out.

"Women, always determining blame," Nicholas shook his head in dismay. "Just read the numbers, joker," he teased.

Emma read the numbers. "327114."

She held her breath as her husband clicked the numbers around, until they all locked into place. He tried the lock--nothing.

"Oh," Emma breathed out a defeated sigh.

"Wait," Nicholas exclaimed. "Walden had a habit of reversing his numbers." He asked her to read the numbers again, but backwards this time.

She read aloud. "411723."

He dialed the numbers in place and this time there was a loud - 'click!'

Nicholas looked up with a surprised look, as if he had just won the lottery. It was a look of, what do I do now? Goosebumps ran up and down her arms. For what seemed like an eternity, they just stared at each other and then back down at the unlocked briefcase.

She was beginning to feel even more overwhelmed about what was transpiring. She reached out and placed her hands on his. Together, they opened up Walden's briefcase.

Emma gulped.

"Holy…!"

"Oh-my-god, Walden," Nicholas murmured.

They were both staring at an official looking document written in German with a swastika letterhead. It looked like a classified report. At the bottom of the page, there was a signature beneath the words Heil Hitler. They both stared at the weathered document, horrified by what they were looking at. Neither of them was able to move at first.

"What the hell was Walden up to? Was he a Nazi or was he a spy?" Emma finally voiced what they were both thinking.

"I don't know," Nicholas, whispered, "this doesn't make sense."

"Spy," she decided.

"He was half Asian, so he couldn't be a Nazi. Not Aryan enough," Emma paused. "Oh… the Japanese were allied with the Nazis in World War Two. Nicholas, a logical explanation please… What the hell was Walden doing with these files?"

She turned on her husband and demanded, "Did you know any of this stuff about Walden?"

"Not to this depth."

"What do you mean *not to this depth*?"

"Emm calm down I am as surprised as you are. Turning on me doesn't help us figure this out." Nicholas picked up the document and placed it on the desk with a distasteful and disdainful look of disgust.

Emma knew that Nicholas could read and speak five different languages including German.

Feeling a little embarrassed by her outburst she asked her husband, "What does the letter say?"

Ignoring her question, he began to flip through the thick stack of files that he had removed from the case. There were neatly organized files, which included faded newspaper clippings along with official looking documents. The content of the briefcase was emotionally overpowering; there was so much information that was not making any sense.

Emma was of the opinion that Walden had just thrown a thousand puzzle pieces in the air. She had no idea where any of the pieces belonged, and she did not like what she was seeing and feeling. Emma had a feeling that by the simple act of opening this briefcase, they were both in great danger. She hated Walden for trusting them.

She decided that the only way to overcome her emotional overload was to avoid the documentation contents and to study the briefcase instead. The case was expensive and beautifully designed with a black metallic exterior with a light grey, soft leather interior. Emma searched the pockets, and found a Mont Blanc pen, a leather-bound pocket notepad, and an envelope.

Pulling the pocket contents out and placing those items on the desk, seemed less scary than going through the files. Emma was wrong.

Nicholas peered over her shoulder to see what she was looking at. In Walden's handwriting, it read, "Emma Lange," on a white legal-sized envelope. They exchanged looks of alarm.

The room was silent for a moment. Walden giving Nicholas the briefcase for safe keeping in the first place was one thing, however, locating the combination to open the briefcase based on a dream was something else. Although, finding these Top Secret files in the briefcase was confusing enough, but this note addressed to Emma, this was really beyond explainable.

Why was Walden doing this? She did not know him well enough for this type of involvement. Even though he invited them during the summers to spend a few days with him and his

VIBRATIONAL PASSAGE

family at their cabin in Southampton, Emma and Walden never exchanged any meaningful conversation. There was no feasible explanation for Walden to be addressing something to her in his attaché case.

In fact, the only time she and Walden did exchange anything meaningful was the first time they met. He had been friendly and kind. Emma even would say he was actually entertaining that night.

They were attending a fundraising event for Autism, one of many hosted by Walden's wife's family. It was a very discreet private party with a few major celebrities, but mostly heavy hitters on the political scene and wealthy executives and their wives.

Nicholas had mentioned to her on the car ride home, that he was pleasantly pleased at how Walden had been gracious with her. Her husband clarified that Walden made it a policy not to discuss his work with anyone outside his research lab. He pointed out to Emma that for Walden to have taken the time to draw a diagram on a cocktail napkin to explain his genetic specialty was his way of welcoming her.

"Well, aren't you going to open it?" Nicholas startled Emma out of her thoughts and her initial memory of Walden.

"What?"

"Open it, honey."

Emma walked around the desk and pulled out a letter opener from the top center drawer. She used it to slice the thick envelope open.

Nicholas stood next to her, eagerly waiting to see what was inside.

Something slid out of the envelope, landing on the desk with a thud. It was a watch.

Nicholas picked up the timepiece and examined it. He played with the buttons. Then Nichols showed her some of the features on the watch. On the face of the timepiece, there were three circular settings. One was a compass, while another jumped five seconds every time one of the side buttons were pressed, and the last one seemed to count the passing of 15-minute intervals.

Instead of just the usual two digits for the date, there was a box of two digits on the left of the watch, and a box of two digits on the right.

"This looks really expensive," Emma observed.

"My guess is, it's worth a little over twenty grand, easy."

"Why do you think Walden put it in there?"

"I don't know."

She had poured out on the desk two other remaining items. Emma picked up a square piece of paper with something in it. The paper, secured with clear tape, appeared as if done hastily. She pulled back the wide piece of adhesive tape to expose a gold coin. It had numbers and symbols with Latin words all over it on both sides.

She held it up to Nicholas. "What do you think this is?"

Nicholas studied the coin. "This," he pointed to a series of numbers, "is the Fibonacci number."

She interrupted Nicholas' train of thought. "What does that mean?"

"The Fibonacci numbers are a mathematical series of whole numbers in which each number is the sum of the two preceding numbers. Beginning with 0 and 1, the sequence of Fibonacci numbers are, as you see here," he pointed to the numbers etched into the coin, 0, 1, 1, 2, 3, 5, 8, 13, 21, and 34. And the sequence continues on," he explained. "Divide any number in the Fibonacci sequence by the one before it, and the answer is always close to 1.61803. It's also known as the Golden Ratio."

"What's that?"

A sheepish grin washed over his face. "For one, the DNA molecule is based on it. It measures 34 angstroms long by 21 angstroms wide for each full cycle of its double helix spiral. 34 and 21 are of course, numbers in the Fibonacci series and their ratio, 1.6191476 closely approximates Phi, 1.6180339."

"That's just way over my head. Can you just say it a little bit simpler?"

Nicholas smiled and nodded. "Well, think about flower petals, pineapples, and snowflakes, their shapes are all based on Sacred Geometry. It's the numerical patterns of everything in nature." He turned his attention back to the coin. "There appears to be a pattern with the groupings of numbers," he hypothesized. He placed the coin back into the briefcase and turned to Emma.

She was holding the last item, which was a letter from Walden; Emma began to read it aloud.

Dear Emma,
Once Nicholas has thoroughly read the files, contact Michael Zeiss.
Retrieve his phone number from page 7 of file 3.
He will have a key for you alone.
That key when placed in the right direction will guide you.
Do not trust anyone other than Nicholas; your life depends on it.
There are three files missing.
Find them.
Walden

P.S. Do not underestimate Martha. For your own safety, stay as far away from her as you can.
I am entrusting you to seek the light of truth and save these children.

She placed the letter down on the desk and took a deep breath in. Emma turned to Nicholas, who had pulled out a file from the middle of the stack of documents and was now examining it.

The file was marked in English, "Genetic Probability."

Her husband opened it up for both of them to see. There was a photo of Walden's daughter, Zoe in the file, stapled to a summary of a series of DNA test results.

"What's Zoe doing here?" Emma demanded to know.

Nicholas, flipping through the papers, suddenly stopped. Ignoring her question, he stated, "I think the more appropriate question we should be asking is what Hitler and Mengele are doing in Zoe's file?"

Emma wanted to throw up. "Oh no…! Wasn't Mengele the monster who did all those human experiments at the concentration camps?"

Nicholas let out a deep, disturbed breath. "They called him the 'Angel of Death,' he specialized in eugenics."

"You-what...?"

"Social genetic engineering," he explained. "It is when a society makes a decision to eliminate certain traits from their genetic pool."

"You mean, like creating an Aryan race?" She retorted.

"Right," he responded. "That's what Hitler was trying to do. Mengele did many experiments with twins. Although they say none of his experiments led to any concrete genetic advancements. He was just using humans as lab rats because he could."

"That just makes me sick," she scowled.

He continued to explain. "Mengele was never caught. They say he fled to Brazil or somewhere down in South America."

Emma felt like her head was going to explode. She was unable to focus. Thoughts were running through her head, as she tried to figure out a connection between Zoe, and these files. What did this all mean? "Is there a file on Wally?"

Nicholas flipped through the papers.

"No, it doesn't look like it."

"Isn't Zoe diagnosed with Autism? Please... please... Nicholas, tell me Walden wasn't using Hitler's research on Zoe."

The color had drained from Nicholas' face. "I don't know. I need more time to look through these files."

CHAPTER 20

Emma was staring off into space, when the whistle of the kettle brought her attention back to the cup of chamomile tea she was preparing in her kitchen. With the tea bag still floating in the cup, Emma threw on her favorite sweater before walking out onto the balcony. She looked up at the clock, noting it was just before midnight.

It was Emma's habit of going out on the balcony at night with a cup of tea to clear her head whenever she woke up from an unsettling dream. The scent of the brisk night air and the faint sound of the city tucking in for the night calmed her. There was a chill in the air on this eve of the month of May.

The iridescent moon was slowly rising above the trees lining the street. Emma smiled to herself as she pulled her sweater tightly around her to ward off the chill. Leaves shivered in the wind, creating a shadowy dance in the dark puddles from a brief rain shower earlier in the evening. It was the eve of Aunt Gertie's birthday.

Her aunt had always joked about the interesting nature of her birth date, of its symbolic timing aligning her for eternity with Walpurgis Night. According to the ancients, this night's objective is to be the last chance for witches to stir up trouble before the reawakening of spring. Goethe once described in *Faust* how the coven would gather at the highest peak in the Harz Mountains.

In fact, on this night, huge bonfires burned in many European cities to ward off the witches. In America though, it was just another April night. Not for her, it was much more.

For Emma, it was a magical night. Her aunt had once told her that it was a time when the barrier between worlds became transparent. Never-ending possibilities were abundant on such nights... good and bad. Neither mattered to her aunt, change was always embraced as something eagerly in the making, to influence her own personal compass.

According to Aunt Gertie, the connecting moment linking thinner veils between worlds, concocted a perfect recipe for mystical energies, female power to be precise. This was Mother Nature's birthing of a new season or as her aunt put it... magic with a woman's touch. Each year on the eve of her aunt's birthday, she would try to spend some time beneath the night sky.

She loved the enchanting stories her aunt told. It was harder on Emma when Aunt Gertie died, than when her mom had passed away. It happened during her first year in college. If she did not have her studies to throw herself into, Emma would still be floating around to this day. To her, Aunt Gertie was her mom.

Emma shivered, and pulled her sweater tighter. Still disturbed by a reoccurring nightmare she had had earlier made it hard for her to relax even with her chamomile tea. Each instance she relived the dream, Emma would remember more and more particulars. It always commenced with women around a cauldron chanting.

This time a robust woman stepped forward and directly addressed her.

"We've been expecting you."

Startled, Emma remained silent.

The female's voice altered to a very comforting quality, which soothed Emma's fear away.

VIBRATIONAL PASSAGE

"You have been called forth to take your place. Some of the most powerful minds have gathered this evening to protect mother England from invasion. This is neither our first program nor our last. Our job is not to stop the darkness, but rather redirect its attention." Looking directly into Emma's eyes, she flatly stated. "It is your job to stop the monster from resurfacing. Know that there are world events that cannot be altered because they have been put forth to awake the consciousness. Face your inner fears, see the truth for what it is, rather than what you want it to be.

Your faith will lead you. I am not speaking of organized religion where unachievable rules are shaped for controlling the sense of worthiness. The truths deeply hidden in all the imposed rules keep the masses asleep and unaccountable.

Listen to your heart. Remember, your faith will pull you through."

Emma, not sure exactly how to respond, nodded to the woman. She knew she received a significant piece of information, but did not know how to apply it.

The woman went on to inform her that the military control - their adversaries, were the Nazis - Hitler to be precise. She explained how an assembly of females similar to her had deciphered a means of utilizing Hitler's own vanity against himself. When Hitler, blinded by his power became godlike, he no longer needed to seek counsel from those who were most loyal to him.

His flaw along with his undisciplined vanity is what shortened his reign and sealed his fate.

Emma could see all this unfold before her eyes as if watching a movie. It revealed the fatality of Hitler's choices.

His fate sealed, by ultimately turning his back on the loyalty of his inner circle. Hitler was nothing more than a fractured human being who was not regimented enough to ensure that his loyal friends remained beside him – protecting him. In the end, by annihilating his inner support, he opened the door to defeating himself leading to his own demise.

It was an epiphany for Emma, who now saw this angry man, portrayed in history books as this larger than life manifestation of evil, in a different light. He was nothing more than a broken, weak man, who could not hear those closest to him who had his best interest in mind. Instead, the voices that guided him were self-prosperous. Furthermore, Hitler lacked the control to contain them so in the end, they were too powerful and he was too isolated.

Tonight, Emma wondered if the world had gotten it all wrong, and perhaps Hitler was content with this mistaken portrayal. His defeat was his own undoing. An illusion presented to him by these enchanters, became his fatal decision in the end. The illusionist had now become stuck in his delusional state.

Emma trembled more from the hallucination she had been experiencing than from the chill in the air. As much as they drew her in, she was uneasy with the women around the cauldron. The way they were able to manipulate any form of energy to their own bidding. It was dangerous.

Hitler served himself, whereas these women appeared to be in service to humanity. However, what stopped these women from ever misusing their powers? Emma could not forget the haunting words the robust woman had spoken before she awoke.

"All of you have been brought back. So, pray tell you get it right this time."

CHAPTER 21

After a night that seemed to go on forever, Emma found it hard to connect to the outside world. She was distracted to the point where she forgot it was her husband's birthday today. If Emma had not preprogrammed their luncheon appointment into both of their BlackBerries, she would have totally forgotten.

She was so thankful that she had already made reservations for their lunch date, earlier that week. The restaurant she wanted to take the 'birthday boy' to generally required reservations, otherwise they could be waiting forever to get a table at lunchtime.

Emma had dropped little hints earlier in the week to spark his interest. As a result, Nicholas had only planned to work in the morning. When his BlackBerry's alarm went off on his way into the city, instructions would be provided on when and where to meet her for his birthday luncheon.

The five blocks north from their apartment to Nicholas' favorite restaurant was a brisk walk for her. She was on automatic pilot, making her way on the busy sidewalks by memory, not noticing anything around her. Her thoughts were whirling in every different direction.

When she arrived, she hoped that she had beaten Nicholas to the restaurant. Recognizing her, the host led her to the table she requested. There he was, seated at the table. Her handsome husband stood up and greeted her with a hug and a kiss on the cheek.

"Well, are you surprised, birthday boy?" She paused, noticing that he looked upset. "What's wrong?"

"Gabriela was found dead. They say it was a heart attack."

"What... a heart attack? I cannot believe that. Gabriela is the last person you would expect to have a heart attack. She clearly kept herself in shape."

"You're right... I'm finding it hard to believe, too."

Emma's stomach began to turn and it was not due to being hungry. Nicholas just looked down at the table. She stared at him not knowing what to say at first. Emma was about to say something to break the silence when the server interrupted by offering them menus.

Being regulars had its advantages because they already knew what they wanted. After placing their order, Emma was relieved that Nicholas changed the subject. As awful as she felt about the young woman's fate, she did not like discussing her.

To Emma, Gabriela represented every married woman's fear of her husband having an affair. She knew it was wrong only blaming the woman in an affair. Somehow, it was easier to blame the woman. Even so, it did take two for an affair to occur.

"So how are things at the bookstore?"

"Same as always," she kept her voice even. Emma pointed to the freshly baked bread, positioned between them on the table.

"Thank you so much for the surprise, honey," he smiled. Nicholas sliced two pieces for the both of them.

He had that look on his face as if he wanted to discuss something, but did not know how to approach the subject matter. This made Emma feel a little uncomfortable. She did not want to rush into any deep conversations, after all this was a birthday luncheon.

Emma was buttering her piece of bread, when Nicholas shifted in his chair and leaned back, pulling something out of his pocket. He opened his hand, presenting the gold coin to her.

She gasped, not expecting that this was what was on his mind. Looking around, she leaned forward and whispered, "Is that the coin from the briefcase?"

Nicholas nodded and without hesitation placed the coin in her hand.

"What are you doing with that?"

"I took it to work with me this morning," he began to explain.

She observed as her husband reached into his other pocket and pulled out the paper that had earlier protected the gold coin.

Ironing it out on the table with his hands, he showed that it was part of an advertisement. Nicholas started to read to her some of the details. It touted the coinage as a healing coin. There were statements describing 'ancient symbols' and something written in Latin.

"Is this what you did at the office this morning?"

He smiled and began to recall his morning activities to her. "I spent the morning obsessed with decoding the symbols and numbers. I scanned both sides of the coin, and initiated an internet search."

Emma cut him off by showing Nicholas what was occurring with her hand that was holding the coin.

There was a circular blister on her right palm, radiating enormous heat.

Nicholas's mouth dropped open and he immediately grabbed the coin out of her hand.

"That doesn't make sense, the coin is 24 karat gold, and you're not allergic to gold."

"I don't understand either, but my hand is just on fire. Nicolas it's hurting."

He scooped ice from his water glass and wrapped it in his napkin. He gently applied it to the palm of her hand.

"That's it," he grunted. "We need to get the bottom of this - now."

Emma recognized that look in his eyes.

Nicholas was furious and determined.

Without asking her for input, he pulled out his phone. Her husband began to dial the phone number, which was on the paper protecting the coin. Seeing what Nicholas was up to, Emma pulled her chair around the table next to him. He placed his phone between them so she could listen.

A man answered the phone after two rings.

He sounded irritated and annoyed.

"Hello?" The man demanded.

Nicholas spoke. "I'm calling about the coins you sell, the ones with the symbols on them."

Slightly changing his tone, the man replied, "Yes?"

"I need to come by and ask you about it in person."

There was silence.

Emma glanced over at her husband.

The man broke the silence. "Is your coin gold or silver?"

"It's gold."

The man's voice loosened up. "I'm available now."

Emma stared at Nicholas and nodded, indicating agreement.

Nicholas checked his watch.

"I am at the location indicated on the piece of paper you have been provided with."

"What are your cross streets?"

The man began to provide directions. Emma immediately grabbed a pen and the back of a receipt from her purse and wrote down the directions. The man lived right on Broadway, in the heart of the Upper West side neighborhood.

"We can be there within a half-hour."

"Then I will be expecting you then."

They skipped dessert. She left a generous tip on the table, and paid the check. Unnerved by the fact that she received $9.11 in change from Nicholas's birthday luncheon, Emma kept her focus on the up and coming meeting. Once outside, her husband hailed a cab.

CHAPTER 22

They exited the cab, into the hustle and bustle of Broadway Avenue, which was always busy. Nicholas paid the driver and motioned for him to keep the change. Emma reached out to hold her husband's hand for comfort and security. They left behind the busy street and proceeded through a large archway into a quiet courtyard.

The Heritage Building appeared residential, pre-war was Emma's guess, and it held the ambiance of a place for someone who wanted the best of both worlds- providing privacy at a prime location. They weaved their way through the courtyard to the main lobby where a sharply dressed door attendant met them.

It just dawned on Emma that they did not have the name of the man they were meeting. She had mixed emotions when the door attendant asked for their names rather than who they were visiting. Everything was as if in a daydream. *This must be what it is like having an outer body experience*, she thought.

Before Emma could add anything besides their names to the door attendant, the well-dressed man was on the phone announcing their arrival. He then pointed out with his left, white gloved hand where the elevator was located. Both she and Nicholas followed with their eyes, his nonverbal direction.

"Your party will meet you on the fifth floor."

"Thank you," Emma offered.

The walk to the elevator was direct and short. As soon as Nicholas pushed the button, the elevator's doors opened with a cheerful chime. The ride was quick and present.

When they reached the designated floor, a middle-aged balding man who was shorter than Nicholas was there to receive them. Without saying a word, he led them to an apartment, where Emma could hear what sounded like a small dog barking from one of the other rooms.

Emma spoke first. "Thank you for seeing us on such short notice. I am Emma and this is my husband Nicholas."

"Could I have you repeat your names, please?"

"I'm Nicholas."

"Emma."

The man only made her repeat her name again. This time, he leaned in and closed his eyes. He listened to her say it once again, although she had already clearly said it at least three times.

The man looked European, but Emma could not be sure. He did not offer his name. Her attention focused on his severely chapped lips, no matter how hard she tried not to stare at them. It appeared that he had attempted to apply lip balm to alleviate the bleeding.

"And you are?" Nicholas asked.

Without hesitation, the man answered, "That's not really important right now. What's important is your gold coin."

Before they could speak again, he directed them through a foyer. The man led them to a living room, which was in the shape of a perfect circle. Floor to ceiling windows looked out onto the busy street. The room screamed eccentricity to Emma.

The man gestured towards a beige leather sofa for them to sit down.

On one side of the room, there were stacks of books and a computer table. While on another, there was a massage table surrounded by an assortment of vials and some kind of machine. Emma tried not to stare or look too nosey.

VIBRATIONAL PASSAGE

The room, filled with various things, appeared to be a cross between an office and a science lab. Everything was orderly. However, the room felt as if it was on the verge of turning into out of control clutter.

"Sit, sit," he commanded.

The dog continued yapping in the background. The man offered an apologetic smile and then turned to Nicholas.

"May I see the coin?"

He passed the coin to the man who eagerly began studying both sides of it.

At this point, he turned to Emma.

"So you must be the one who had the reaction to the coin."

Emma was stunned.

They had not disclosed why they were there, nor that it was her hand, which received the burn. Yet somehow, he knew. She held her hand up revealing the red welt.

"Yes, I see," he nodded, leaning in and studying the burn.

"What does this all mean?" Nicholas quizzed.

The man smiled and sat up with pride.

He started in on a long-winded explanation as he pointed to the front and back of the coin.

"Each number has a vibration, and when the numbers are placed in a specific order, each set of numbers creates a specific pulsation. Vibrations open the doorway to the different levels of human consciousness. The different levels of consciousness hold knowledge. That knowledge can further humankind or control it.

The vibrations occur at an individual's molecular level. These molecules continue to vibrate at a certain manner unless enhanced by the pulsation of numbers and symbols. When we do not vibrate at the correct level for our consciousness, we are unable to experience this dimension as we are meant to, causing all sorts of problems, such as mental illness or physical diseases.

Small children, when correctly guided, can access deeper consciousness. However, due to their limitations are unable to translate any useful information. The use of precious metals along with a specific series of numbers and symbols can provide access for the individual that vibrates at a certain pulse to be able to heal, jump between dimensions, or even time travel."

The man calmly stared back and forth between them. It was as if he had just read them his shopping list for the week. Emma kept blinking to slow things down for her. She had just mentally gone from zero to one hundred and twenty miles in less than two minutes.

Unable to process all the information thrown at her, she decided to focus on one very current personal question. She wanted to know why she kept seeing the same number patterns.

"Why am I always seeing the number 911? It keeps coming up in different ways in my life." Even though she was feeling a bit self-conscious by her question, she still leaned forward and continued. "Could you please explain why I keep seeing 911 or 1111 throughout my day?"

Emma could feel Nicholas staring at her but she avoided his eyes.

The man seemed amused by her question, making her feel even more exposed.

"We find ways in which to communicate to each other through dimensions. This can occur by using words, gestures, symbols and shapes – even numbers. It is just a form of communication. I do not know what your belief system entails, but it appears that someone, or something, is trying to communicate."

"What?"

"I am sure you have watched the movie *Ghost*, you know with Patrick Swayze. Just because we do not see something, does not mean it does not exist. We do not see or feel radio waves but they exist. Correct?"

"Correct," Nicholas, agreed.

"Communicate what?" Emma quickly asked.

The man shook his head and smiled. It was clear he was not going to be providing an answer to her question. Maybe he did not have one, she thought.

There was an uncomfortable silence until Nicholas redirected the man to explain the meaning of the numbers and symbols on their gold coin.

"Ok, so what do the numbers and symbols represent on our coin?"

Instead, he explained to them how he used to be a renowned educator on the vibrations of symbols and numbers. Until one day, he received very clear instructions to discontinue.

"What do you mean by discontinue?" Nicholas raised an eyebrow.

The man did not answer, but instead held up his hand to protest any further questioning.

Trying to be sympathetic, Emma did her best to convince him that they needed him to translate the coin to them. "I am so sorry for what has happened to you, but I need some answers. I cannot believe I was sent to you for nothing."

The man studied her for a long moment, and then finally nodded.

He examined the coin for some time, flipping it back and forth.

"What appears to be on your coin is the vibration of accessing the consciousness with children." He paused. "To be more specific, children diagnosed with Autism."

Nicholas interrupted and asked him to clarify what he meant.

The man smiled, and his eye sparkled, clearly enjoying the chance to share his knowledge.

Emma had a fleeting thought of pity for this man; there was a strong sense of solitude about him.

The man faced Nicholas and began. "Children who are born extremely sensitive have access to higher vibrational intelligence. This gives them the ability to utilize the passage of non-linear time, which means they are aware of our past, present and future all at once. They also hold the capability of healing others at the molecular level.

Therefore, it makes sense that these children do not process information the same way you or I would. Just imagine, having a child who has the natural ability to tell the future, and heal others. What do you think that would do to the pharmaceutical companies and Wall Street alone?"

The man raised an eyebrow, and then continued.

"Add to that, these children cannot be emotionally manipulated to fit into a society that is kept sick. If a society remains sick, it has no choice but to remain dependent, which makes it vulnerable to control by those who hold the power. People know at their molecular level that life is more than eat, sleep, and die.

There is a reason for being. Every soul has a purpose for their life. Although, this purpose generally eludes them most of their lives. Society as a whole is presented with illusions, which provides human beings with ways to numb themselves to their truth."

He sighed and went on.

"So, here you have these children coming in who can heal, as well as see the future but cannot be manipulated in the normal way. The objective would be to find a way to control these children. Control them... and in essence, you control the world."

He dramatically paused.

Emma glanced over at her husband who was in as much shock as she was. As she turned back to the man, he took her right hand without notice. She still had red blistering on the hand that held the coin.

"There's a reason why the coin burned your hand," he offered.

She was glad when he let go of her hand. He pointed to a series of numbers and symbols on their coin.

"You see this line here, this represents the angels. It's also the reason why the coin did not burn your husband's hand or anyone else's." He hesitated. "It is your vibration. The coin was specifically coded for you, indicating you were the one I needed to share this knowledge with."

Emma was baffled. "How does someone put that into a coin?"

He laughed, "That's where the real secret lies."

Emma was perplexed. She did not understand what this man was getting at.

However, he continued.

"Angels have a hierarchy. Furthermore as with all hierarchies, each level has a number designation. Each angel is accorded a specific vibration. Remember everything in the world has a vibration, whether we can comprehend it or not. If you can pinpoint the vibration of anyone or anything, it unlocks the path of mental communication. In fact, that's how whole societies have been controlled." As though he could see right through her, he added. "Take Hitler for example. He controlled a whole nation and was on his way to controlling an entire continent. If it had not been for his lack of trust within his inner circle, which lowered his vibration, he would have been able to maintain and increase his mental control, making him unstoppable."

Emma's head was spinning now. This was so much information to be taking in at one time. She felt overwhelmed.

Ignoring the man's comment about Hitler because she felt so closed to shutting down, Emma asked, "Why would something representing angels' burn me?"

"If you're sensitive enough to the angels' energies," he pointed to her burnt hand. "Then this means your vibration is elevated enough to communicate with them. You're just unaware of it."

Emma, feeling vulnerable, lied. "Well, I just don't believe in angels."

The man burst out laughing, as if she had just said the most absurd thing. He obviously knew she was lying. Emma turned to Nicholas for support, but he was staring at a picture, clearly unaware of what had just transpired in the conversation.

She looked at the photo on the wall he was studying, which was of a big round ball with lights attached to it. Nicholas looked like he had just seen a ghost. She gently touched him on his leg, which made him jump but drew his attention back to her.

Nicholas blinked a few times and stood up. He reached over and grabbed the coin out of the man's hand, sliding it safely into his front pocket.

"Thank you very much for your time, Sir. We need to get going."

Startled by her husband's abruptness, Emma thanked the man and followed her husband out of the apartment. Nicholas refused to speak to her until they were back out on the busy street.

He turned to her and blurted out, "*That* is a dangerous man."

Mystified, she asked, "What do you mean? Are you talking about the outrageous stuff coming out of his mouth, or the photo on the wall you were staring at?"

Nicholas rubbed his chin, looked over his shoulder and lowered his voice. "That photo is a top secret military engineered mobile radar station. The only reason I know about it is that a person involved with the military from secret ops approached Walden. A man who called himself Mr. Brown on the project asked him to consult. I know there is a connection with another top-secret project up in Alaska called WOLF. I do not know all the details, but around that time, Walden was becoming even more secretive. That's when it got to the point where Peter and Walden couldn't be in the same room without verbally attacking each other."

She stopped him. "I can't take any more; my head is swirling too much. I, we need a cup of coffee. We need to slow this down."

CHAPTER 23

The man who would not identify himself watched from his window as the couple who had just been in his living room walked down the street. He reached for the phone and began to dial a series of numbers. He waited for the dial tone to click three times before entering the next set of numbers.

Mr. Brown answered the phone, clearly agitated. "This better be important."

The man who placed the call responded, "They've made contact."

Mr. Brown leveled his voice, "They?"

"Yes, a man and a woman."

"Interesting... Did they have the coin?"

"Yes," the man replied.

Mr. Brown let out a heavy breath. "Do *you* have the coin?"

"No, they took it with them."

"Do they know what they have?"

Keeping his tone even, so Mr. Brown would not detect his lie, the man countered. "No."

"What did you tell them?"

"Everything you instructed me to say."

"Their names are?"

"Nicholas and Emma Lange..."

"Nicholas...?"

Mr. Brown laughed. "Well I'll be damned. Nicholas Lange."

When the man hung up the phone, he closed his eyes and sighed. "May the angels protect you on your journey, Miss Emma," he whispered aloud. "Whether you know it or not, you have been chosen to lead the children to safety."

He was relieved that Mr. Brown had assumed it was Nicholas. He liked Emma. He felt kindness from her, and he had not felt kindness from another person in a long time. His was a world where compassion would lead to being murdered.

He walked over to the guest room and let his dog out. Grateful for his freedom, his dog obediently sat at his feet, waiting for a treat.

CHAPTER 24

Emma circled her car around the arrivals area at JFK airport until she spotted her brother waving at her. It was their routine that as soon as he was out on the curb, she would stop the car and he would get in with his carry-on. This way they could be on their way quicker and without having to pay the airport's outrageous parking fee.

As much as she was happy to see Jake, it was hard for her to focus because of the distraction of everything going on in her life recently. Emma could feel Jake's eyes studying her as she drove.

"So, what's going on?" He inquired. "Don't tell me things have gone sour with you and Nic."

"No," she smirked. "I'm just a little stressed." She sighed. "Better question yet, what's going on with you and Helen?"

She looked over at Jake, who casually swatted the air in front of him, indicating he was not in a place to talk about it yet. Emma knew not to press the subject.

"Well, both of us can't be messed up at the same time, soooo I will be the strong one," Jake teased.

This made Emma burst out laughing. It was so ironic coming from him, the 'mature' one.

"I think you should tell me what's going on," Jake invited, his tone of voice turned serious.

"Jake, I'm fine."

Mocking her, he stated, "Well Ms. Fine I think you're not. Start talking."

She could hear the note of concern in his voice. He could easily read her emotions and she knew he just wanted to help. Where to start, she could not even think of how to begin telling him what had happened during the past few days.

Jake pressed and probed her, asking as well as making statements about their marriage. She could not let him believe something that clearly was not true, anymore. Emma trusted him. Taking in a deep breath she slowly began to recount the strange occurrences since Walden's memorial service.

Emma conveyed to him everything, as much as she could remember. Jake would stop her now and then, asking her to clarify certain details, but otherwise he remained somewhat silent.

As soon as she finished divulging to him everything, which she could recall regarding the man with no name concerning the gold coin, Jake let out a deep breath. Finally, he leaned back in his seat, stretching his legs out in front of him. It was not until he did this, that she realized Jake had been at the edge of his seat, rigid, and intensely hanging on her every word.

Her brother leaned his head back and did not say anything initially. He was lightly tapping his fingers, playing imaginary piano keys on the car door. It was something he did whenever he was trying to figure something out.

Decisively, he finally smacked his hand against the dashboard. "Alright, I'm in," he announced.

She was grateful for the lightness and seriousness in his tone. Her last few days had been unimaginably stressful.

He nudged her shoulder, just as he used to do when they were younger and he was trying to annoy her.

"Stop that," she giggled. "You are such a pest."

Jake reclined his seat back and sank back into his chair, becoming more comfortable. He then shoved his hands into his pockets.

"Ems," he started. "That stuff you were talking about - about Pentecost and that dream you had with the Birch trees. As I recall, you mentioned something about 3,000 souls baptized. Don't you think that is a strange coincidence that about 3,000 people died in 9/11? I mean is it just me, or do you see the connection?"

Emma did not answer right away, so Jake went on. He loved a good conspiracy theory, and she could see the wheels turning now. However, Jake liked to process information on a slow simmer. "You know what didn't sit well with me since 9/11," he stated. "On a typical day, more than 50,000 people worked in the towers. Another say, maybe 200,000 visitors passed through. I mean, the place had its own zip code, for God's sake. So why were the towers only half filled that day? No one really talks about that. Isn't that an interesting fact?"

"Maybe they're just grateful that that's all who died," Emma offered. "You know, 'it could have been worse.' It was an election day and first day of school."

"Oh, come on, Ems." Jake shot back. "Don't insult me."

"So what are you getting at?"

Jake sat up in his seat and began to recount details he remembered from that awful day, half a year and a world away. He had always been spouting conspiracy theories about the events surrounding the attack. "Okay," he said, gesturing with his hands as he spoke. "So here's what we know - Terrorists hijacked American Airlines Flight 11, from Boston to L.A. and parked it into the northern facade of the north tower at 8:46, hitting the building's 93rd to 99th floors."

Emma shook her head in awe. Her brother and her husband both shared only one common trait, and that was a photographic memory. Even knowing this, she still asked, "How do you remember all of this?"

Jake shrugged. "It's the only thing they kept playing on the news for weeks. They pounded the information into us, don't you think?"

"Uh, no," Emma laughed. "I don't recall all the details. I could not have told you the exact time of the attack on the first tower. I just knew it was in the morning though."

"Seventeen minutes later," he persisted, "a second team of joyriding terrorists steer United Airlines Flight 175 from Boston to L.A. into the south tower, taking out the 77th through 85th floors. In the north tower, above the impact zone, over 1300 people trapped with no way to escape. While in the south tower, less than 700 die or become confined. At 9:59, the south tower collapses. The north tower falls at 10:28 after about 102 minutes of suffering, what I can only image as pure hell on earth. If I remember correctly, your husband's boss, Dr. Sinclair, was on one of the floors just above the impact zone in the north tower, right?"

Emma had shivers run up her spine as she nodded. "Correct."

Jake resumed. "Within 30 minutes of two planes hitting the twin towers, American Airlines Flight 77 departs D.C. bound for L.A. and attacks the Pentagon. The fourth plane crashes into a field near Shanksville in Pennsylvania. Nearly 3,000 victims and 19 hijackers died in the September 11th attacks. Don't you think that's a bit coincidental given the fact that you were shown the connection between the Birch trees and Pentecost in your dream, sorry nightmare?"

"Jake, I don't know what I'm even doing." Emma readily admitted this fact.

"Well, if 9/11 was in fact connected with the Pentecost," Jake sighed, "which is believed to be the birth of the Christian church, and the terrorists were Muslim... was 9/11 a purging, a cleansing of some sort? Let us say, a baptism by fire. Was someone trying to sacrifice 3,000 souls, to reverse the original 3,000 which included the Apostles?"

Emma felt a chill run up her spine again. Not wanting to believe something like that was possible she kept her eyes on the road. She remained quiet for a while.

Breaking the silence, she asked. "Don't you think that's a bit farfetched? How would they know they were going to kill 3,000 people, there were several targets, how can you *plan* that kind of collateral damage?"

Jake shrugged. "Well sis, you have your theories, and I have mine."

For the rest of the ride into the city, neither of them spoke. Emma, frightened by the possibility that her brother could be right, enjoyed the quietness.

Jake clearly digesting their conversation, remained deep in thought staring out the window.

When they arrived at her apartment, Emma directed Jake to one of the guest rooms. By the time Jake settled in and cleaned up from his flight, Nicholas was home from work.

Emma had prepared one of Jake's favorite dishes, so as soon as she got home she put the Shepherd's pie in the oven.

Over dinner, Jake who was no longer deep in thought asked probing questions about the briefcase and its contents. Nicholas did not seem the least bit surprised that Emma had already confided in her brother. Nicholas cleared his throat and placed his napkin down on the table.

"I think it's time you called the contact Walden named in his letter."

Emma, taken aback by this, blinked her eyes several times. "You've gone through all the files? What have you learned?"

"I don't want to get into that right now," Nicholas added. "I still have to check out a few things. I think our focus right now should be to find out what sort of key this Michael Zeiss holds. We need more information."

Jake leaned forward in his chair. "Who's Michael Zeiss?" Jake, clearly lost, glanced from Emma to Nicholas, waiting for an explanation.

Ignoring his question, her husband carried on. "I'm not going to be able to go with you until Saturday, and I think that's too late." Turning to face her brother, he requested, "Jake, can you go with her?"

Jake did not answer. Emma understood how her brother processed. She knew he needed an explanation.

Emma rubbed her forehead and explained to her brother that Zeiss was the person Walden had named in his letter to her. She was to contact him once they had read the files in the case. Zeiss supposedly was to provide her with some kind of key.

"It just so happens, my schedule is open tomorrow," Jake was doing what he did best, trying to keep things as light as possible "Let's give this guy a call and find out what's behind door number two."

They all laughed.

The rest of the evening included small talk about nothing in particular. She was so grateful because Emma needed a break from all of it, whatever 'all of it' meant. For one brief night, she felt normal again and slept without those dreams.

The following day, Emma and Jake found themselves in a small, tidy building around the block from Union Square. They climbed a flight of stairs and entered a waiting room that looked more like a conference room. There was a small kitchenette off to one side, and two offices side by side.

Emma had spoken to Zeiss over the phone earlier that morning. All she had informed him of was that Dr. Walden Sinclair had referred her. The man tried to get more information out of Emma, but she held her ground.

He agreed to meet her within an hour.

When she and Jake showed up, two men were joking together in one of the offices. The younger of the two men quickly straightened up when he noticed them. He smiled and nodded, and without uttering a word exited out the door, Emma could hear his heavy footsteps descending the stairs.

Zeiss stood up, and introductions occurred. He pointed to some chairs in front of his desk and urged them to sit down. Once seated, he politely took his seat. He held the persona of the typical downtown executive.

His suit was gray, understated, with a plain tie. He was a man who could easily get lost in a crowd. As she studied him, what came to mind, was Walden's warning not to trust.

Mind you, he was referring to his wife but somehow it seemed to fit here as well. Emma had once read in an espionage book that the best spies were the ones who looked ordinary, the ones who looked harmless. So was he dangerous?

This line of thinking was only scaring her even more. Something she did not need right now. Emma focused on the task, getting whatever this key was.

"So, you knew Walden?" He flashed them both a wide smile. "He was a good man, complicated, but nevertheless, a solid man. You said on the phone, he referred you to me?"

As politely as possible, Emma got straight to the point "I believe you have a key for me."

The man cleared his throat, and then glanced at Jake. He returned his attention back to Emma, and proceeded to stare at her. She began to feel uneasy, as his eyes moved up and down her body. She could not be certain, but he seemed to be staring at her chest.

Clearly uncomfortable with what the man was focusing on, Jake snapped. "Mr. Zeiss are we wasting our time, or do you have the key we came for?"

Zeiss pulled something out of the inside pocket of his blazer and slid it across his desk towards Emma. "Walden and I go back a long ways," Zeiss offered. He stared at Emma. "I have been instructed to expect a woman wearing a fleur de lis."

Emma was astonished. She could not believe that Walden had remembered. The first time they had met, he had asked her about the gold pendant she was wearing. Emma confided in him that the fleur de lis pendant was a family heirloom. Her mother had given it to her when she turned 16, and she had never taken it off since.

Walden had told her that it was also a symbol for the Archangel Gabriel.

"Do you know the significance behind this key?" Zeiss asked, pulling her back from her thoughts.

Emma let out a big sigh. "I have no idea."

He met her gaze and offered what seemed to be a severe warning. "Once you leave this office, the luxury of your anonymity will be gone. Only awareness to detail will provide you safe passage."

Emma's eyes widened and she laughed nervously. "What are you saying, we're being watched?"

Zeiss looked away and did not respond.

Trying to gain some form of control Jake asked. "Do you know what this is all about?"

Zeiss stood up, indicating that he no longer wanted them in his office.

Responding, they also stood and followed Zeiss to the door.

Not answering Jake's question he turned and stated. "I believe our business is done here. It was nice to meet you Ms. Emma and Mr. Jake."

Emma thanked him for the key and they promptly left his office.

She and Jake decided to walk a few blocks before hailing a taxi. Emma enjoyed walking in the city. Amid the noise, craziness, and intensity of those who surrounded her - she could always find pockets of peacefulness. Perhaps it was that comfortable feeling of being anonymous in a crowded city street.

Emma thought about Zeiss's warning, about losing the luxury of anonymity. She looked over her shoulder, to see if anyone followed or was watching them. No one in particular seemed to be paying any attention.

Jake was doing the same. However, it was too noisy and crowded for them to talk about what had just happened. So instead, they just weaved their way through the crowd, staying close together. Emma tried to shake off the terror creeping towards paranoia. What had Walden gotten them into and how were they going to get themselves out?

When they reached a part of the avenue where the sidewalk was less crowded, Emma dialed her husband on her cell phone.

"Hi, honey it's me."

"So how did it go, what happened? Did you get the key?" Are you okay?

"Slow down one question at a time."

"Sorry."

She told Nicholas that she and Jake had just picked up the key that Walden had instructed them to get. Zeiss had not provided any additional information. After Emma mention Walden's name, a distinct click occurred on the line followed by a static feedback. It sounded like she was speaking into a tin cup, with a digital echo.

Then their call dropped.

Confused, Emma called Nicholas back. "Did you hang up on me?"

"No, Honey, I thought you hung up on me," Nicholas sounded troubled.

Emma proceeded with their conversation. The connection was fine until she spoke Walden's name again. The phone line clicked again, followed by the same feedback she experienced earlier.

"Can you hear that?" she asked.

"Hear what?"

Emma had an idea. "Nicholas, I need to talk to you about dinner."

"What?"

"Honey, trust me."

She changed the subject completely and began to discuss what they were going to eat for dinner. Another click occurred. Afraid that the line would go dead again, she quickly added that she would see him at home shortly. The line went dead again.

Her heart began to race.

Emma started walking faster. "I think we need to get out of here. We need to find a taxi," she nervously told Jake.

He nodded, and flagged one down in a short amount of time. This was unusual. Normally getting a cab required a great deal of patience especially at this time of the day.

"How would you know if your phone is being tapped?" Emma whispered as Jake slid in to make room for her in the back seat of the cab.

Jake ignored her.

Emma realized Jake was watching the cabdriver's eyes, as he was studying them through the rearview mirror. Feeling unsafe, she gave the driver directions to drop them off, several blocks away from her home.

Jake paid the cabdriver as Emma slid out of the backseat. All she wanted to do was get home, lock her door and pretend none of this was real. The few blocks took forever to walk.

She was so exultant to see her door attendant, then her elevator, followed by the unlocking of her apartment door.

Once inside, Jake and Emma each chose a chair to sprawl out on in the living room. They were both emotionally exhausted. After a while, her brother sat up in his chair.

"Why do you think your phone is tapped?"

"I heard a click and then static... twice. It was when I mentioned Walden's name. Do you think I'm just being paranoid because of what Zeiss said?"

Jake ran his fingers through his hair and shook his head. "I don't know. Who would want to tap your phone anyway?"

Emma laughed. "That's a good question. I want to peek at the briefcase again. Maybe I missed something."

Nicholas had taken out the files from the attaché case, so there was no need to lock it in the safe any longer.

"Yah I'd like to finally see this case for myself."

They made there was to the study. Emma and Jake found the briefcase, unlocked, sitting on the desk in the study. Jake began searching the pockets of the briefcase. As for Emma, she re-read the letter from Walden in case she or Nicholas had missed anything.

Jake slid out a postcard from one of the compartments. "Have you already seen this?"

Emma put down the letter. "What do you have there?"

Looks like a postcard. The return address printed on it was from an art gallery in SOHO. Jake flipped it around, and on the back of the postcard, there were no words. Instead, there was a sketch of a key.

"Oh-my-god," she gasped. "That looks like an outline of the key we got today."

Without too much thought, Emma placed the key she received from Zeiss down onto the postcard. She jumped back. Surprised, elated, and relieved they had solved one piece of this vast puzzle. It was a perfect match. Emma energized instantly.

They had figured out the next clue. Impatient, she did not want to wait until tomorrow.

"We need to go to this art gallery now," Emma blurted out.

Jake was slumped in the leather chair and clearly appeared exhausted. "Well, maybe we should call Nic first."

"I don't want to distract him again," she argued. "He has a really heavy caseload now that he's been left in charge of the lab. Plus, we'll be back before he gets home anyway."

Jake laughed. "Right, Emm. You just do not want Nic knowing what you're up to, besides he'll probably tell you to wait."

Emma grabbed her sweater off the back of the chair next to the desk and headed towards the door. "And that, too," she conceded.

CHAPTER 25

She was fidgety during the entire journey because her mind was racing a mile a minute. At about half way there, Jake placed a hand on her shoulder and gave her that look to relax. So Emma replaced her fidgeting with squirming around in her seat. Jake just shook his head in defeat.

As the yellow cab pulled up to the curb, Jake turned to her. "Emm, are you going to be ok? You really need to chill a bit."

"I know." Taking a deep breath in, she paid the cabdriver and they both got out. There they were, standing outside the front doors of the Blue Stone Gallery. The building looked more like Fort Knox than an art gallery.

Emma took a deep breath in through her nose and slowly exhaled. "Well here we go Jake."

He laughed nervously and opened the main smoky, beveled glass door for them. She went in first. The camera located in the left corner instantly activated and shifted to peer down at them.

A man's voice announced out of nowhere, "Please place your key on the glass."

She glanced over at Jake, who just shook his head and shrugged his shoulders. Subsequently, Emma looked around the small entrance lobby and noticed what she had first assumed was an art piece clearly was not. This blue stone rock carving had a

VIBRATIONAL PASSAGE

glassy surface covering, while in the center, a light baby blue square lit up on the smooth exterior.

"Please place your key on the blue square," the man requested.

"Emm I bet you it's the key..."

Emma fished the key out of her coat pocket. She placed the key down as requested. Together they watched as a red laser just appeared out of nowhere and scanned her key. The laser completed its scan within a few seconds. Afterwards, the light baby blue square turned emerald green.

"Thank you. Please retrieve your key."

The sound of a buzzing noise droned, followed by a loud echoing click. Jake first glimpsed at her before pushing open the next set of thick glass doors. Once through, she found herself standing in an elite art gallery with not a soul in sight.

Emma was anxious. The exclusiveness of this art gallery, the inaccessibility to it was not normal. If something were to happen to them behind these, in all probability bulletproof double glass doors, no one would ever find out.

"Maybe you were right. We should have told Nicholas where we were going."

"I think it's a little late now Emm."

Classical music played softly. There was no receptionist. It was the two of them among all these beautiful paintings. Emma was about to turn around and try to leave, when a precisely dressed younger man in a black suit and tie entered the room.

He stood facing them. Emma was not sure where to look first. The young man had a short haircut with a streak of bleached hair that swiped across his forehead. It looked as if his jet-black hair had been paint brushed with white paint. In his left hand, he held an unlit cigarette daintily held between his fingers.

"Trying to quit," he waved the cigarette.

Emma realized she had been mostly staring at the object, trying to figure out what it was. She thought it was a cigarette, but she was not sure. Emma smiled, mostly because of the way he had addressed her rudeness with kindness. People had a way of including her in their private struggle all the time.

Without another word, he turned on his heels, indicating that they were to follow him. Emma and Jake swapped looks, while keeping pace with him. The journey ended at a lavishly decorated suite one floor up.

Their guide led them to an older man who seemed to be in charge. The distinguished elderly man sat at an exquisite Koa wood desk. He appeared to be absorbed in paperwork.

Just as her friend Maddy had taught her how to calm herself, Emma focused on her surroundings rather than the individuals in the room. Her focus was the desk. She knew it was Koa wood because of its distinct characteristics, which she had learned about while living in Hawaii. This desk was made of curly Koa, meaning it was on the pricier end of the cost spectrum for this expensively rare and endangered wood.

It was working. She was feeling more relaxed and her breathing was deeper, meaning she was not so freaked out anymore. *What would she ever do without her best friend Maddy?*

Noticing their arrival, the man put his pen down. He came out from behind his desk to greet them. With a smile, he glanced back and forth from Emma to Jake.

"Good afternoon, how may I be of service?" He had a distinct British accent.

"Good afternoon," Emma countered. "Dr. Walden Sinclair has sent me."

She noticed a slight shift in his demeanor.

He paused. Holding eye contact with her, he stated, "Yes, of course. I will be right back."

She peeked over at Jake with a puzzled look.

The man disappeared and returned within seconds with an art portfolio book. He raised his right hand motioning for them to have a seat in a sitting area.

"You should be more comfortable here."

The younger chap, who had originally met with them, still holding his unlit cigarette, asked if they would like a beverage and began to list several items.

"No thank you," she politely declined

"I'm fine, thank you," Jake added.

The young man smiled and disappeared.

Not wanting to expose the fact that she had no idea of what she was doing, Emma began slowly flipping through the leather-bound portfolio.

It was page after page of exquisite photographed oil paintings, mostly from the Renaissance period, with just a few modern art pieces. Emma sheepishly smiled and looked to the British man for guidance.

Returning her smile, he suggested, "Mr. Sinclair preferred the masters."

He halted briefly. "Durer, Cranach, and Raphael, I believe, have been selected for you. However, only if that meets with your approval, of course?"

"Yes... those will be fine."

Emma relieved by this man's graciousness.

"Please allow me to prepare these items and arrange their transportation. If I maybe so bold to recommend?"

"Yes," Emma evenly responded.

"Of course, please." He pulled something out of the inside pocket of his blazer. "All that is left are your particulars."

He handed Jake an antique fountain pen along with a cardstock form for Jake to fill out on her behalf. Emma noticed Jake smile, apparently amused that this man had assumed he was her personal assistant. This made Emma smile with amusement inside.

She could feel herself breathe deeper. They were one more step closer to figuring this all out.

CHAPTER 26

Nicholas could not take the morning off so he would not be there when the paintings arrived. It was Saturday morning, which meant he worked until noon. She still felt remorse for not informing him of the visit to the Blue Stone Gallery. Nicholas was right, she could have gone missing, and he would have never known where to look.

Both she and Jake received a strong lecture last night during dinner. Emma was embarrassed that Jake also received a scolding, along with her regarding her safety. However, she secretly thought that her husband took his concern for her protection as an opportunity to vent his frustration over Jake's latest botched wedding plans. After all, Nicholas did have to go to a lot of trouble to get that time off. As for the plane tickets, it was - what it was in Nicholas's eyes.

Three paintings promptly arrived, each one wrapped in a light baby blue cloth. The deliverymen carried each painting individually. Emma thought they looked and behaved more like security guards. Nevertheless, she directed the men to place the paintings in the study, where Jake was waiting.

After they all had coffee together, and as soon as Nicholas left for work, she and Jake spent most of the morning in the study. Their goal was to make sense of the symbols on the gold coin and the watch that Walden had left for her in the briefcase.

The deliverymen were fast. They were in and out of her apartment within ten minutes. After closing and locking the entrance door she race back into the study.

Emma looked at Jake. "Well, should we wait for Nicholas, or should we at least take a peek at one of them?"

"You know what; it feels like Christmas morning to me." He rubbed his hands together; he could never resist an unwrapped present. "Oh, come on, Ems, if there's a bad dog talk to be taken, I'll take it," Jake reassured her.

"Remember, I was there last night, too. Nicholas was on a rampage and you threw me under the bus to save your own skin. In fact, I felt the bus run me over several times and you were driving it," she teased.

"Don't be such a baby!"

They both laughed.

"Alright let's do this then," Jake slid the gold coin into his front pocket.

"Alrighty then…" Emma fastened the watch she had been examining to her wrist, rather than putting it down on the desk.

Now with freed hands, they leaned one of the paintings against the desk. Jake held the painting with both hands while Emma pulled the cloth off.

"It's a Durer," Jake announced with awe. He pointed out the initials "AD" etched beneath the date "1500". "It's an Albrecht Durer; I believe it's a self-portrait, if I am not mistaken." When he adjusted one of his hands so she could remove the rest of the covering, Jake's hand accidentally brushed the front of the painting.

Rather than sweeping over the painting, his hand disappeared into the canvas.

Emma held her breath and stared at him.

Then she finally gasped for air. "Jake, what have you done?"

"What the hell," he snapped. "I can't get my hand out. Emm, help me. Quick…"

Without a second thought, she grabbed his wrist. Emma felt a piercing pain in her skull that blinded her. There was indescribable throbbing throughout her body; it was as if a vacuum cleaner was sucking her in.

Then it stopped.

Emma's breathing was erratic and her skin felt tingly all over.

As she blinked away the oily residue from her eyes, a queasy feeling overcame her, forcing her to reach over for Jake. They exchanged a look of horror. What had just happened here?

Clearly no longer in the study, they were now standing in a cement, walled-in room which had a low ceiling, with the musky, heavy smell of being underground. There was a dusty haze as if a bomb had just exploded. The smell of bad body odor mixed with smoke burned at Emma's nostrils. She covered her nose. Candles provided the only lighting in the room.

A group of men dressed in old-fashioned military uniforms assembled themselves around a tactical table at the center of the room. A man was leaning on the table, holding the map out with his hands.

His mouth was sewn shut with what looked like thick, white shoelaces.

Emma pinched herself to make sure she was not dreaming. "Ouch!"

Everyone in the bunker turned and looked straight at Emma. They acknowledged her, but seemed unaware of Jake.

"You will help us," one of the men commanded.

A younger man holding a German pistol in his hand appeared between them and the Durer painting. Emma's mind filled with questions. Did they have the same Durer oil painting that she had? Had Walden's painting brought them here? Somehow, as the questions ran through her mind, she knew the painting had sucked them through to here.

Yet, where was here?

Emma stared back at these men. She fought back her overwhelmed need to cry. Emma felt trapped and powerless.

"What do I do...? What do I do...?" She thought softly aloud.

Then inside her head, she could hear her last conversation with her best friend Maddie again, just like when she was at the Blue Stone Gallery. *"Breathe and focus on what makes you feel strong."*

"Right then," she reflected.

Emma began to visually scout out the bunker; being aware of her surroundings always made her feel stronger.

Collected around the right side of the tactical table were four men. There was a man with thin-rimmed eyeglasses, wearing a German military uniform, a man wearing a white coat, who appeared to be a doctor, and next to him, was a stout, overweight man, whose face had patches of eczema.

Ok it is working, she thought to herself as her breathing deepened. *I am feeling more in control.*

She continued scanning the command post.

A man with bushy eyebrows, wearing a brown uniform, pushed his way to the tactical table. He was struggling to inhale, clutching his chest. When he looked into her eyes, for a brief moment Emma saw rolling hills and could hear bagpipes inside her head.

Jake whispered, "Holy shit, that's Hess."

Emma had completely forgotten about Jake. "What...?" His statement confused her.

He paused and quietly let out a deep exhale. "All the players are here."

Emma stared at her brother with a puzzled expression. "Did you hear bagpipes, too?"

"What...no..." Jake answered, coming out of his own deep thoughts.

Speaking made Emma fearful so she wanted to limit her conversation to a very soft whisper, because when she spoke the men in the room seemed to hear her. While, when Jake spoke, no one seemed to hear or see him.

"Rudolf Hess." Jake clarified. "He was Hitler's confidante. That man flew over to Scotland right before the Germans invaded Russia. Supposedly, he tried to broker an alliance with the Brits. Hess was caught and ended up in the Spandau Prison in Berlin where he committed suicide in '87."

Emma had never understood Jake's interest in World War II history, but she was grateful he was able to provide invaluable context to their current situation. Another man moved towards the group, he had a bullet hole right through his temple.

She felt dread, anger, and darkness from him. He had black, oily, combed back hair with a feminine quality to him. With his slender fingers, he was unsuccessfully trying to figure out a way to get the laces out of the map-reader's mouth.

"Joseph Goebbels," Jake sucked in air. "Goebbels was infamous for being the Minister of Propaganda. He was with Hitler in his bunker until the gruesome end. According to history books he had his six children murdered, then he and his wife, committed suicide. Their bodies were found charred to a crisp."

Even though the topic was not her favorite, hearing Jake's voice right now was calming.

Emma followed Jake's eyes; he was looking at the man in the white doctor's coat.

"You know who that is, right?" He kept his voice down to a whisper.

Emma shook her head. She did not recognize any of the men in the room.

"Josef Mengele, the Angel of Death, himself, known for doing inhumane experiments on identical twins at Auschwitz to create a master race. They say he escaped to Brazil. It's believed he never stopped his experiments."

"That name... oh...my...God... Jake, the files..." A look of recognition and shock washed over Emma's face. His name had been in Zoe's file.

Emma exchanged an uneasy look with Jake.

"Calm... breathe... in and out..." Emma coached herself. "Ok that's not working... look around..."she continued coaching herself.

"Em it's going to be alright," Jake offered support.

She began to look around the bunker.

Emma turned her attention to the sweaty, fat man.

"That's Hermann Goring," Jake, breathed out. "He was head of the Luftwaffe. Big art slut - Goring was sentenced to death at Nuremberg, but committed suicide with a cyanide pill instead."

Goring was walking around shouting at anyone in the room who would listen. "The only way to jump into another body is to commit suicide. Death is nothing," Goring insisted. "Wish, Kiss, Suicide," he repeated the words, chanting them and laughing like it were all one big joke.

"Wish, Kiss, Suicide, that's what Walden said in my last conversation with him. Jake this bunker is connected to Walden somehow."

"Ok, so let's get as much information as we can Emm, and get out of here." Jake drew Emma's attention to the other man at the table and provided as much knowledge as he could to help her.

"That's Himmler," Jake murmured. "Architect of the Holocaust, he was a huge follower and activist in the occult. This guy was one big whack job."

It was hard to make out the short man standing in a darkened corner of the room. He was a slender man, with a small, protruding belly. Even though his jacket was undone, his pulled-together appearance established sophistication.

Almost responding to Emma's thinking, he stepped out of the shadows. This man slammed his fists down on the map. Now Emma could see his face. Goosebumps ran all over her body. She was now staring into the face of the world's most renowned murderer... Adolf Hitler.

Emma took a step back. She shot Jake a look of disbelief. Emma's stomach began to churn.

Hitler was furious and frustrated because he clearly was not getting answers he was seeking. He looked impatient. She did not know why, but she was getting the sense from Hitler's disposition, that he was running out of precious time. The monster marched back into the shadowy corner of the bunker. Emma guessed he wanted to continue to be alone with his sinister thoughts.

Copying Hitler as if unable to think independently, the man who had black, slicked back hair struck the tactical table with both of his fists. He then turned his anger to someone behind the group of men. These men quickly moved out of Goebbels' line of rage, exposing a robust woman seated in a wooden chair.

Emma recognized her immediately from a book she had read. Madame Blavatsky was a famous Russian psychic who once lived in New York. Blavatsky waved her fists in the air and yelled back at Goebbels while remaining seated.

No one had noticed including Emma, that Hitler was now standing back at the tactical table. Without warning, his voice boomed out. "Stop it!"

Everyone's attention in the room, together with Emma's, was now on Hitler. Even though he was speaking in German, Emma could understand what he was saying.

In a demanding tone, Hitler stated, "Goebbels and Blavatsky, you must work this out, we are running out of time."

Watching the events unfold, it dawned on Emma that Goebbels and Blavatsky could not put their energies together because of their selfish personalities. In truth, no one in the room was a team player. Each of them was seeking individual glory. They could not work to align and frame their abilities to get out of their situation. Their addictions trapped them.

She observed as these monsters held the key to their own isolation. What they needed was someone to frame and piece together their talents, so that a bridge between realities would allow them to travel. That someone was not going to be her, she reflected.

Goebbels shifted his attention to Emma. "You're from New York," he stated. "Are you part of our re-emergence?" Goebbels eyes bored into hers.

Emma could feel his threatening question wrap around her throat.

Without warning, a large, canvas painting hanging on the wall behind Goebbels began to shimmer.

Jake, trying to distract Emma from Goebbels's verbal attack, pointed at the painting. "Do you see what's happening to the Raphael?"

Emma watched in awe, as the Renaissance painting for a brief moment shimmered, giving way to what looked like a live television feed of 9/11. A man jumped forward out of the painting, landing on his feet next to the tactical table. His skin was blistered and peeling.

Immediately, Goring began questioning, "Did you find it?"

"No," the man answered.

"Why are you back here?" Goring snapped.

"It wasn't there."

Goring smacked the man's head with the back of his hand, "Well, then find it!"

This time the man chose a painting next to the Raphael and without a thought touched the canvas. It was just like what had happened with Jake, as soon as the officer contacted the oil painting, his hand disappeared into it, and then he was gone. The painting flickered; an image instantly appeared in the frame. The view was that of the Deutchbank building, located across the street from the burning twin towers.

Impressions played out in the painting frame, providing everyone in the room with a live feed of what the officer was viewing. At first, he was following men dressed in business suits down a narrow hallway of an office building.

Without warning, a static screech filled the bunker; it was the identical noise that could be heard when a radio receiver is stuck between channels. This high-pitched noise was excruciating, forcing Emma to plug her ears.

Goring began to laugh at her. "You are a very stupid Fraulein. It is not by accident you are here. We have been observing. Know that Dr. Sinclair decided on you just before we did. You Americans, you covet our technology, and believe you can command our secrets. You think you are so clever, but you are barbaric."

The fat man paused to relish the moment, and when he smiled, his round cheeks glowed with pride. "Yes, we were the ones who prevented Dr. Sinclair and his group from jumping into their selected bodies. Now they are just as trapped..." He gestured towards the exhausted men and one woman in the bunker. "Just as we are..."

Not stopping, Goring when on to brag. "The difference between us and the WOLF group is that we know how to fix it, they do not... making our situation temporary, where theirs will soon become permanent."

He pointed to an oil painting, explaining that they had captured and imprisoned others, which also included children, through these paintings. He lectured that they were changing their fate by mining knowledge from the past and future to set up an untouchable Nazi regime in her timeline.

"The children, these must be the children Walden..."

Goring cut her off.

"That is correct. But that is not the entire picture." He went on to brag. "9/11 was necessary," Goring, grinned with delight. "An army of Nazis was searching for a specific art piece housed at an undisclosed location at ground zero, which would bridge realities so that everyone in the bunker could pass through to obtain their new bodies."

Looking insulted by the manner she was examining him, Goring locked his jaw and railed into her. "You view me with ignorant eyes. I am not dead. I am merely waiting for my new body. You still live a two-dimensional life, where we were working in a four-dimensional reality that still eludes you vulgar Americans. While your country was obsessed with the nuclear bomb... we... Nazis... perfected a way to exist outside of time. Your scientists continue to be infantile in the field of quantum physics. That is why we will rise again within your borders, to take over your country."

Emma watched as Goring verbally exploded.

"You fools... call it 'looted' Nazi art." Goring angrily waved his fists in the air at her. "We did not pillage, we 'acquired' art. It was better for the world to have someone like us possess these works of art. Yes, we understood their true value. The artists would be proud to know that we recognized their genius. The Third Reich comprehended the creative vibrational process.

These 'Masters' channel a higher level of consciousness by transferring the elevated vibration into their artwork, creating portals between time and space. We see passages. You see paint."

No matter how much Emma's mind was spinning, she held her poker face. She did not intend to reveal her lack of understanding of what Goring was ranting and raving over.

"You self-righteous people accuse us of looting, and look at you." Goring pointed at her wristwatch. "You stole that anti-gravity watch from us."

He pointed at himself. "We, we were the ones who trekked into Tibet to discover and develop the science behind the symbols."

Hitler, who had been pacing like a caged animal in the shadows, finally stepped forward again. "Enough!" He commanded.

Goring, respecting Hitler's authority, folded his hands behind him, clicked his heels, and stepped aside, making room for the Fuhrer.

Emma felt Hitler's intense, icy eyes bore holes through her skull as he fixed his gaze on her. All she could think about was that his eyes were supposed to be blue, as recorded in history, not the hazel ones that now stared her down.

She sensed Hitler's thoughts in her head, a prickly sensation of a thousand needles ran across her skin. She wanted to scream and run, but she stood her ground. It was at that point, Emma realized, Hitler was the only one in the room who could 'sense' Jake's presence. However, he could not see him. Hitler must be aware of Jake's presence through her thoughts, she reasoned.

Confirming Emma suspicions, she felt him searching and trying to read her thinking process. Hitler was trying to figure out who and where Jake was in the bunker. Emma could discern him sizing up both of their characters as well. It felt to her that he could sense their inner darkness and at the same time, their level of discipline within their personal blackness.

This made Emma grin, because Jake did not have a problem having his dark side unleashed should he need it. She continued smiling to herself, realizing that Hitler could not figure out how to motivate them.

Hitler needed them to do what Blavatsky and Goebbels could not.

Jake began to nudge Emma.

She kept her eyes locked on Hitler.

He whispered, "Emma, while you've been talking to Mr. Charismatic and Mr. Crazy here, I've been studying the map on their tactical table. Look, the symbols on the map are right here on the coin."

Breaking the fixation Hitler had on her, she stepped forward towards the tactical table to get a better look at what was on their map. Emma narrowed her vision to focus on the details. To her amazement, the map was altering, responding as if commanded by her desire to see more. She was no longer just looking at ground zero; the map was alive - zooming out to show her the entire island of Manhattan.

Emma looked up to see the map-reader staring at her. His eyes were wide. Even though his mouth was sewn shut, she could feel what he was thinking. They were the only two in the room who could activate the map.

Somehow, this man believed she was the answer.

She turned her attention back onto the tactical table. Jake was right, the same symbols from the coin were on this map. In the middle of the map was the word, Fitzgerald. There were drawings of buildings accompanied by symbols, some appeared to be hieroglyphics, but Emma could not be sure.

The map danced with energy similar to heat radiating off the pavement on a hot day. A number of building locations throughout the city shimmered. Emma gasped. The building she owned and lived in was one of the points on the map shimmering.

Looking up, astonished, there staring back at her was Hitler, with a sly smile of acknowledgment; she had just confirmed her value to him.

VIBRATIONAL PASSAGE

She stumbled backwards away from the map, bumping into Jake, knocking the gold coin out of his hand. In a flash, everyone began shouting at Jake. His cloaking was gone. There was a great commotion and agitation in the bunker.

Emma kept an eye on Jake as he reached down to retrieve the coin from the floor. Without hesitation, he bolted upright, punching the confused guard square in the face knocking him down. Jake grabbed Emma's arm and pulled her back with him into the Durer painting.

CHAPTER 27

Emma landed on her side as Jake slammed against the wall in what appeared to be her study. Jake was in a pile on the floor, his groans unexpectedly turned into peals of laughter. It was so like him to find humor in every situation.

"I can't believe you find this humorous," she protested.

He just continued laughing.

It was contagious; Emma began to chuckle, as well.

Jake rubbed his shoulder where he had struck the wall. "That was one bad trip Em."

She stood up and rubbed her eyes. Amberish-orange radiance lit up the room, however Emma could not locate where the glow was coming from. There was not a sufficient amount of lighting, so she reached over to turn on her desk lamp, but it was not there.

At that moment, she was instantly conscious that something was not right. As her eyes took in her surroundings, she discerned that everything was a bit off. It was all the same furniture, except her filing cabinet was missing. Nicholas' favorite artwork was gone from the wall; in its place were black and white photos of different New York City structures.

Nevertheless, the Durer painting was there, leaning against the desk. Yet, the other two paintings from Walden were nowhere in sight.

"Jake, there's something wrong."

"You think?" Jake plopped himself into a deep, brown leather chair.

She inspected the room, trying to curb the panic building inside her. "Jake, I'm serious."

"Okay, Emm," he said to appease her.

"Jake, we're... not... in...my... study," she articulated slowly, trying to emphasize her point.

"What are you talking about? Of course we are," he argued.

"I can prove it." Her brother jumped to his feet and tried to open the door to the study. "It's locked." Jake spun around and faced her. "When'd you put a lock on the door?"

She stared at Jake with terror in her eyes. "We've never had a lock on our study."

Jake tried the door again. "What the hell?" Puzzled, he turned back to her. As their eyes met, she could see that the whole weight of their current situation had finally become apparent to him. When Emma saw the flicker of fear in his eyes, her emotions burst into uncontrollable sobs. Tears poured out.

"I'm so sorry," Emma, cried. "This is all too much."

Rushing over to her, he took her hand. Jake soothingly led her to a chair next to the one he had been sitting in. Emma could see Jake talking to her but she could not make out his words. All she could think was that she needed to get control over her emotions. She closed her eyes and recalled the breathing exercise Maddy had taught her to calm her in times of stress.

Gradually, she gained back her composure. She began to hear Jake's words at last; it was no longer a drone of noises.

"Don't cry, Emms," he soothed. "Everything will be okay, I promise."

Jake was holding her hand, patiently waiting. Embarrassed, she asked for a tissue, her nose was leaking mucous everywhere.

He scanned the room and then shrugged. "Sorry Sis, you're going to have to be a boy and use your shirt."

Unexpected statements like this from Jake always made her laugh. However, this time it triggered her to shoot even more snot out of her nose, which increased her humiliation, as she laughed even harder. Now she felt crazy, laughing and crying in the same moment.

Taking her brother's advice, she sheepishly blew her nose on her sleeve.

"I'm sorry. I don't know what I'm doing."

"Oh, whatever, Goring is boring, and Mr. Anger management issues can kiss my..."

"I hate this. I hate all of this. Those men are the foulest individuals I have ever met."

"As Voltaire responded when asked to forswear Satan on his deathbed... *'This is no time to make new enemies'*."

"Quoting Voltaire... really?" Emma knew Jake was trying to lighten the situation.

Jake hesitated. "Come on Emm...you gotta love a guy with a sense of humor, right?"

Emma half way laughed. "So, what do we do now?"

Jake shook his head. "I don't know. I think we need to figure out a way to get back to *your* study in *your* home, and *not* back to that carnival." He shifted in his leather chair. "Speaking of the carnival, what was going on with you and Mr. Crazy at that tactical table before you knocked the coin out of my hand?"

"I don't know. I was thinking I wanted to see more than Ground Zero, and it was as if the map was alive and responding to my thinking. Whatever I wanted the map to show me it would. This is going to sound bizarre, but I saw lines that looked like an energy grid hovering above the map of New York City."

"That's not that unusual. Have you ever heard of ley lines?" Jake asked.

"Sorry not really, I mean I know a little."

"Well, Hitler and his gang of merry men were deep into the occult. The term Aryan race is actually an occult term. All the symbols they utilized originated from ancient mystical beliefs. Hess... now that man was into ley lines big time. He believed in them so much that he had a map created of them.

VIBRATIONAL PASSAGE

You see, shamans, spiritualists, and even scientific groups believe that there's an electric magnetic grid wrapped around the earth. At different specific points on that grid, there is an intense cluster of energy. I have even read somewhere that some consider these locations vortexes." Jake paused. "I wonder if they're using these vortexes to make these jumps."

She interrupted him. "What's the difference between a portal, like Walden's painting, and the vortex you're talking about?"

"From my understanding, a vortex is a stationary concentration of energy in a set location, like Stonehenge in England. While the Durer painting is different, it's a mobile bridge between dimensions of time and space." Jake dithered again. "You know what, I have a thought. Can I see that watch?"

Emma slipped the watch off her wrist and offered it to Jake. He clutched the gold coin and the watch next to each other.

She rubbed her forehead, trying to erase her tension. "Jake, they couldn't see or hear you until you dropped the gold coin. I believe the only one who could sense you were in the room was Hitler. Goring pointed out that my watch was stolen. He also called it an anti-gravity watch. Do you think the gold coin and the watch have something to do with the jump? What if they activate the paintings, making them portals?"

"I think you're right," he agreed. "In fact, I believe they activate, and better yet, protect. Remember that officer who jumped out of the painting? His skin was chafed and peeling as if he had a damaging sunburn. But look at us," he touched his face and his arms. "We're okay. Maybe these two items," he held up the coin and watch, "protected us somehow during the jump."

Emma took a deep breath in and nodded. Thinking aloud, she began to piece together what she had just experienced in the bunker. "Jake, what do all those people have in common other than their Nazi connection?"

"Well, they all killed themselves," Jake retorted. "Except for Blavatsky, I'm not sure about her."

"Okay... what else?"

"Well, they're obviously all trapped, and they're trying to find their new bodies, according to Goring. It's more like they're looking for their hosts, 'cause they're such parasites."

Emma smirked. "They're dead by our standards, but in a way, they're not really dead. You saw them they are trapped. The gang can jump in and out of our reality, yet they can't stay for long."

"Another thing they have in common," Jake added, "is that they all seemed to be fascinated with you."

"As creepy as that sounds, you're right, they really became fascinated with me when the map started responding to me."

"It's got to have something to do with your vibration, Ems."

"What do you mean?"

"I think it has to do with them finding a host. I think you have the right vibration, if they are going to be jumping into bodies, that vessel has to have the right vibration for them to jump into and take it over. Otherwise, it would be like plugging a toaster into the fridge power socket. Wrong appliance plugged into the incorrect power source, we are talking fried..."

Emma cut her brother off. "They require my body?" She wanted to vomit.

"Yes, I'm beginning to believe the piece of art they're searching for is not activated until the right person holds it or touches it. Therefore, that person's touch vibrationally activates the item for them to be able to use it. That person must have to have a certain pulsation that can also control the map as well. After what you did they're thinking you're the one."

"Vibrationally activated?"

"Emm before you totally lose it, hear me out. There is a theory that gifted people can comprehend and create from the abstract. If you or I looked at clay, we would just see clay. However, an artist sees what it can become. Let's say these paintings have their own vibration, matching the artists who painted them. Making those perfect portals… are you still with me?"

She took a deep breath in and nodded.

"What do all the artists have in common? Albrecht Durer, Lucas Cranach, and Raphael Sanzio… they were all masters in their field. They were all brilliant artists working on a higher level than the rest of us."

"So why is my vibration different? You've seen my artwork," she countered.

"Yes I have, but that's not why you're vibration is higher." He hesitated. "You're a healer."

"What are you talking about?" She scoffed. "Maddy yes… but me… no way."

"You were a pivoting aspect in my recovery when we were younger. You healed me by reframing the way I viewed the world." Jake went on. "Our thinking is our steering wheel to what we will experience in our reality and what you showed me was how to take control over my steering wheel. Remember when I was younger and in and out of hospitals all the time? I lived in constant fear. I was letting fear take over my thinking, my world. Then you helped me reframe that, and take back the power in my life. That was the only thing that got me through."

"That's not quite true," Emma, argued. "You really suck at relationships Jake. If I'm such a healer, why haven't I healed that part of you?"

"It's not you, Emms. I get myself into these situations. You know that I am attracted to strong, opinionated women. The relationship always starts out balanced and equal, but then when the women stop being strong, that love becomes a dog collar."

Emma raised an eyebrow. "A dog collar…?"

He shook his head up and down while continuing. "It all starts off with the romantic pursuit. I show them how I adore them and love them, but then it turns into 'it's not enough.' If I love them…, *I would call them at noon every day*, if I love them… *I would do this*… if I love them… *I would do that*… so it is a constant proving of my love. It is exhausting. That type of love is about control, about their fear of losing something.

That controlling of me, rather than trusting that I love them is depleting. Their fear just sucks me emotionally dry. They want constant confirmation, which bleeds the life force out of me. I have never given any of the women I have been with reason to doubt my feelings. This endless verifying saps the joy out of being in love. It ends up more like being in prison. When we reach that point, the only way I can preserve a sense of myself is to end the relationship." An indignant darkness covered Jake's face as he spoke.

Emma realized that this was the first time Jake had been able to verbalize his relationships regarding the females in his life.

She studied Jake compassionately. "Jake I had no idea how angry you are. Every time you have a breakup, you always act as if it does not matter. I am so sorry..." She paused, debating whether to continue, and then she took a leap of faith. "Remember... what Aunt Gertie always told us when we were young?"

Jake nodded. "What do you think got me through? Whenever I got so angry and thought my head was going to explode, I would hear her words... *when we are full of rage, we are forgetting that someone loves us deeply and that someone was she; her love sees and remembers our worth even if we do not. We are never alone or abandoned on our journey through life.*"

Neither of them talked until she finally interrupted the silence. "And here Nicholas and I were thinking you were just allergic to the altar."

A slight, grateful smile spread across Jake's face. "What's your opinion on all of this?"

"I see it as, when you fall in love, each person is a different harmonious note," she articulated. "People forget this and they try to influence the person they're in love with to become the same musical note that they are. We are attracted to people because of how they make us feel... like pleasant-sounding notes complementing each other. Nevertheless, because we are afraid of losing them... we force them to become the same tuneful note as ourselves. Then it is just noise... or fighting, rather than harmonious music. The truth is that in order to create beautiful music together, a couple must learn to appreciate and work with each other's uniqueness."

Jake burst into laughter "Ems, you're such a romantic. So why did you choose someone like Nic? Don't get me wrong I like Nic, but..."

Emma took a profound breath and looked down. After a few seconds, she began, choosing her words carefully. "I know you couldn't bear watching Aunt Gertie die. Then again, when she asked me to be with her because she wanted to pass on at home instead of in some sterile hospital, I could not say no. I had no idea what I was getting myself into when I said yes. Bearing witness to someone's death remains the most painful thing I have ever done in my life to date.

Watching her suffer towards the end when the pain medication was ineffective was hell. I felt so helpless, useless... and isolated. I would stay up all night with Aunt Gertie, to make sure she did not die alone. I was drained and lonely - all that was left of me was a dark, twisted black hole of nothingness. That's how I felt for a very long time until Nicholas came along."

"Ems, I had no idea." Jake cleared his throat. "I'm sorry. I should have been there." He halted briefly and cautiously asked. "Is that why you have been the way you've been? I thought it was Nic all this time."

"What do you mean?"

"You used to be so adventurous, full of life, and you just had a way with people. Now, you are so careful, so old... You do not let anyone new into your life. The only time I see the real Ems, is when you're around children."

Emma shrugged, fighting back her tears of sharing the pain she still felt in her innermost being. "You are right, I know."

"So why haven't you and Nic had kids? What are you guys waiting for?"

She had been able to circumvent all these questions from Jake for quite some time. Each occasion he would verge towards these topics, Emma always found a way out. However, being trapped she guessed it was about time to finally address it.

Emma gazed down at the floor for a second time. "It is just not in our cards."

She was grateful that Jake did not push this topic any further, but rather he transferred the focus of the conversation to what she saw in Nicholas.

So grateful by Jake's shift, Emma smiled. "I assure you. Having Nicholas in my life is amazing. It took a long time for me to get out of that deep, dark, black tar after we lost Aunt Gertie. Nicholas stuck by me through it all. I really love that man. I do not know what I would do without him."

"Emms," Jake interrupted her. "Look at the painting, look what is happening."

She observed as the painting began to shimmer. A light started to glow around them, causing the portal to open. A beautiful, red glow pulsated from the canvas. It was an amazing auric field of glistening stars... nothing like anything she had ever seen in her life. Sparks of thin, pink and red electric tendrils reached out from the canvas; connecting to her heart.

"Keep doing what you are doing." Jake instructed her. "Keep talking about why you love Nic. Here, take the watch and put it on your wrist."

Looking back and forth between the painting and Jake, she continued expressing why she loved Nicholas so deeply. The more and more she communicated her love for her husband, the more the portal opened up in the painting. The lightning sparks intensified until it saturated the space with tones of pink and red.

As she continued on, she fastened the watch on her wrist. She concentrated and imagined the details of her husband's face, his smile, and the way he squinted his eyes, the way he laughed...

"That is it!" Jake shouted. "It's focus and intent. That is why we ended up here and not in your real study." He grabbed her arm and directed her. "Stay focused on your love for Nic."

He lightly touched the Durer painting.

Nothing happened.

"Emm, you've got to focus."

"I can't. I am too tired."

"Concentrate on a favorite moment... that time you guys went to Europe for your first vacation as a couple... your honeymoon in Hawaii... Emms think... think about happy memories. Think about what you love about him."

She closed her eyes, and focused on her husband's face, on his voice, she could hear his laughter... and finally, she could feel the air shiver around them.

Sucked and swallowed into the painting, all Emma could see were an array of colors - a beautiful patina of shades.

Jake and Emma emerged from the frame, shivering, cold, and damp. She knew this was her study.

They were home.

CHAPTER 28

It was raining outside. A flash of lightning glowed through Wally's bedroom curtains.

He tossed and turned in bed, and could not seem to find a comfortable position. It felt like eternity before he was able to fall sleep.

Wally was not sure if he was conscious and hallucinating when he found himself standing in front of a porthole of some kind. He could not be sure, whether it was more like one of the portholes he had seen on cruise ships, or if it was a porthole from a submarine. The opening was dark, and the air seemed to move and glisten like there was water all around him.

Seeing a light coming through the porthole, Wally moved closer to get a better glimpse. When he gazed into the opening, a hand slapped against the glass. Wally jumped and let out a scream. The face blocked out the light behind it. Wally had no idea who this man was because he did not recognize his face.

The blistered skin on the man's face made him look horrifying, just like in the horror movies Wally sometimes liked to watch. Another desperate face appeared. It seemed like they were taking turns looking out of the porthole.

None of it made any sense, until Wally finally saw a face he recognized. It was his father. His dad looked determined, his lips were moving, and Wally desperately tried to hear what his dad was uttering.

Wally screamed for his dad, but nothing came out, he had no voice. There was a dampened silence, and a murky darkness filled with shadows of different faces mixed with intermittent light coming from the porthole.

His father's face appeared back in front of the opening. He was motioning for him to come closer, but Wally was unable to move at first. Desperate to reach his father, Wally focused every ounce of his energy, pushing himself forward. When Wally reached the opening, he was able to witness a group of men in business suits panicking.

Yet, he could not see his father. His dad was somewhere there with the other scared men who were trapped in such a tiny space and unable to get out. Wally just wanted to help.

Then the porthole vanished. Wally found himself sitting on a rock looking out onto a peaceful lake. He recognized the place. It was his favorite vacation spot. He liked this lake because it was calm and everything always felt safe. He watched as a white swan slowly swam by.

Wally heard his Dad's voice.

He looked around, but could not see him.

"Dad, where are you?" Wally yelled.

"I'm here, Son."

"I cannot see you."

"But you can feel me," his dad assured him.

Wally's thoughts were full of emotions, questions, and confusion.

Interrupting his train of thought his dad spoke. "Wally, we do not have much time. I need your help."

Wally sat straight up, obediently listening to his father.

"There are some very bad men who want to hurt Zoe," his dad warned. "You need to protect your little sister. Do not trust Uncle Peter and this man that you have not met whose name is Mr. Brown." His Father commanded Wally to repeat Mr. Brown's name a few times before he went on. "You did a good job getting that book from my study to Aunt Emma. You are going to need to help her again. Very bad men are planning to hurt children like Zoe."

"Dad, did you make the book fall and why were the paintings changed in your study?"

"Yes I did. What was the last painting you noticed?"

"Your copy of the Durer painting... How did you do that Dad?" Walden hesitated.

"It took a lot of energy and focus. When I move objects in your reality, I become vulnerable making it easy to be located. I hid a very important message for your Aunt Emma in that book before I left. The Durer painting, even though it is a copy helps me. It is too much for me to explain to you right now son, but one day I will... I promise."

"Okay Dad... so does that mean I can talk to you in your study?"

"Not anymore son. I am proud of you, Wally, I have always been proud of you. You are a good son. I love you. I'll be seeing you again soon."

A cool breeze blew across Wally's face as tears slowly flowed from his eyes.

His father continued. "This is going to be hard for you to believe, son... but I am not dead. Wally, I am trapped in a place between where you are and where death is. I am working on finding my way back to where you are. Except, I'm going to look different the next time you see me."

A shimmer followed by a flash on the lake occurred just in front of the rock Wally was sitting on. He could see the reflection of a church he could not quite recognize, although he knew he had been there before. He watched as a movie played out on the watery surface. The picture show was of an older groundskeeper watering a bed of roses.

By some unexplainable means, he could smell the fragrant roses. Glass chimes sparkled, from the touch of the sun. Wally felt the gentle breeze that set the chimes dancing. He leaned forward towards the lake while remaining on his rock.

Wally was hoping to get a better view of the groundskeeper. The man unexpectedly turned his attention from watering the roses, to look directly at him. He was now staring straight into his dad's eyes.

Wally shot up in his bed, shaken and shivering, as the storm outside raged on. He felt robbed once again; he did not get to tell his dad how deeply he loved him...

CHAPTER 29

Peter Sinclair settled into his chair. He was starting to feel the fatigue after his turbulent flight into England followed by a lengthy chauffeured ride to the Castle. He was the last to arrive, and as soon as he took his place, the meeting came to order. Peter could not recollect when the last meeting had occurred. But then again, he really did not care.

The secretary, seated at the head of the long table read back the minutes from the previous gathering. Peter sat impatiently; he despised the formality of these encounters. He would much prefer it if they could forego the rituals and just get down to business.

The Global Peace Organization (GPO) met quarterly at different classified locations around the world. Every aspect of this organization was secretive, from its members to its corporate affiliations. The protocol behind the gathering of the representatives who belonged to the five wealthiest families in the world was just as enigmatic. The knowledge of the time and location of the meeting only occurred 24 hours prior. There had only been two emergency meetings that Peter attended since he entered this group, one of those was during the 9/11 situation.

Peter found his membership to be just another burden inherited from his late father. Being a part of the discreet family dynasties that globally controlled the world's banking, mining, trade and real estate holdings, did not come without a price to his personal agenda.

He was barely listening when the doors opened to the castle's chamber. Mr. Brown walked in and stood at the end of the long, ebony table - facing the secretary. Standing at attention, he waited for the secretary's permission to brief the attendees.

Receiving the nod, Mr. Brown reported.

"After the investigation at WOLF, I was able to determine that the 33 assets from the twin towers have been intercepted by the German group. Our initial tracking of ten assets is still under investigation. As everyone is well aware the loose ends at WOLF, no longer exist. The location of the 33 assets has not been determined. However, it appears that Dr. Walden Sinclair has left behind information despite warnings against such actions."

Peter perked up in his chair. He concentrated on controlling his excitement that the file he had been looking for had been possibly located. *Maybe Mr. Brown was useful after all,* he thought.

He slowly and precisely chose his words when he fired his questions at Mr. Brown.

"Why has it taken you months to determine this? What has Dr. Sinclair left behind, and to whom?"

Even though questions came from different individuals at either side of the table, Mr. Brown was required to address only the secretary with his responses. Never permitted to make eye contact with any of the members at any time, Mr. Brown demonstrated he knew his place.

He maintained his gaze at the secretary and stated. "It is unclear at this point what Dr. Sinclair has disclosed. Nonetheless, Sinclair had sent classified information to unknown sources. As agreed upon by this group, we monitored one of those possible sources for several months, this ex-female laboratory employee. The one he had a sexual affiliation with to verify and intercept if Sinclair posted something to her.

My team has recently ascertained directly from her, that she did indeed have a post office box. Confirmation through a source within the Federal postal service indicated that she refused a package prior to 9/11. An attempt made to corroborate the identity of the sender encountered a dead end.

Nevertheless, Dr. Nicholas Lange and his wife, Emma, are the persons of interest. Lange was employed as Sinclair's assistant at the Mendelrose Corporation."

Mr. Brown did not attempt to answer Peter's first question, which was more of a statement.

Peter could feel the scrutiny of the other representatives at the table creep upon him.

Mr. Brown resumed. "The surveillance install is complete. A hundred percent... phones, landline, cells, computers, residence and workplaces for both subjects."

Another member at the table interjected. "Are there any others we should be aware of, or concerned about?"

"Not at the moment, Sir," Mr. Brown's tone remained even and he went on. "However, we discovered that the phone line and computer at Dr. Lange's workplace was already under surveillance."

Peter kept his composure as four sets of eyes looked over at him. He slightly bowed to indicate he was listening just as intensely, not giving away the slightest clue that he was the one monitoring Nicholas' computer and office phone. "I will have my I.T. team look into it immediately," he assured them.

"We are having someone from RVI investigate," Mr. Brown added.

Peter kept his composure, though he was seething with anger. *Who do you think you are, Mr. Brown?* He deliberated. *Challenging me... you are just an ant who I will squash when the timing is right.*

"In addition," Mr. Brown hesitated, "we detected a molecular signature which indicates a jump has recently taken place at Lange's residence."

"Are you sure? Was it Dr. Lange who made the jump?" A member interrogated.

Mr. Brown gave a brisk response. "Yes, we are sure about the molecular signature. No, it is unclear who the individual was."

After several minutes of silence, the secretary thanked Mr. Brown, who then, exited the room.

VIBRATIONAL PASSAGE

All eyes shifted to Peter, who had now become next on the agenda due to Mr. Brown's statements.

The newest member of the group was sitting across the table from Peter. It was only his second meeting, after inheriting his membership from his mother, who had died just recently. Peter hoped he would keep his mouth shut this time. That man was always posing so many ridiculous questions. He was nothing more than a time waster in Peter's mind.

Peter refused to stand as required by protocol. He knew no one would push him to comply.

From his light blue leather chair, he commenced. "Based on our latest findings, our research demonstrates, it takes only seven of our young subjects to do what it takes billions of our dollars at WOLF to achieve."

"Have you found your seven?" Someone cross-examined.

"We have a group of five," Peter replied, sternly. "I'm searching through some files left behind by Dr. Sinclair. I believe he unearthed something that will accelerate my search for the remaining two."

"How long before you find a way to control the subjects?" Another member queried.

Peter sighed. "You cannot rush science. We are talking about the culmination of over sixty years of research... where the genetics are the final key to unlock what we have been working towards."

The newest member spoke up.

Peter worked hard on not rolling his eyes.

"Mr. Lyceum, please indulge me and explain how it works with these young subjects."

Peter, controlling his temper, thought, *this is going to be the last time I am going to break it down for him.* He was no longer going to overindulge this new member.

Peter clarified. "As you recall from the briefing at your first meeting, the information that we gained as a group from Hitler's scientists and the files they left behind, provided us with the technology to jump between time and space. Through Mengele's files, we were able to ascertain exactly why he was conducting experiments on twins. Hitler's scientists figured out that certain children, due to their brain processing, possessed intense psychic skills. Once these subjects are controlled, we could then manipulate them into accessing and controlling consciousness.

From the groundbreaking research, our group, which you are now a part of, has developed a means towards genetically modifying the DNA of children while in the womb. First, we experimented with the morning sickness pill, which created a generation of offspring with the brain processing disorder known as dyslexia. We verified the dyslexic progenies were intuitive and empathic.

The conclusions of that research led us to an understanding of the unique skills of subjects under the Autism Spectrum. We were able to introduce a stabilizer concealed in a particular category of Mendelrose antibiotics, which enhanced a generation of children with extreme sensitivity and psychic awareness, but they were too unstable to utilize.

The variation of the brain processing occurring in the Autism Spectrum is too broad. We cannot control the subjects... yet. What my research team acquired from the dyslexics' findings, we applied to the autistics. Now, we are on the cusp of constructing an innovative generation of manageable subjects who possess the skills and abilities necessary for tapping into and controlling the world's unconsciousness."

The newest member interrupted. "Is not what we are doing crossing the line into crimes against humanity?"

Peter retorted. "Please do not confuse us with the Nazis. Hitler constrained the consciousness of the German population. If we succeed in controlling a group of undeveloped subjects who can alter the unconsciousness of humanity, there would be compliance without wars or weapons or bloodshed. Do you really have any other questions?"

The man shook his head.

After a moment of silence, the secretary moved the group forward to the last item on the meeting's agenda. As the secretary outlined the last topic, the neutralizing of the 9/11 conspiracy theorists, Peter lost interest. He started to fiddle with his cufflinks, which Peter had inherited from his father.

The cufflinks provided safe passage and protection. Most people mistakenly thought the symbol hand engraved into the cufflinks were the caduceus, representing the Lyceum legacy of medical research. In actuality, the family sought protection from the symbol of the Greek god Hermes to gain access to safe passage with their inventions, commerce, and connection to the underworld consciousness.

Walden… Walden… Walden… Peter thought to himself as he slyly smiled. *The file does exist.*

Well, it seems Dr. Lange…we are going to be spending some quality time together.

CHAPTER 30

Nicholas discovered Emma and Jake in the study when he arrived home from his half-day at his office. He did not seem to perceive how traumatized they were when he found them sitting in separate leather chairs. Mind you, he had only poked his head into the study quickly.

"Let's go guys; we are going to be late. I've got the car in the loading zone downstairs." Nicholas shifted his gaze to Jake. "I was able to get a hold of Olivia and they are expecting you as well. Come on people, we gotta go. Let's go…"

Emma peered over at Jake and groaned to herself. "Oh, damn, the barbeque."

There was no way she could get out of their evening plans. Nicholas would never forgive her for missing the anniversary party. They had RSVP'd months in advance.

Nicholas only had a handful of people he respected on the level of Dr. Steven Waterford. His favorite college professor was the pivoting mentor steering him into his specific field of genetics. Nicholas continued to confer with him throughout his career. The man was still a respected member in the field of genetic research, and the esteemed name of Waterford was renowned.

"Honey, give us five minutes, and we'll meet you down in the car," Emma promised.

Pulling out of the chair too quickly, she had to steady herself because her body ached everywhere. She made her way to her bedroom where she quickly rinsed in the shower and brushed her teeth. Emma then selected a simple black dress with a pair of black kitten heels and a pair of pearl earrings.

With a spritz of her Chanel perfume, she was out the door in record time. The elevator ride to the lobby was swift and in no time, she took her seat in the vehicle. Nicholas drove while her brother sat in the backseat.

She was grateful that the journey to the Waterford's was traffic-free, so she could keep Nicholas focused on small talk about his day. Jake remained quiet for most of the journey, he only asked a few questions here and there about Nicholas's day. Emma knew that she needed to share with her husband everything that had just occurred, but now was not the time.

When Nicholas pulled the car up to the front door, two young men met them. One opened Emma's door, while the other opened Nicholas' and Jake's car doors. Her husband then handed his keys over to the valet.

The 25th Anniversary of Steven and Olivia Waterford occurred at their Sands Point Estate. Even though the invitation stated that it was a barbeque, the event was a black tie affair. Jake immediately wandered off and found his way to the open bar. Meanwhile, Emma and Nicholas each nursed a glass of champagne they had selected from a server's tray passing by. They made their way through the crowd mingling among the other guests.

In light of what they had just been through, Emma was nervous that Jake would prescribe a generous dose of alcohol to settle his nerves. Jake had a talent for attracting single women; they too, would soon become an alternate distraction for her brother. Nicholas seemed to notice this after about forty minutes, as well, and retrieved Jake. Her husband redirected him upstairs with them where an elaborate oyster bar was set up on the balcony.

She found herself zoning out, unaware of the conversation that was taking place on the balcony until Nicholas gently touched her arm, flashing a concerned look. Their eyes met, and Emma could see that her husband noticed she had been withdrawn throughout most of the evening.

When the guests of honor began to speak, Emma was thankful when Nicholas shifted his attention towards Dr. Waterford and his wife. Since it was the couple's 25th Anniversary, it was only appropriate that the theme of discussion was the recipe to a lasting relationship. It was in answer to someone's request from the crowd.

Dr. Waterford chuckled and his voice boomed in response. "I see it more like the exact opposite of theory of mind... I respect that my lovely wife might disagree, but let me first present my hypothesis."

Steven raised his glass to toast his wife and then commenced his lecture. "The proposed theory of mind assumes that one is able to translate thoughts, desires, and intentions of others, in order to predict and comprehend behaviors. The speculation is that those who do not possess the capacity to see things from a perspective other than their own - are unable to rely on social based assumptions, and fall under the umbrella of cognitive impairments such as Autism. I, too, felt these impairments years ago as a newlywed."

His wife interjected. "You have such a way of making everything sound so romantic, Sweetheart."

Someone who had just joined the crowd that was slowly growing probed. "Tell us about your impairment."

The crowd laughed.

Steven grinned and persisted. "Just wait; I can decipher this for you all. You contemplate you know what your partner is really thinking - but that is just an erroneous myth. We attach experiences to words, and we have an assumption that the other person shares in our muscle memory... our experience.

When my wife and I were first married, some of our arguments consisted of the simple task such as unpacking groceries. She would ask for my assistance, which I would readily give, nevertheless it would end up with her being exasperated, rendering me a failure.

Let me illustrate a typical event. My wife would invite me to acquire the groceries from one of her hands, and of course, I would select the hand I perceived versus the hand she meant. This led to several heated discussions over a guessing game that required resolving. There is this ambiguous conviction in relationships that love postulates insight into a partner's expectations."

The crowd gathered around the guests of honor was growing even larger.

"Well doctor, what did you prescribe?"

This set the group into loud laughter.

Dr. Waterford smiled and raised a hand to his audience and continued. "At this point, the only way to resolve the impasse of hurt feelings was to create our own language that consisted of details of meanings. One might say the creation of a collective muscle memory between us. Therefore, if my lovely wife asks me to take the groceries from her hand I now know she usually means her left, which is her weaker arm. If she wants me to purchase oranges, unless otherwise specified, I would know that she means Navel oranges."

Jake burst out laughing. "Just what we need, more step by step details from women. Like they don't give us enough already…"

Dr. Waterford snickered. "Ah, we clearly have a bachelor among us."

This made the audience roar.

"Sweetheart, as much as we love to hear your passionate interpretation on relationships," his wife interrupted. "I believe it's time for our guests to enjoy our freshly made gelato which is now being served downstairs."

Dr. Waterford raised his champagne flute to his wife and gestured for everyone to follow her.

Before the gathering trailed behind her, there was a round of applause for his speech. Dr. Waterford basked in the appreciation as he too, shadowed his wife downstairs.

The whole ordeal of the day had finally caught up with Emma. She felt light-headed and quickly grabbed for Nicholas' arm.

She could hear Nicholas whispering in her ear. "Em, are you okay?"

She only managed a nod.

"I need to get you home," he gently spoke in her ear.

She watched as her husband motioned for Jake to come over.

Nicholas turned to Emma. "I'll be right back. I am just going to thank our hosts and we will be on our way. Jake, please stay with your sister."

Emma achieved a faint smile.

CHAPTER 31

Peter sat in his vehicle impatiently anticipating Martha's return home from dropping Wally off at his Saturday morning swim lesson. Seeing Martha's light baby blue Lexus pull up, he sprang into action before the valet could maneuver her car away. Peter desperately needed to get his hands on Zoe.

Over time, he had been able to pinpoint a few of the laboratory assistants that had been working with Walden. The trickiest aspect was convincing them that Walden and he had been functioning jointly. Peter had ascertained sufficient knowledge from his female spy to frame a likely enough story regarding Walden.

Mind you, it did take some undertaking because each colleague on Walden's team felt he was rogue within the corporation because of his secrecy. His work focused on his daughter, therefore protecting Walden's daughter was something they would not betray easily, but Peter had them all convinced they were all on the same team.

Walden had selected wisely with his inner team, although not good enough, he contemplated.

Peter could overhear and see Zoe screeching while kicking the driver's seat, as he approached the SUV. Martha did not look happy to see him. Her face flushed with her eyebrows knitted together, she was obviously annoyed and distressed.

Running various scenarios in his mind, Peter derived several techniques to persuade Martha to give Zoe to him for the next two hours. It was unproblematic to fabricate to her, especially when she was so irritated. Martha was always unable to think clearly when rendering a decision in her current state.

Standing beside the SUV, he indicated to Martha to roll down her window.

"Martha, it is so good to see you. Please forgive me for not calling."

"Uncle Peter, how are you?"

Disregarding her small talk, he got right down to his rehearsed explanation for needing Zoe.

"As you know, there is a world-renowned expert who is providing training at the center. It came to me earlier today that he could possibly see Zoe before he leaves New York later this afternoon. He was tough to get here in the first place with his schedule. In fact, it may take us some doing to get him back."

Peter had to elevate his voice to counter Zoe's commotion in the backseat. "I am so sorry for the short notice,'" he lied.

Martha appeared puzzled by his request. Peter had to act fast to move his request along. He ventured into the second part of his plan, getting her to talk about the good old days with Zoe.

"Zoe sure is growing. I remember when she would sit quietly and play with her toys."

Peter knew she would jump at his shift in conversation. Embarrassed by her lack of control with Zoe, Martha would welcome his focus in the discussion to a status where she felt less of a failure. It worked.

She recalled to him in a nostalgic tone. "I miss those days. As you can see, all she does now is screech. What is this expert's name again? I wonder why Dad didn't say anything when I saw him yesterday for lunch."

"You are not going to believe this, but all of Zoe's screaming has made me forget his name. Let me think... You know what Martha, let us just skip it and the next time he is in town, we can arrange something – not so last minute. I believe he will be back in the fall of next year... possibly. Well I have to get back to the center." Peter turned and slowly walked towards his car.

"Wait, Uncle Peter. Maybe it would be good for Zoe to see someone. I can follow you to the center."

Knowing that the nanny did not work Saturdays, Peter agreed with her, and then pretended. "That will be great to have you there. So, will the nanny be picking Wally up?"

Martha quickly responded. "Oh, that's right."

Peter observed, as she comprehended that she would not be able to drive out to Long Island and return in time to pick up her son.

"Would you mind driving her there? I can pick her up after I retrieve Wally. It would be good for Wally to see you."

"That would be perfect. How is the little man doing?"

"I am not sure these days."

Peter smirked to himself. "He is a good boy," he assured her.

"Thank you, Uncle Peter."

He had been influencing Martha her entire life on what to do and what her place in the world was. Peter received little resistance from people like her, who were too afraid to make mistakes. He was enjoying seeing himself in the image of the hero through Martha's eyes.

What a senseless woman, Peter reflected to himself.

With the assistance from the door attendant, Zoe's car seat was positioned in Peter's black Bentley, while Martha held onto Zoe tightly so she could not run away. It took all three of them to fasten Zoe into her car seat.

Peter was losing his tolerance with Martha when she began to brief him on Zoe's latest behaviors. He just did not care that Zoe had become obsessed with light blue strings and ribbons. When Martha went on to explain that Zoe had boxes overflowing with them, he wanted to stop her. Yet, he knew better, Martha needed her guilt appeased. He listened for another three minutes before cutting her off. He let her explain how Zoe would take them out and organize them across her bedroom floor, from longest to shortest or in order of color from darkest to lightest.

"I am sorry Martha, I need to get going."

"Yes, of course. I will pick her up in about an hour-and-a-half."

"Possibly give us two hours, you know, just in case."

"That sounds fine. I will see you then." Martha waved to her daughter who was beginning to rip at something in the backseat. He waved his hand and began to drive.

Peter watched in the rearview mirror, as Martha waved goodbye to her daughter. While Zoe did not care one bit, her focus was more on trashing his backseat. During the entire drive, Zoe screeched and kicked at the passenger side of the front seat.

He philosophized to himself that he would particularly enjoy this session as the half-human, half-child continued pounding and kicking at his tan leather seat.

As they got closer to the Brookstone campus, he activated his car phone while he drove, using the buttons on his steering wheel, placing a call to his assistant.

"Hello. I need you waiting for me. My ETA is four minutes. Make sure everything is prepared so that we can begin immediately upon my arrival."

He did not wait for a response. Peter clicked his car phone off just as he felt Zoe's flying tennis shoe collide with the back of his head.

Peter was enraged and yelled at her. Zoe giggled.

They drove to an off-limits area of the research campus where the Center for Advancement of Autism Research (CAAR) executive offices was located. A level four clearance was required for entrance. Peter pulled into his designated parking stall next to the private entrance, where he encountered one of his assistants who assumed the challenging task of getting Zoe inside.

"We are all prepared, per your request, Dr. Lyceum, the other children are already in their observation rooms."

He marched ahead, as he heard a yelp from his assistant.

It sounded like Zoe had bit him.

Peter was in the observation room in no time. He watched as Zoe was being ushered into the therapy play suite complete with dollhouse, toys, and picture books. Two assistants strapped Zoe into what looked like a dental chair, securing her legs, ankles, upper arms, and forehead down, while leaving her hands free.

From the observation area, Peter could view several rooms at once through TV monitors, which recorded the experiments.

He tapped the intercom button. "Zoe, my dear," he flatly stated, "You know the drill, just like you did it for your daddy."

He ordered his staff. "Begin stage one of the tests. Remember I want it done just the way Dr. Sinclair performed the tests. Is that clear?"

There were several nods.

An assistant standing next to Zoe interrupted. "Dr. Lyceum, the subject has urinated in her pants."

"Unbelievable," Peter mumbled. He pushed the intercom button. "Take care of it. Wash her clothes and make sure she is back into them before her mother gets here. We only have an hour-and-a-half left people…"

Peter turned his attention to Zoe. "You are not going home until you are done, Zoe. The sooner we get through this, the sooner I will let your mother take you home."

He drummed his pen on the countertop.

Within ten minutes, they resumed.

"Begin," Peter, commanded.

In Room A, fastened into a similar chair to Zoe's, a picture of a zebra was displayed to a young boy, about Zoe's age. The boy refused to look at the photo at first, pain applied to his left hand changed his mind. An assistant did this by placing a pencil between the boy's fingers and applying pressure until the child screamed from the torture and complied.

The laboratory assistant was cautious, so as not to leave any marks on the child's skin. Peter was pleased to see that the lab technician administered his negative reinforcement meticulously, especially in light of what happened to a subject in this trial a few months ago.

A boy's heart had stopped during the testing procedure. This episode had decelerated the process. Nevertheless, with the credentials of all the experts surrounding him, Peter was able to minimize the responsibility for the child's death while remaining on course with his experiments.

When the subject looked at the photo, Peter pressed the intercom button to the room where Zoe was located. "Show Zoe the pictures, please," he specified.

There were three photos revealed to Zoe, a zebra, a flower, and a truck. Peter witnessed as Zoe quickly selected the correct answer, pointing to the image of the zebra. An assistant offered her a choice of different sized baby blue ribbons. She chose one and began to play with it for a period of three minutes while remaining strapped in the chair.

When the timer sounded, the experiment resumed without Zoe holding the ribbon. The process resumed however with the girl in room B. This continued for a set of five trials each, alternating between the two subjects.

Every aspect of the experiment adhered to precise timing. It was imperative. Consequently, the children could recover and be in a '*happy place*' by the time their parents or nannies picked them up from their therapy session.

All the photos used during the testing were set down in the child's play area, once the completion of the examinations occurred. Peter had included this procedure to remove any negative associations regarding those pictures. Each child participated for fifteen minutes in the play area while listening to manipulated Beta wave music. Subsequently, the subjects appeared refreshed when retrieved.

Peter watched the testing taking place, enjoying the accuracy of Zoe's answers, recognizing he was close to having his seven. Initially, Peter had been reluctant when he found out Walden had been using Zoe for his trial. Walden had had no idea the complex issue he had opened up.

From the file he did have on Walden's research, Peter was able to learn about Zoe's unusually high psychic ability. It made Peter honored that the pivotal subject of the seven was a descendant from his own bloodline.

Zoe remained the mentally strongest out of all the subjects tested, making her the perfect team leader.

VIBRATIONAL PASSAGE

Peter knew that Hitler got it wrong, concentrating on the physical packaging of a person, such as blonde hair, blue eyes, for his Aryan race. Yet, Peter was grateful for the petri dish created by the Nazi organization. He viewed Lebensborn, which was a breeding program based on eugenic selection of only those considered racially pure - as a structural scaffolding to his own current work with the children.

He grinned to himself, thinking, *the past is always influencing the future.*

Peter believed Hitler's scientists did get a vital piece of it right, through their work manipulating DNA, Autism was a byproduct, a miscalculation of a failed attempt to create an elite society. Peter was sure that Walden had discovered the numerical marker for Autism on the DNA strand. Once this marker was located, they could tell while still in the womb, through amniocentesis, the potential of a subject's psychic ability.

Peter beamed with delight from the success of the findings today. They were finally able to select the seventh child.

CHAPTER 32

Nicholas unlocked the apartment door letting her, and then Jake, into their residence. Emma was never so pleased to be home. The barbeque was a beautiful event and she would have wanted to stay longer under different circumstances.

A pure exhaustion washed over her as she plopped into a chair in the living room. Nicholas disappeared into the kitchen telling her that he was going to make a pot of coffee. During the ride, back home from Long Island, Emma and Jake had filled Nicholas in on what had transpired earlier that day. Emma was still unsure how much he believed them.

Jake slid into the sofa next to her chair. "So, do you think we freaked out Nic a bit?"

Emma snickered. "Just a bit, I think."

"Well, do you think he believes us?"

Emma rubbed her forehead. "Well, I think it is a lot to take in."

Nicholas entered the living room and inquired, "Take in what?"

"You are kidding, right?" She smiled at her husband.

Jake jumped to his feet. "I just remembered something I learned at the party tonight. It has something to do with the paintings," he said over his shoulder as he raced off to the study.

VIBRATIONAL PASSAGE

"Hold on Jake," Nicholas swiftly trailed after him.

Emma, not wanting to get up from the security and comfort of her chair, reluctantly followed Jake and Nicholas to the study.

"Before you get started Jake," Nicholas turned to Emma. "Where are the coin and the watch?"

Jake fished the coin out of his pocket and handed it to Nicholas, whereas she walked over and pulled the watch out of the desk drawer. She held it up for her husband to see. Jake, bursting at the seams, redirected their attention to the back of the Durer painting, which he had flipped over.

He pointed to a series of numbers handwritten on the canvas. "Look at this. You are not going to believe what this is."

"Lot numbers...?" Nicholas offered, as he played with the coin in his hand.

"No... That is a logical assumption, however, no... I had a conversation with someone at the party tonight, about how the Nazis looted art like maniacs. They had a method to their thievery. You see, this is a code used to inventory stolen art.

According to a very attractive museum docent, I met by the oyster bar tonight, this R here, stands for Rothschild. The numbers here," Jake pointed, "represents the sequence in which it was stolen. This is just one of thousands of items that were taken from this family."

Nicholas frowned. "After everything you have told me tonight, now you are telling me Walden owned stolen Nazi art?"

Jake turned to Nicholas, "Uh, yup, that is about right." Her brother held a small card in his hand. "Check this out, I found this shoved in the corner at the back of this painting."

Jake held the card out to Emma, but she wavered. Her husband took it instead, describing it and reading it aloud. It was just slightly larger than a business card, and had a symbol of a caduceus engraved in the left corner of the exquisite card.

In handwritten calligraphy script it read:
To: Walden & Martha on Your Wedding Day...
Love, Uncle Peter.

Nicholas turned to Jake.

"Now *that*... I can believe... Dr. Lyceum is not someone I have ever had the luxury of trusting. In fact, before 9/11, he and Walden could not even be in the same room together without getting into some kind of verbal altercation."

Emma was feeling somewhat fanatic, acid burned at the pit of her stomach. "So... what are you saying? We have artwork stolen by the Nazis. Can this get any better? We could go to jail for this! This has crossed the line from being twisted to now being against the law." She could feel herself being irritable and irrational, but could not stop herself.

Jake snickered. "Emm, you are worried about getting arrested? I think your focus needs to be more on trying to figure out what to do about this gate to hell you have inherited."

Emma stared at Jake, frustrated with his flippant approach to the situation.

Nicholas stepped in. "Let's calm down and figure this out together."

Emma watched as Jake, heeding Nicholas' advice, turned his attention back to the painting.

She chose to take a seat next to the desk, where her husband and brother were. They continued to study the back of the painting.

Emma listened as Jake motioned towards something. "Nic, look at this, we have another set of numbers here." He pointed to the position on the bottom right hand corner of the canvas it was where the card hid in the frame. Nicholas, grabbing a pen and pad asked Jake to read him the numbers. Just as Nicholas wrote the last number down, she witnessed the look of epiphany cross over her husband's face.

"What is it, Nicholas?" She enquired.

Her husband just looked back and forth between her and Jake without uttering a word before he finally spoke. "I cannot believe I did not make the connection. This was the combination for Walden's briefcase, and this is the number that Walden discovered." He paused, turning pale as blood drained from his face.

VIBRATIONAL PASSAGE

His mouth dropped open as he stood in awe. "This is also the number I found in Walden's research file, which was stored in the briefcase. It is associated to the Birchwood Project; I was working on parts of it with Walden. From studying the files, I came to the conclusion that what Walden discovered was the specific marker for the actual Autism gene."

Due to her exhaustion, she was having a hard time focusing and following the conversation. Whatever he was getting at, it was clearly huge. "Nicholas?" She gently touched him on the shoulder, but he did not move or respond. "Nicholas, are you okay?"

Finally, he let out a deep sigh. "No," was his emphatic response. "These six numbers are being sought after by some of the world's most powerful players in the genetic field. Now I understand why Walden was so secretive towards the end. Because if these set of numbers had fallen into Dr. Lyceum's hand..." Nicholas seemed to shiver at the thought.

"So this Dr. Lyceum is quite the boss-hole."

"Jake!" she scolded.

"Rumors have surfaced surrounding the Brookstone lab," Nicholas intensified.

Emma interrupted. "You mean Glacier Bay? Aren't you based out of there right now?"

"Yes to both of your questions. Even with my level four clearances, my badge will not get me through security in the area of the offices for the CAAR executives. You remember Em, the Center for Advancement of Autism Research. The rumor circulating for years is that Dr. Lyceum has been conducting unethical research with children diagnosed with Autism. Supposedly, the trials are conducted without parental knowledge, disguising it as treatments."

"Oh-my-god," Emma whispered, "Zoe."

Jake looked confused. "Slow down, I am not quite sure what you are getting at..."

Nicholas took a deep breath. "You know what... I need a cup of coffee."

Jake got up, indicating that he was going to get the coffee that Nicholas had made earlier. It would be ready about now.

He turned to her before leaving the room. "Do you want a cup, the usual way?"

She nodded, and watched as he left the room; it felt good to be alone with her husband at last. He always had a way of making her feel safe.

Emma noticed that Nicholas had been fidgeting with the gold coin ever since Jake had returned it back to him.

"By the way, did you ever figure out any of the symbols on that coin?"

Nicholas looked over at her and suddenly realized he had been flipping the coin back and forth across his knuckles. "I was not able to figure out all of the symbols, but I was able to determine this one," he pointed at a symbol on the coin.

Emma moved closer to Nicholas to get a better view of what he was pointing to on the coin, accidentally knocking the painting. Her husband leaned forward, and propped it back up against the desk.

The intensity of the Durer painting now commanded their attention. She wanted to tell him to turn it back over, but was too interested in what he had to say about the coin. Forgetting the painting, she focused on the mysterious symbols.

He continued. "This is from the Kabbalah, while this one is derived from Tibet," he flipped the coin over again. "Whereas this here dates back to the days when alchemy was practiced, and I also believe some of the numbers represent elements from the periodic table." He paused. "I'm very close to establishing a connection between one of the files from Walden's briefcase containing research on Nikola Tesla and this coin. That file also included a reference to the number sequences on this coin."

Emma held up the watch. "Did you have a chance to take a look at any of the symbols on the watch?"

Without even looking at it, he shook his head. "No. Sorry. I have not gotten around to it yet."

Unexpectedly, the ceiling light flickered.

Nicholas stammered, "What... the...?"

VIBRATIONAL PASSAGE

With a pit in her stomach, she noticed the Durer painting beginning to shimmer. The colors danced, vibrating in waves off the canvas.

Her husband was now curiously leaning forward to get a closer look.

Emma tried to pull his hand away.

"No, Nicholas! Don't touch it!"

Their hands were about six inches away from the canvas when Emma felt that familiar, dreadful pull followed by a piercing pain in her head. One heartbeat later and she was back in the dusty, dank bunker, but now with her husband.

The man with the laced up mouth was still at the table looking at the map. Behind him, there was the same group of men arguing. To the right of the room was Hitler. He was no longer in the shadows and somehow appeared stronger and healthier now.

He did not speak aloud, but Emma could hear his voice in her head again. It was different this time. His tone was quiet, even, and his words were hypnotizing her into a paralyzed state as he thanked her for healing him.

Nicholas was beside her, he slid the coin into his pocket while looking around the room, frantically.

"What the... Where are we?"

She held her index finger up to her lips, silencing him. Fortunately, no one seemed to care that she was back, except for Hitler.

With precision, Hitler was making his way over to her. His voice slithered in her thoughts as he calmly asked her for her assistance. His words hypnotized her as he pointed out that his men were no longer able to take direction from him, they just kept arguing. Blinded by their anger, it made it impossible for them to do what they needed to do.

All she could think about was how she had inadvertently ended up helping this monster in the first place. He was closer now, continually inching forward as he reasoned with her. Mesmerized, imprisoned by his intent. Somehow, she knew that if he touched her, she was dead, no longer existing in any reality.

It happened so rapidly, it did not seem like any of it was real. Startling her out of her trance, Nicholas stepped in front of Emma blocking her from Hitler. Her husband was glowing, a golden light illuminated off his skin as he held his hand out.

All of a sudden, Hitler thrown back hit the wall in the back corner of the bunker.

This broke the hypnotic state imprisoning Emma. She turned around and was confused when Nicholas grabbed her hand pulling her into the nearest painting.

The tension in her head replaced with that familiar vacuuming sensation, pulled her in every direction. The colors blinded, whereas the sounds raged within her.

"Now where are we going?" Emma moaned.

They landed in a laboratory centered on a magnificent coil. This coil framed the entire wall, visually blocking any signs of the barrier to the outside world. A man with streaks of white hair and a beard who was dressed in a white suit to match held onto an object that had sparks flying from it. A dark-haired scientist, his hands folded behind him, looked on with an expression of delight.

They were two schoolchildren playing with a new toy.

Emma could not help but wonder whether Nicholas and Walden had worked together in their lab in a very similar manner. She and her husband watched as the scientist with the dark hair and mustache turned his attention to a cylindrical tube.

Sparks of electricity crawled over as well as around the object, like little fingers of lightning hopping back and forth over the metal. The light beams started getting bigger and longer. Then the ground began to shake beneath them, stirring everything in the laboratory.

The man with the dark hair tried to shut the cylindrical tube down, but was having trouble stopping what he had just started. Meanwhile, the other scientist with the bushy white hair was laughing with glee. Once aware of the seriousness of the situation, his hooting turned into more of a nervous laugh.

Two police officers stormed into the room, turning everyone's attention to the door they had just barged past.

VIBRATIONAL PASSAGE

One of the men screamed, "Shut it down, Mr. Tesla!"

Invisible to the others in the lab, Nicholas mouthed in awe.

"Nikola Tesla and Samuel Clemens... unbelievable... we are in Tesla's New York lab. We just experienced an artificial earthquake created by that cylindrical tube over there. Projects like WOLF are based on Tesla's research."

Nicholas pointed. "I need a closer look at the spiral coil."

"No, Nicholas," she protested, but he was not listening to her.

She shadowed him as he excitedly explained that the spiral coil was actually a high-frequency transformer. It had the capability of creating artificial lightning. Emma fastened the watch she had been carrying, onto her wrist. She then linked her arm into Nicholas' to make sure they remained connected in light of all the commotion around them.

Nicholas examined the wall, running his right hand across the huge coil in what looked like a large fan or a metallic spider web with neat concentric rows of coils. Sparks flew when Nicholas' hand made contact with the coils. Fingers of electricity engulfed them. Emma had the sensation of falling.

Pulled towards and through the metal coils, Emma screamed. She lost her grip of her husband's arm, grasping, reaching to grab hold of him, but his shirt slipped through her fingers.

Every part of her body ached, bones prying apart, aching joints and muscles, she was out of breath, feeling a heavy weight pushed up against her heart. She concentrated, trying to breathe, willing her heart to keep pumping despite the apparent possibility that it was about to give out and give up.

Emma found herself in a white-walled reception area; an expensively dressed, exotic young woman was standing at a white podium.

"Where am I?" Emma stammered.

The woman just beamed back at her without giving a response, making Emma wonder if she even spoke English. She scanned around for Nicholas. He was nowhere. Emma became frantic when she realized she could not locate him anywhere.

Whiteness surrounded her.

"They have been expecting you," the young woman finally communicated. She gracefully stepped to the side, to reveal a door behind her.

"Who's expecting me?"

The woman did not look back at her. Instead, she remained focused on the door and gave no reaction. Emma had had enough. She was so over being emotionally tortured.

A surge of energy forced its way through the exhaustion of everything being so cryptic. She was now aware that she steeped in fear for days. Emma refused to be scared anymore. If she walked through this door to her death, so be it.

She would not do it afraid, not anymore. "Fine, I will just see for myself," she snapped, trudging through the door, with raw determination.

Emma entered a room she vaguely recognized.

She had seen this place before once in her dreams. It was a boardroom filled with ten men dressed in business suits. Just like in her hallucination, they all looked sickly, as if they had caught the flu. Dr. Walden Sinclair, situated to her right, did not speak.

A bald man stepped forward. "Are you ready to pull us all out?" His tone of voice was more a demand than a question, which Emma found annoying.

"What are you talking about?"

"Well, you are here to get us," he affirmed. "It's about time WOLF got its act together. We are running out of time."

A muddle of barking ultimatums descended upon her, as each man, in his own way tried to take control over the circumstances. The only one who remained silent was Walden, who was still standing beside her. Emma scanned the area of executives, seeing them, but too tired to comprehend their faces entirely.

They were just a blur of bullies endeavoring to dominate over her. There was bellowing and shrieking while pointing in her direction about how infuriated they were that someone had botched this all up. They moaned that they had been part of a deception; she was to fix the circumstances immediately.

Emma could not believe the way they were speaking to her, as if she were some subordinate they could command. They were stuck, yet they still saw themselves as in charge. The insanity of it all was just too much.

When it was apparent that Emma was not responding to their directives, a tall, rotund man with a deep voice held his hand up. The other men gradually stopped shouting. The man's voice was calm and buttery.

He did not apologize for their behavior. Instead, he commenced cajoling her, proposing large amounts of money, asking her what she required from them, working her over as though this was a deal he was about to negotiate.

Emma stared blankly at the overweight man, who was now slowly making his way towards her.

Then he unexpectedly paused. "You are with WOLF, I presume..."

She shook her head, "Nope..."

A dark haired man quickly asked, "Then who sent you?"

The bulky set man moved forward rapidly, looming over her. "Understand this, young lady. Everything that has happened in your life has led you to this moment. Seize it!"

"You all assume I am here to help you. Yet you think you can bark orders at me. You have got to be kidding, right?"

The room was silent.

Finally, the bald man spoke up. "You are obviously here because someone sent you. We do not need to know whom, and there is no reason to get emotional. We need to complete our jump. So, let us just get started."

Emma began to chuckle uncontrollably. "All of you are dead. Yes, your bodies were not found, but your families have buried all of you."

Walden took a deep breath and sighed.

He finally spoke. "All of us are confined between that place you call death and being alive. We were all promised bodies in different timelines so that we could undo our own personal atrocities."

Emma could not hold back. "You narcissistic group of men, every one of you is self-centered. You lived self-absorbed lives, and now you are going to go back and take someone else's body?

You think because of your power and wealth that you are all above the rules... that rules don't apply to you?"

She halted briefly. "They do... I will make sure of it."

Tears were running down Walden's face. "Emma, you are right. You are right about all of that. Please understand I chose this because I have to undo what I did to Zoe and children like Zoe."

Emma stared deep into his eyes and then over to the door that was now shimmering. "You are right Walden; you do need to fix what you have done."

She grabbed his arm and jumped.

Still furious with the selfishness of their actions, Emma fought the mental throbbing and focused her intent on permanently sealing the door shut. Not only would it be sealed shut, no one will ever know where to look for them.

Emma felt satisfied, knowing that these men's actions sealed their own fate. They were prisoners in their space for eternity.

All she focused on was being at home in Nicholas' arms.

What made her angry was the realization that it was not over.

Just like Walden, Emma knew that she had to reverse what she had accidentally done as well.

Hitler's scheme had to be undone.

CHAPTER 33

Emma could hear Walden's voice repeating: "Wish... Kiss... Suicide..."

She discovered herself surrounded by white again; it felt as if she was back where she started except now there was an extended hallway lined with doors. Emma was not sure which way to go, and then she caught a flash, a glimpse of someone moving from one entranceway to the next. Emma went over to the doorway someone had just entered.

The door was still open.

Walden was standing there, waiting.

"Where are we, Walden?"

"You still have something to do, Emma, before you go back."

"Yes, I know," she retorted. "Now that I know how to, I have to seal in Hitler."

Walden challenged her. "Do you know how to do that?"

"I'm not quite sure," she confessed. "But I know that I can."

"Then you are going to need the help of the sisters sub rosa," Walden offered.

"Who are they?"

"The women you keep seeing in your dreams."

"You mean the women around the cauldron? I thought those were witches."

"Because of your own reference point, you see them as that," Walden clarified. Toying with her, he continued. "Why do you interpret them as witches?"

"Because it was just like the scene from Macbeth," she justified.

"So were the witches in Macbeth good or evil?"

"Walden, I have not changed my opinion from the last time we had that conversation. I still believe in free will. I would not allow others to decide my fate based on a prophecy." She glared at him. "By the way, what is with this wish, kiss, and suicide?"

Walden smiled. "It has everything to do with intent."

"You are going to have to do better than that."

"'Wish' refers to the desired outcome," he explained. "While 'kiss' is intent and focus, whereas 'suicide' is about letting go."

"Is that why you ended up where you did? Since you speak in lousy metaphors?"

Walden roared with laughter. "Not quite. We had the assistance of the men in the bunker. They were able to alter our final destination, just like what happened to Hitler's gang by the sisters sub rosa.

As long as the intent is not at a hundred percent, there is the opportunity to alter it. That is what makes these children diagnosed with Autism so powerful. They can maintain a hundred percent of intent because they are not dictated to by social norms so that their focus is not distracted by emotions or feelings; especially fear and lack of worth."

Emma was afraid to ask, but she had to know. "Walden, what were you up to with your daughter, Zoe?"

He looked down, ashamed. "Something that I must undo with your help…"

"What were her DNA results doing in the same file with Hitler and Mengele?"

"Nobody knows this," he countered, "but she's not my biological daughter. Did you not read the file? Her father was deceased before she was even conceived."

"What?" Goosebumps ran up and down her arms.

VIBRATIONAL PASSAGE

"I discovered by accident when Zoe was eight months old... what Martha's family had contrived under the direction of Peter." His voice softened. "After Martha's betrayal with the conception of Zoe, our marriage was over because I could never trust her again. Still, I had a responsibility to protect Zoe. Even though she was not of my DNA, she was still my daughter."

"So, who is her father?"

Walden did not answer her question.

In a way, she was almost glad he did not tell her. Emma had a feeling whatever the answer was going to be it needed to remain unspoken.

He went on. "Mengele was the genetic engineer responsible for gathering and storing Hitler's DNA. Peter made sure Zoe experienced exposure to a specific type of Mendelrose antibiotics along with selected vaccinations when her immune system was overloaded. This all occurred before her first birthday.

This sent up a red flag for me, and that is when I started investigating what Peter was doing. All of a sudden, my typically developing daughter started demonstrating characteristics of Autism.

I was able to manipulate Peter for a short time, into believing that I had discovered a way to reverse her diagnosis. However, when he found out what I really uncovered, I had to attempt a jump back. Peter wants the numbers I have entrusted with you and Nicholas. Know that he will stop at nothing in obtaining it."

"What do the numbers mean?"

Walden gradually breathed in before carrying on. "Well, I discovered the specific subsections of DNA that can be built upon for the next generation of children without the uncontrollable side-effects of Autism. Peter believes this information will progress the psychic abilities within the human brain, while not hampering the necessary social skills for survival.

Human beings, like honey bees, require the social aspect to thrive. My objective to 'cure' autism changed when I discovered that instead, there was a way to allow these children to maintain their unique abilities, while providing them safe passage. I found a way to trigger their DNA so they would acquire the social and communication skills they need. This would enable them to balance the enormous amount of information they have access to…"

Emma became silent. "I don't quite comprehend what you are getting at Walden."

He persisted. "This may be a little complicated to comprehend. During my research, I learned so much from the honeybee and their system of social behavior, which I then applied to my research with Zoe. To clarify one I must explain the other. Let me begin with honeybees first.

The master regulator genes involved in the nervous system development are used for behavioral functions in honeybees. Young bees change jobs in response to needs of the hive, so much so that the bee's DNA structure changes with it. This involves changes in thousands of genes in the honeybee's brain.

This is where the connection between the honeybees and their genetic social structure, and the social structure breakdown that occurs for children diagnosed with Autism Spectrum Disorders (ASD) began for me.

In an isolated experiment, I was able to suppress the social regulator genes in half the bees of a hive. The result was disastrous for the collective, however.

Some of the bees had mysteriously escaped, proving disastrous for the honeybee population in the geographical proximity to our lab. Fortunately, damage control stopped the mistake from spreading and ultimately devastating honeybee populations worldwide.

I had hypothesized that once I found the social regulator genes in the human genome, I could find the short strings of DNA that lie close to the gene, I then could switch on for example, as in a light being switched on, the social regulator genes for a child with ASD.

When the correct transcription factor latches into the binding site, the gene when switched on, would allow the child with ASD to have the needed social and communication skill, similar to the needed social and communication skills necessary for the survival for the residents of a beehive.

This involves the actual change of the honeybee's DNA. Switching genes on and off by manipulating strings of DNA that lie close to the gene is not as simple as it sounds. The strings serve as binding sites for particular molecules called transcription factors and..."

"Walden, I am sorry you have lost me."

"Alright... Let me put it this way...The world is shifting on its access. No matter what we as scientists hypothesize, we do not know the reason why. I believe these children, like Zoe possess in their DNA the ability to mentally communicate as well as the ability to read the earth's magnetic grid. Just like honeybees, these children have altered DNA, which I believe will save the future of humanity.

Emma, we have a group of children that hold our future in their thoughts. Now combine that skill to the capacity to focus intent. You have recently learned firsthand the effects of intent..."

"How do you expect me to help these children?"

"With the help of Nicholas, you will get the word out to parents on how to protect their children. Parents paralyzed with fear can no longer make simple decisions on whether to immunize their children or who to turn to for guidance. Immunization is important but the amount at one time is wrong.

Today a small infant receives over 30 shots before their first birthday. Their immune systems cannot overcome that, and these children become suppressed at the DNA level. Therefore, the shots must occur over longer periods, giving their tiny bodies time to adjust. However, what is transpiring is either a child is not receiving inoculations, which is opening the door to diseases such as polio. Or these children's systems are overloaded with vaccinations to the point they leave their bodies making them an open vessel to be taken over by someone or thing else."

Emma worked hard on wrapping her mind around everything he was revealing to her but she was getting confused, "Walden..."

He held up his hand and continued, "I am going to make it very simple for you. When you drink alcohol, it impairs your body, as well as impedes your brain processing. The more alcohol at one time the greater impairment, now replace alcohol with immunizations and alter the age."

"Walden parents are not going to listen to me."

"That is why you will need Nicholas. I left him a file with all the proof needed. Inform parents to remain involved with their child's therapy, so individuals like Peter cannot hurt them."

She could feel that Walden was not telling her everything, but she still felt bad for judging Walden so harshly.

It was unimaginable what she had now ascertained about Walden. He was a father first, trying to protect a child who he considered his own. At that moment, she knew she had done the right thing by pulling him out of the chamber.

"So, back to my initial question, what do the numbers actually mean then?"

Walden turned to her and assured her, "All in due time."

Shifting the subject, he asked. "What about my colleagues trapped in the boardroom? What is your position with them? Are you going to help them?"

She stared into Walden's eyes and emphatically said, "No," indicating it was not up for discussion.

Emma beamed at herself for her newfound confidence.

In the past, Walden dictated terms, but now...

"Well," Walden added, "that still leaves us with your unfinished business with Hitler."

Emma was silent for a moment, thinking about that bunker. "The map that they possess, it is everything," she murmured. Her voice was weary and hoarse. "It can give you unimaginable power, anything you can dream of, it will provide. I saw and felt what it can do. I know why Hitler wants to use it, and I know that he cannot."

Walden nodded.

She persisted, "It is no different than a mythical sea siren luring sailors to their death. The promise of infinite promises can destroy worlds."

Walden interjected. "So, this still brings us back to what and how are you going to do it. My suggestion as a researcher is, you start with what you do know."

"I witnessed that they have access to three portals in their bunker leading to New York. If they succeed in escaping, it may be the end of my world's reality. Those sick men are only after dominance. Death and anguish follow them; even genocide is somehow justified in their minds. There is a growing sentiment who would support them at all costs should they make the jump here. I would not be able to live with myself knowing that I did not do something to stop it because I was too petrified and shattered to deal with it.

I do not think Hitler's team intends to use an object this time like the map. Instead, I think they are searching for a human vessel. I have to stop them before they find that person."

Walden knowingly smiled at her. "There is so much you have not figured out yet."

Emma grinned back and thought, *I have figured out I am the vessel they seek*. "At this point, I like it that way because I do not need any added responsibility. Walden, I need to know about the gold coin."

"Yes... the gold coin, it is complicated. We do not have enough time for me to divulge to you everything. However, I can tell you that *everything* has a vibrational reason for being. The coin was on a course to find you and to assist you in remembering who you are as well as what you can do. Emma you have the capacity to communicate to those in different realms. This also opens the door for you to mentally connect to children lost to autism and bring them back to the here and now. The coin provides a vibrational gateway. I know I have not answered your question completely, but there is no more time left."

He stared at her with such intensity, while changing the subject. She was careful to listen to his words. "The sisters sub rosa, whether good or evil, represent temptation... when you step up to the pot, *know thyself, or you will surely lose yourself.*"

Emma, puzzled by where Walden was going with this, nodded.

Walden opened the door and stepped aside.

He offered her a long, thin piece of Birch bark, as well as a shard of burnt wood.

There were the three women chanting, laughing, and dancing around a fire. They were blurry figures now; Emma could not see their faces, just fuzzy outlines of their shapes as they moved around the cauldron.

Emma approached them, and they continued what they were doing, as if expecting her. She could smell and hear the burnt Birch wood crackling in the fire beneath the pot. Thin tree trunks surrounded the women, in this forest of Birch trees that glowed in the dark and reflected the light from the flickering flames of the fire.

Emma could not believe that she was now whispering, "Wish... Kiss... Suicide..."

She wrote down her wish, then kissed the thin layer of bark, approached the dark pot, and leaned down to set the bark on fire.

A sharp pain ran up her arm. It felt like an electric shock. A gust of wind blew through the trees, rustling the leaves on the high branches above her.

"You still have not found your answers," a voice hissed in the wind.

The wind blew her hair around her face, tickling her ears.

"We know the cure for Zoe." A voice behind her, mocked very softly.

"What if you are making a mistake?" The voice seemed to echo, and questions of doubt began to reverberate and bounce off the trees.

"Are you sure you know what you are doing? What about Zoe?"

Then in a hushed voice, "Will you turn your back on the child?"

A book hovered over the large, black pot. It was a thick, old book. Murmurs of the same word quietly, gently echoed around her. "Grimoire... Grimoire... Grimoire... The Key of Knowledge... You can slide back in time and cure your mother and your aunt; they did not have to suffer so. Only you can help. If you want to..."

A flicker of guilt shot through her at the mention of her mother and especially her aunt. The smoke from the fire seemed to thicken, burning her eyes and choking her. Emma stepped back, and she could see Nicholas' face.

He looked annoyed. "You are making a mistake!" He yelled. "Knowledge is our only hope. Do not throw it away."

The smoke billowed up into the dark sky, the gray turning to black as it rose higher and higher into the air.

"They have a cure for Zoe." It was Wally's voice.

He sounded so sad and hurt. "You could help her if you wanted to."

Emma started to cough; the smoke was all around her. She squinted through tears, her throat was so dry, and she could barely breathe. Everything around her was swirling, spinning, as she gagged for air and reached down, struggling to light the bark with the flame.

The wind picked up, sending the flames away from wherever she held the bark. A sudden lethargy washed over her. Emma did not know if she had the strength to even stand up, let alone finish what she had begun. Doubts, guilt, confusion made her want to crumple into a ball and rest. She felt so alone, it ached. Maybe this was a miscalculation.

Emma closed her eyes for a moment, and she saw words shimmering on a piece of lined paper. They were typewritten words from an old typewriter. She could not quite read the words, but it broke her away from the moment long enough for her to regain enough strength. She needed to focus her intent.

She speedily lit the bark on fire and held the burning papery Birch over the cauldron, waiting for the words to burn away. Emma whispered a prayer of protection and love, calling upon Archangel Michael. She thought of the statue of the archangel Michael that her brother had given her when she was so depressed when Aunt Gertie died.

Once the words were gone, she threw the burning bark into the pot. The flames hissed in the pot and a terrible stench of white smoke arose from the boiling liquid.

The smoke cleared leaving blurred figures, which took shape. They were not monsters or terrible creatures. They were not the scary, ugly creatures as described in Macbeth.

Three beautiful women looked up at her and nodded in unison.

"You were 'the one.' Now it is done," then they were gone.

A loud door slammed shut, a mighty gust of wind pushed her back, shoving her down onto her hands and knees. The woods... the cauldron... all of it gone. Emma was standing in the middle of her kitchen. Only the glow from the clock on the stove provided enough light for her to know where she was.

Emma burst into uncontrollable sobs. Her eyes were still burning from the fire. The tears stung at her cheeks, which were dried and chapped from the fire beneath the cauldron.

She had sealed the portal.

Emma's focus was now to protect these children.

END OF BOOK ONE

EXCERPT FROM THE DRAGON KING SAFE PASSAGE TRILOGY: BOOK 2

Wally ambled down to the subway platform trying to keep up with his nanny. Rather than thinking about the unaware adults pushing and shoving past him, he focused on seeing his Aunty Emm. Normally, Wally would be at his Saturday swimming lesson, but the pool, closed for unexpected maintenance, left him free for the day. His mother had persuaded the nanny into taking him with her on her errands. Wally completely comprehended why his nanny was grumpy today. In fact, he felt guilty that she had to watch over him on her day off. He always felt the same way when he was stuck minding Zoe.

He appreciated that she was trying to make the best of it. Wally did not understand why his mom had decided all of a sudden this morning that it was Zoe's day for a haircut. Deep down, Wally suspected that it was a way of punishing Zoe for her latest antics. Zoe's haircuts were an excruciating experience for anyone within a one-mile radius.

Wally was halfway through the latest *Dragon Kingdom* book. That book was still so popular getting a copy was next to impossible, even on the internet. Aunty Emm had handed him a signed copy, which he clutched tightly beneath his arm. So much shoving occurred until the train doors could finally shut.

At last, a friendly female's voice announced their destination and the train halted to a stop. The doors slid open, and his nanny gave his hand a slight tug indicating it was time to get off. Hot, stale air surrounded them as they made their way up the stairs from the platform. Wally did his best to keep up, careful not to trip, fall, or touch anything.

He had made a deal with his mom that if he helped his nanny with all her errands, he had her permission to go to Aunty Emm's bookstore on their way home. Zoe and his mom would pick him up at the bookstore after the haircut debacle.

Within a few minutes, they arrived and he was giving his Aunty Emm a huge hug, hello. Aunty Emm, positioned next to Zoe on the rainbow rug, was flipping through Zoe's favorite picture book quietly together. Zoe looked up and smiled with pride. Wally stifled a laugh, her bangs were uneven; she obviously won this round against Antoine's scissors.

The nanny waved at Aunty Emm, as she left him to join his mother who was settling her nerves with a cup of coffee in the store's cafe.

"What's up, little man?" Aunty Emm inquired.

Before answering, he made sure his nanny had established herself next to his mom at their usual spot in the corner. Aunty Emm gazed at him, anticipating his answer.

Wally leaned forward and uttered, "I had another one of those dreams about my dad. You know, where it is a dream, but it is not a dream?"

He looked about; making sure no one was listening in on the conversation.

Aunty Emm did not say anything. He could feel the compassion from her, giving him confidence to share his dream.

"Dad showed me this church and it's like I know this church, but I am not quite sure where I've seen it."

Wally went on to explain the details from his dream, recalling the glass chimes and the gardener who had his dad's eyes.

He watched as Aunty Emm's eyes lit up.

"Wally, I know where that place is."

He immediately asked. "Aunty Emm, can you take me there?"

"Okay, but we are going to have to clear it with your mom, first."

Wally was worried. "We are not going to tell her what I just told you, are we?"

"No," she whispered, "don't worry Wally, we are not, I will just tell your mom I am going to take you for a quick snack at that new place everyone is raving about." She leaned over to Zoe. "Zoe, you in the mood for some French fries?"

Zoe slammed the book shut, startling a few people around them. "You... betcha...!" She excitedly jumped to her feet, taking Aunty Emm's hand in hers. Zoe placed the book she had been reading in her aunt's other hand, indicating she wanted to take it home with her.

Together, the three of them walked over to the cafe. Wally listened patiently as Aunty Emm made small talk with his mom. He was nervous as he waited and wondered how his aunt would get permission for them to leave the bookstore without his mom and nanny in tow.

It was Zoe to the rescue. She helped Aunty Emm when she began screeching and patting her head with her left hand, drawing her mom's attention to her newly acquired hairstyle. Wally watched as Aunty Emm redirected Zoe, getting her to stop screeching and stand quietly as she continued to talk to their mom. Wally felt sorry for his mom because it could not be easy for her to not have control with Zoe and watch how easily she responded to Aunty Emm.

His mom was massaging her temple, which meant a migraine was coming on.

Wally was captivated as he heard Aunty Emm easily convince his mom that she would take them to this new place, *Fry Frenzy*, for some gourmet French fries. Moments like this made Wally miss his dad. His dad had that identical ability as Aunty Emm. When his mom offered to pay, Aunty Emma showed her a buy one get one free coupon she was holding in her hand.

She assured her that she would walk them directly home afterwards.

They easily made their way out of the bookstore. Holding hands with Aunty Emm in the middle, they strolled towards *Fry Frenzy*. She walked them down a side street he did not recognize, when he started hearing the glass chimes he instantly recognized from his dream. They turned a corner and approached a church courtyard from a side entrance. Wally promptly noticed the groundskeeper, who had his back towards them, while watering rose bushes. He felt a wave of shivers wash over his body.

Unexpectedly, Zoe yelled out, "Daddy!"

She broke free from Aunty Emm, darting towards the groundskeeper.

Wally's skin was prickly everywhere from his head to his toes now.

Without hesitation, Aunty Emm was rapidly in pursuit of Zoe. Everything was happening so fast, it was as if a chain of events was set off. Wally watched as Zoe hugged the groundskeeper from behind. Time seemed to slip into slow motion.

A van door slammed, pulling Wally's attention across the street where two men in black suits were looking directly at him while advancing towards them.

The groundskeeper turned around, hugged Zoe, while looking straight into Wally's eyes. He was looking at a stranger, who was staring back at him with his dad's eyes.

Aunty Emm yelled, "Wally! Hurry...!"

The two bulky men in the suits were closing in on Wally.

Wally sprinted over to Aunty Emm, Zoe, and the stranger with his dad's eyes.

"You are not safe," the groundskeeper uttered. "I need you to follow me."

He maneuvered them through a side door into the church and bolted the heavy wooden door behind them.

Wally was apprehensive in asking if this was his dad, just like in his dream. Nonetheless, he listened, and followed single file, up a winding staircase. The journey ended in front of another heavy looking wooden door, which the man opened with a key he had hidden under his shirt on a chain. Once inside, he locked that door behind them. Wally found himself in a long narrow room filled with a musty smell, likely from the aged books lining the walls. A faint light streamed in through stained glass windows.

The groundskeeper was now speaking to Aunty Emm, giving her directions. She was listening carefully and nodding her head every few seconds. Wally then saw her pull out a watch from her pocket. She fastened it on her left wrist.

Aunty Emm turned to Wally and pushed a gold coin with etchings on it into his right hand.

"Wally I need you to hold this tightly. Do you understand?"

Unable to answer her, he nodded.

Zoe was holding the groundskeeper's hand. *She hates holding everyone's hand except dad's hand. Even when she was angry with him, she still held his hand.* "What is going on here?" Wally reflected.

The groundskeeper placed Zoe's hand on Aunty Emm's wristwatch. "Do not let go of the watch." He instructed. Zoe nodded.

"These old churches hide rare gems," the groundskeeper nodded towards a large oil painting hanging on the wall they were all facing. "This is an original from Lucas the Elder. Perfect alchemy…"

Wally felt emotionally overwhelmed, so he focused on the coin in his hand. He stared down at it in awe. It was then that he realized his Dragon Kingdom book was missing.

"Aunty Emm!" He screamed. "My Dragon book, I don't know where it is!"

He was frantic, panicking; nothing was making any sense, when the groundskeeper placed a steady hand on his shoulder.

The stranger looked straight into Wally's eyes, and spoke, "I love you, son."

Wally jumped as a loud pounding on the other side of the door grew louder and louder. Someone was trying to break the door down to get in.

The groundskeeper turned to Aunty Emm. "We're running out of time. Are you ready?"

She nodded while taking his and Zoe's hands, gently pulling them towards the painting.

Sharp blurs of light, finger-paint swirls of colors swished the air around him. Wally grabbed his head; it hurt as if a million bees covered his head and were simultaneously stinging him. A loud, slurping sound wrapped around him as if a giant vacuum cleaner was sucking him in. Wally was petrified as an ocean of light engulfed him.

ABOUT THE AUTHORS

Jennifer Dustow holds a Doctorate in Education and is a Cognitive Behavioral Learning Specialist. She runs a successful private practice in Hawaii.

Kimberly Miyasaki Lee is a freelance writer. She is a former TV News Producer and community relations specialist who now lives and writes in New York.

Connect with us Online:

http://kimandjenn.blogspot.com

Made in the USA
Charleston, SC
07 May 2011